DEVIL'S GULCH

D0956242

*Look for these exciting Western series from bestselling
authors William W. Johnstone and J.A. Johnstone*

The Mountain Man

Luke Jensen: Bounty Hunter

Brannigan's Land

The Jensen Brand

Preacher and MacCallister

Fort Misery

The Fighting O'Neils

Perley Gates

MacCoole and Boone

Guns of the Vigilantes

Shotgun Johnny

The Chuckwagon Trail

The Jackals

The Slash and Pecos Westerns

The Texas Moonshiners

Stoneface Finnegan Westerns

Ben Savage: Saloon Ranger

The Buck Trammel Westerns

The Death and Texas Westerns

The Hunter Buchanon Westerns

Will Tanner: U.S. Deputy Marshal

DEVIL'S GULCH

A Devil's Gulch Western

WILLIAM W. JOHNSTONE

AND J.A. JOHNSTONE

PINNACLE BOOKS
Kensington Publishing Corp.
www.kensingtonbooks.com

PINNACLE BOOKS are published by

Kensington Publishing Corp.
119 West 40th Street
New York, NY 10018

Copyright © 2023 by J.A. Johnstone

This book is a work of fiction. Names, characters, businesses, organizations, places, events, and incidents either are the product of the authors' imagination or are used fictitiously. Any resemblance to actual persons, living or dead, events, or locales is entirely coincidental.

To the extent that the image or images on the cover of this book depict a person or persons, such person or persons are merely models, and are not intended to portray any character or characters featured in the book.

All rights reserved. No part of this book may be reproduced in any form or by any means without the prior written consent of the Publisher, excepting brief quotes used in reviews.

PUBLISHER'S NOTE: Following the death of William W. Johnstone, the Johnstone family is working with a carefully selected writer to organize and complete Mr. Johnstone's outlines and many unfinished manuscripts to create additional novels in all of his series like The Last Gunfighter, Mountain Man, and Eagles, among others. This novel was inspired by Mr. Johnstone's superb storytelling.

All Kensington titles, imprints, and distributed lines are available at special quantity discounts for bulk purchases for sales promotion, premiums, fund-raising, and educational or institutional use.

If you purchased this book without a cover you should be aware that this book is stolen property. It was reported as "unsold and destroyed" to the Publisher and neither the Author nor the Publisher has received any payment for this "stripped book."

Special book excerpts or customized printings can also be created to fit specific needs. For details, write or phone the office of the Kensington Sales Manager: Kensington Publishing Corp., 119 West 40th Street, New York, NY 10018. Attn. Sales Department. Phone: 1-800-221-2647.

PINNACLE BOOKS, the Pinnacle logo, and the WWJ steer head logo Reg. U.S. Pat. & TM Off.

First Printing: May 2023
ISBN-13: 978-0-7860-4973-8
ISBN-13: 978-0-7860-4977-6 (eBook)

10 9 8 7 6 5 4 3 2 1

Printed in the United States of America

CHAPTER 1

OUTSIDE DEVIL'S GULCH

1868

John Holt looked up from his campfire when his roan started fussing.

He knew the animal could see and hear things in the darkness. It could be an animal attracted to the smell of the bacon he was cooking up as his supper. Maybe a wolf attracted to the scent of his horse.

But Holt knew there was a good chance it was a critter of the two-legged variety drawn by his campfire in the hopes of a meal or something worse.

That was what he hoped, anyway. It was why he had camped out on the outskirts of town rather than riding in and spending the night in the warm bed of a hotel.

Holt drew the Remington .44 from his belt and wrapped his blanket tightly around his shoulders. No reason to show whatever—or whoever—was approaching what he had waiting for them.

His answer came in the form of a shout from the darkness.

"Hello, the camp!" a man's voice shouted. "We'd like to come in."

Holt smiled to himself. His trap had worked. "Come ahead, then. Nice and slow with your hands empty."

"We can do slow," the man responded, "but we ain't got slings for our rifles so we won't come in empty. Can come in holding them by the barrel if that'll suit you."

Playing games already. A bad sign. "Sounds like it'll have to be. Come ahead."

Holt's roan fussed and pulled against her rope as the men drew closer and broke into the clearing. Slow and easy as they had promised. He looked back at the mare and told her to be easy.

Holt watched two men as they entered the weak circle of light thrown off by his campfire. He had learned a man could tell you a lot about himself before he even opened his mouth if you took the time to let him.

Their appearance spoke volumes to him now.

He judged the two men to be in their early twenties. They both had a fair complexion and sandy colored hair, so Holt took them for relations, maybe even brothers. One favored their father while the other favored the mother, though it was impossible for Holt to tell which was which. They looked like the better parts of two different people, which confirmed they were blood. Their clothes were damp and dusty and hadn't seen a good washing in a while, if ever.

Their pants were tattered and torn, but their boots were in reasonably good condition. Neither man had seen a bath or a shave in some time, but the small amount of stubble on their faces showed there was hardly enough reason to put effort into lathering up in the first place.

No, it wasn't their appearance that put John Holt on edge.

It was their eyes.

Eyes that should have been youthful but could not hide

what they had beheld. Eyes that had seen the worst of what men could do to each other when they had no other choice. Eyes that reminded Holt of his own.

The war had done that to him and, by his reckoning, had done the same to these boys too. He could not tell which side they had fought for, not that it mattered. Blood and horror had left its mark on men who had worn either blue or gray.

He watched the young men approach the campfire holding their rifles by the barrels with the stocks forward.

Holt kept his pistol beneath his blanket. He bided his time until he knew who they were.

"Evening, mister." The taller of the two young men smiled. "Thank you for your hospitality."

"Nothing to thank me for yet," Holt said as he continued to eye his new guests. Their clothes might be ratty, but they had taken good care of their rifles. He judged the pistols holstered on their hips to be in good condition too.

His mare fussed again, and Holt told her to be quiet.

"Your animal's a might touchy, mister," the other one said. "If you don't mind my saying."

"I don't mind, and neither does she." Holt tried a smile. "She's never taken kindly to strangers. Guess we have that in common."

The taller of the two nodded down at the coffeepot he had set next to the fire and the pan of bacon beginning to sizzle. "We'd sure appreciate a cup of coffee if you can spare it, mister. We'd be indebted to you."

Holt said, "I've only got the one cup to spare, unless you boys brought your own. There's four of you, aren't there?"

The shorter of the two froze while the taller used his smile as his shield. "Four? Why there's just two of us, mister, standing here as plain as day. Are you seeing double?"

"I'm seeing just fine." Holt nodded back toward the mare still pulling against her line. "Not as good as her, of course, especially at night. She hears better than me no matter the time of day, so I know enough to pay attention when she fusses, which she's doing now. Plain as day, as you said. That tells me you boys have a friend out there somewhere in the darkness trying to flank me at this very moment."

The shorter of the two swallowed.

The taller of the two kept smiling. "Mister, you've got a mighty distrustful nature."

"And you boys have got a choice," Holt said. "Either call him in here—and tell him to be nice and slow about it—or there's going to be a misunderstanding."

The taller man was not smiling any longer. "Come on out, Cleat. He's safe. Come to us, not behind him."

"Smart boy." Holt told the taller man. "That fourth fella can keep tending the horses. I want to keep this a small affair for now."

The shorter of the brothers stammered, "H-h-how'd you know we had horses?"

Holt decided there was no harm in telling him. "Your boots don't look like you've been walking all day and you're not carrying any gear for outdoor living. That tells me you've been riding and, since you didn't bring them with you, nor your saddles neither, I'd say you've got someone watching them."

He did not tell them how he really knew there were four of them. That could come later.

Cleat entered through the darkness on his right side. His rifle in hand but aimed down at the ground. Holt did not have to look at him to know exactly where he was.

"Could've hobbled them," the taller man said. "Or tied them to a tree."

"If you had, that fourth man would be with you, but he's not." Holt's eyes moved slowly from the shorter brother, then to the taller one, and finally to Cleat. He resembled the two brothers, but the similarities were distant. If he was blood, he was a cousin. He was also a follower. The taller of the three was clearly the leader.

"Which has me wondering," Holt went on, "why you'd leave him out there all alone instead of bringing the horses with you?"

His eyes moved back to the taller man. If trouble started, it would start with him. "So how about it, boy? What're you hiding on those horses of yours?"

The tall man's smile was gone now. The flickering firelight revealed the true nature of the youngster before him. "You ask a lot of questions, mister."

"My fire," Holt said. "My grub. My privilege." His eyes narrowed. "You wouldn't be hiding anything that might be draped across your saddles, would you, boy? Something you wouldn't like me seeing?"

The shorter brother took a step back. He might have run away if his brother had not been there. But Holt knew that if it had not been for his brother, the shorter man would not have been there at all. And neither would Cleat.

Holt forced the issue while the taller man glared at him from across the fire. "If I were to walk back there and find those horses, I wouldn't find any money bags from the First National Bank in Devil's Gulch, would I, boy?"

"You wouldn't make it that far," the taller man told him. "And I ain't nobody's boy."

It was Holt's turn to smile. "Then I guess that would make you three big rats, now wouldn't it."

As the taller man dropped his rifle and went for the

pistol on his hip, Holt raised his Remington and shot him in the chest.

Cleat was bringing up his rifle when Holt's second shot punched through his belly. The rifle went off and a bullet struck the fire as Cleat doubled over and dropped the rifle to the ground.

Holt was already on his feet, his blanket shucked from his shoulders, his pistol aimed at the shorter brother who was still making up his mind about what to do next.

"Careful, son," Holt cautioned. "You don't have to die tonight. Just drop the rifle and throw up your hands."

Holt did not know if the younger man had heard him. He was looking down at the bodies of the two Holt had just killed. Thin streams of vapor rose from their wounds in the cold night air. He had seen such sights before—of that, Holt was certain—but not these men. They had already lived through so much. They had escaped death's grip for four blood-soaked years, yet there they were, lying dead on the cold ground around the campfire of a stranger.

It did not seem possible, but there they were.

And here he was. The only one left to do something about it.

Holt knew the look that appeared on his face all too well. The look of resignation.

"Don't do it, boy," Holt warned. "Don't make me kill you."

The shorter man looked at him. The fire casting ugly shadows on his face, making him look older than a man so young had any right to be.

"You in the war, mister?"

Holt nodded. "So were you, I take it."

"Manassas Junction," he said. "Both times."

Holt was not surprised. "So was I."

The young survivor's expression did not change. He

was committed. He was just working himself up to it. "Which side?"

"Does it matter?"

The man took a deep breath. "No. I guess it don't."

He tossed the rifle at Holt, who fired as soon as he saw his shoulder flinch. The rifle tilted into the fire. The man hit the ground with a bullet through his head.

He fell to the ground. His pistol still in his hand.

Holt kicked the rifle free from the flames and walked toward Cleat, who was clutching his belly with one hand while he pawed for his rifle with the other. Holt grabbed the rifle and tossed it on the far side of the fire.

Cleat looked up at him. Defeated. "You at Manassas too?"

"My side called it Bull Run."

"I'm surprised." The dying man's eyes narrowed. "You got a bit of Old Virginia in your voice."

"You got good ears, son." He aimed the Remington down at him. "That belly wound is mighty bad. I'll end it if you want."

Cleat tried to keep his head from shaking as he nodded. His voice quivered as he said, "Looks like we picked the wrong campfire."

Holt thumbed back the hammer. "Looks like."

Then, he granted Cleat his last wish.

Holt did not try to conceal himself as he walked through the overgrowth toward the horses. He had an easy time finding them in the darkness. Whoever the dead men had left behind to watch them was having a tough time keeping them under control. The gunfire and the smell of death had spooked them.

The clouds that had been covering the half-moon for

most of the night slowly parted and showed Holt a young man he judged to still be in his teens on foot, grappling with four horses pulling away from him.

They were rearing back, eyes wide, and thinking about kicking out with their forelegs.

He could read First National Bank of Devil's Gulch stamped on the satchels around their saddle horns.

"You're covered, son," Holt said as he stepped out of the overgrowth. "Keep your hands where I can see them, and you might just live through this night."

But the boy was too preoccupied with the horses to pay him much mind. "If you shoot, you'd be doing me a favor. You can wrestle with these damned things for once."

Holt kept his pistol on the boy while he held his left hand out to the largest of the four horses. "Easy, boy, easy. It's all over now."

The animal reluctantly stopped fussing and its nostrils flared to smell the air. It backed away from Holt's hand as he gently laid it upon its muzzle. "There you go. See that? Nothing to be afraid of. That's a good boy."

The horse blew air and scrapped at the ground but calmed under Holt's touch. The other three did the same.

The boy gave the reins some slack as the fight slowly went out of the mounts. "You know how to handle horses, mister."

"Pistols too." Holt pulled the boy's Colt from his holster and tucked it into this belt. "You'd do well to remember that while you bring this bunch over toward the fire."

The boy did not turn to face him as he got the other animals under control. "You kill them?"

"I did."

"Cleat too?"

"Had no choice."

The boy turned on him and found himself looking down the barrel of the Remington.

"You think that scares me?" Tears streamed down the boy's face, but his voice was steady. "You've just killed all the kin I've got in this world, mister. What makes you think I've got anything to live for?"

Holt admired the boy's courage, but not enough to let him speak to him that way. He brought the barrel across his nose, breaking it easily.

The boy dropped to the ground, both hands to his bleeding nose.

The horses' reins were free, but they did not move.

"Keep a civil tongue and I won't do that again," Holt said. "Next time, I'll break your jaw. Now get up and move these horses to the fire like I told you."

He made no effort to help the boy get to his feet. The horses didn't shy away from the smell of blood and made no effort to fight the young man as he led them through the overgrowth.

Holt held the Remington on the boy as he picketed the horses alongside Holt's gelding. The five mounts quickly forgot about the humans and began munching the grass at their hooves.

The prisoner set the bank satchels on the ground where Holt told him and their saddles too.

His task done; the boy looked down at the three dead men around the campfire. "After all they've been through, they get killed by an old man in Colorado."

Holt grinned. He was not quite thirty yet, but imagined he looked about ready for the rocking chair to a young man of such tender years. "If it takes the sting out of it any, they died as well as could be expected under the circumstances."

The boy looked up at him. "From where I'm standing, looks like you kill pretty well too."

Holt did admire the boy's spirit. "Turn around, get on your knees and put your hands behind you. I'm gonna have to tie you up for the night."

The boy did as he was told, and Holt grabbed the rope from his saddle next to the campfire. He holstered his Remington and bound the boy's hands and feet, giving him enough slack to stretch out his legs if he decided to try to sleep. Holt was nothing if not a considerate jailer.

He dragged over one of the saddles and pulled the boy over to it. "You can use that as a pillow if you want."

"And what about my damned nose?"

Holt kicked some dirt in the boy's face, which made him cough. "Remember what I told you about a civil tongue. Any more swearing, and I won't be happy. Get some sleep. We're heading back to Devil's Gulch at first light. You'll need all the rest you can get for the ride ahead."

"After you bury the money, I reckon."

"Money's coming with us," Holt said as he got to the ground and found his blanket. "We'll be returning it to its rightful owners. I'll see to it your kin get a proper Christian burial, for all the good it'll do them."

He could feel the boy looking at him in the darkness. "You mean you're just gonna give it back? There's over five thousand in those bags, mister. Free and clear. Why would you go and do a fool thing like that?"

Holt shrugged down until his head rested against the saddle just right. "Because it's my job."

"You a lawman?"

"Not at present," Holt admitted, "but come this time tomorrow, I will be."

He could feel the boy's eyes still on him as he began to think about sleep.

"You sure are a strange one, mister."

"Light sleeper too. You try anything, and I'll put you down for your trouble. Now shut your mouth and get some sleep. We've got a big day ahead of us."

Holt closed his eyes and allowed himself to drift off to sleep. The presence of the dead men around him did not bother him. He had become comfortable with death a long time ago.

CHAPTER 2

H olt saw the townspeople of Devil's Gulch watch him from the boardwalks as he rode past them with four horses in tow. Three of the horses carried dead men slumped across their saddles. The fourth had a sullen young man whose hands were bound behind him.

Holt heard them whisper as they pointed at the money satchels slung across the horses. He knew, human nature being what it was, the attraction of death and money was difficult to resist.

The clock tower of the First National Bank had just struck eight o'clock as Holt climbed down from his horse and wrapped its reins around the hitching rail in front of the town jail.

He pulled the lead rope closer to him and knotted it around the rail before pulling his prisoner down from the saddle. The boy landed on both feet but staggered until Holt held him upright.

"Lucky I didn't fall out of the saddle along the way," the boy said as Holt pushed him up on the boardwalk.

"Sure are. I would've dragged you if you had."

Holt grabbed him by the arm and steered him toward the jail, but found the door was locked. He knocked on the door as a small cluster of townspeople gathered on either side of him, careful to keep their distance.

"Afraid you won't find anyone in there, mister," an old woman told him. "Haven't had any formal law around here for a couple of months or more."

Holt was annoyed. Hadn't they received his letter? "Any idea where I can find Mayor Chapman or Mr. Mullen?"

One of the men on the other side of the group spoke up. "Too early for them to be at the county hall where they ought to be. Best place to look for them is the Blue Bottle Saloon just down the street. The mayor's partial to the breakfast they serve."

"Among other things," the old woman said to the laughter of all.

But Holt did not laugh. He pointed to the man who had spoken up. "You stay here and keep an eye on the money. If anyone so much as touches those bags, I'll hold you responsible."

"I ain't no lawman, mister," the man protested. "Besides, I've got to—"

Any remaining protest died in his throat under Holt's glare.

The man looked away. "I'll look after them. You have my word."

"Anyone touches them, I'll have your hide nailed to this door."

Holt pulled his prisoner along with him as the crowd parted to allow them to pass.

The Blue Bottle Saloon was easy enough to spot. The sign swinging in the morning breeze told him where the place was. The blue-tinged glass of the large window confirmed it. He had never seen a saloon with such thick, oddly colored glass before, but reminded himself that he had never been to this part of the country before.

He opened the saloon door with his free hand and pushed his prisoner in ahead of him. The boy tripped on the threshold and the sawdust on the floor caused him to hit face-first, narrowly missing a spittoon beside the bar.

Holt shut the door behind him and left the young man on the floor as he looked over the customers who looked back at him. Five men sat at a table in the back playing cards. A soiled dove who looked like she wanted to go to bed was rubbing one of the gambler's shoulders. She seemed more attracted to the pile of chips in front of him than his person.

The rest of the tables were occupied by men who appeared to be eating breakfast and enjoying mugs of piping hot coffee.

Holt called out, "I'm looking for Mayor Chapman or Joseph Mullen. I was told I could find them here."

One of the men at the table to the left of the door cleared his throat and wiped his chin with a napkin as he got to his feet. Holt pegged him to be on the north side of forty and wore faded clothes that had once been fancy. They struggled to hide his growing belly. "I'm Chapman, sir. And just who might you be?"

Holt looked at him and the other three men around the table. They all resembled the mayor in their own way. Middle-aged and worn the way frontier life could wear down a man if he let it.

"You sent for me, Mr. Mayor," Holt said. "If you don't know who I am, then we've got nothing to talk about."

The mayor clasped his hands together. "Mr. Holt, I presume."

"Your presumption is correct."

Holt stepped over his prisoner and shook the mayor's

hand. "Delighted to finally meet you, sir. Absolutely delighted."

Holt looked at the other men at the table, who also began to rise in greeting. A stern-looking man with a full head of brown hair and mustache streaked with gray was next to greet him.

"And I'm Joseph Mullen, head of the Devil's Gulch Vigilance Committee. It was my letter that reached you, Mr. Holt."

Holt shook hands with him and found them course and callused. He was a working man, unlike the mayor. "Glad to know you, Mr. Mullen."

Mullen stepped aside and gestured to a thin, balding man to his left. "This is Anthony Cassidy, the owner of the Blue Bottle Saloon. Tony, this is that Mr. Holt we've been talking about."

Holt noted Cassidy's fallow skin and pock-marked face. He looked like a flesh peddler. Holt had never held such men in high regard.

"Welcome to the Blue Bottle Saloon, Mr. Holt," Cassidy said as they shook hands. "Your reputation precedes you."

Holt released his hand. "And what reputation might that be?"

Cassidy tried a smile as he shrugged. "You reputation for law and order, of course. Everyone's heard about 'Gunner Holt,' even here."

Holt did not smile. "You don't get to call me that. Not now. Not ever. Understand?"

The mayor cleared his throat again and tried to break the awkward mood that had settled over them. "And last but not least, this is Dr. Ralph Klassen. The finest doctor this side of the Mississippi. We're lucky to have him."

The doctor was leaner and younger than his breakfast companions. He was clean-shaven except for a pair of healthy black mutton chops that complimented the rest of his hair. "Glad to make your acquaintance, Mr. Holt."

Holt returned his strong handshake as the mayor grabbed a chair from another table and slid it over for him. "Have a seat, Mr. Holt. I imagine you're tired after your long journey. Where is it you came in from again? Chicago, was it?"

"St. Louis," Holt corrected him as he sat down, but offered no further explanation. In his experience, the less people knew about him, the better all around.

"Splendid," Mayor Chapman said as he and the others resumed their seats. "Simply splendid. I was going to say that I hope your travels were uneventful, but your friend on the floor seems to indicate just the opposite."

Dr. Klassen looked around Mullen at the prisoner trying to get his knees under him. "Don't you think you ought to help him up?"

"Why?" Holt asked. "He was with the bunch who robbed the bank last night."

Mullen had picked up his fork to resume his breakfast but dropped it. "How do you know that?"

"On account of them bragging about what they were going to do at every cow town between here and Kansas," Holt told him. "And because he and his friends had satchels with your bank's name stenciled on the side of them across their saddles."

Mullen placed his napkin on the table as if it were an afterthought. "You saw these men?"

"They tried to jump my camp last night," Holt told him. "Got themselves killed for their trouble." He gestured toward the prisoner on the floor. "He's the last of them. You'll find his friends across their saddles in front of the jail along with the money they stole. I left a townie in charge of the money, but I wouldn't put much stock in his 'vigilance' if I was you."

Mullen and Dr. Klassen got up from the table and ran outside, practically leaping over the prisoner as they did.

Holt smiled at Mayor Chapman's stunned expression. "Nothing like found money to ruin a man's appetite." He pulled Mullen's plate over to him and was glad to see the fried eggs were still warm. He could not remember the last time he'd enjoyed fried eggs and began to dig in.

He looked at Cassidy after he downed a mouthful of food and reached for Mullen's coffee. "Not bad, Cassidy. I can see why this place is so popular."

Mayor Chapman laughed and clapped his hands again in delight as Holt continued eating. "By God, sir. You are remarkable. You're not even hired yet and you've already foiled a bank robbery."

"Now let's not get ahead of ourselves, Blair," Cassidy said. "He didn't exactly foil it. He simply caught them while they were on the run." He looked at Holt. "You said they tried to jump your camp last night, Mr. Holt?"

"I did." He drank some of Mullen's coffee. It was luke-warm, but better than the mud he had made for himself at camp. No matter how he tried, he had never gotten the knack of making a decent pot of coffee. "Didn't go as well as they'd hoped."

"There you have it straight from the source," Cassidy said. "He didn't stop them. They practically jumped right into his lap. All he had to do was pull the trigger. Anyone would've done the same under the circumstances."

Holt set his mug on the table. "That what you would've done, Mr. Cassidy? Or are you the type who would've had it done?" He looked over at the saloon owner as if he was making up his mind, though he had already formed his opinion of the man the moment he had seen him. "Don't trouble yourself with an answer. You're the type who'd have it done."

The mayor tried to interrupt, but Cassidy's dark eyes narrowed. "Why'd you camp outside of town instead of riding straight in? Maybe you could've been here to stop the robbery before it happened?"

Holt slid his fork into the fried egg. "Unless I miss my guess, those boys are the Turnbull Gang. They've been bragging about hitting your bank at every watering hole from here to Kansas, like I told you. These boys hit banks at night, hoping it'll cut down on their chances of being shot. I don't know this town, Mr. Cassidy, but I know the wilderness. I knew they'd be hotfooting it out of here after dark, so I built my campfire nice and high, so they'd have no choice but to see it from a distance. I figured they'd see it and ride in, looking for a place to spend the night. Looks like I was right."

Mayor Chapman sat back, looking very pleased.

Cassidy continued to glare. "And if you'd been wrong?"

Holt shrugged. "I don't concern myself much about 'ifs,' Mr. Cassidy. I concentrate on what is and what's right in front of me. Makes life easier."

He took a final swig of coffee and placed the mug on the table. "Take that mug, for instance. It's empty. I don't fret about it being empty for long because I know you're gonna get up and fill it for me. And you're not gonna spit in it, either, because I'll know it if you do. And you won't like what happens after that."

Cassidy pushed himself back from the table and stood up fast enough to knock the chair backward. He glared down at Holt, who continued to chew his eggs unbothered. "Is that so, Mr. Holt?"

Holt nodded as he chewed. "You said my reputation preceded me, so yeah, it's so. Come to think of it, bring the pot and leave it here. The mayor and I have business to discuss, and I don't discuss business in front of flesh peddlers."

Holt watched Cassidy run through the same litany of emotions he had seen dozens of other men run through in his same position. First, they were insulted and given to doing something about it. Holt could not possibly be as good as the rumors had made him out to be. Maybe it was time to put that reputation to the test?

But the longer he looked at Holt, and saw the man did not look away, Cassidy began to remember all the stories he had heard about him. About what he had done in the war and since. About the order he had brought to New Orleans after the war. About the nickname he had earned as The Moses of Missouri for the river of blood he had waded through in Jefferson City.

Even if half the stories he had heard about what Holt had done in Kansas were lies, there was enough truth in them to give a man pause. There were other, more grue-some tales a man like Cassidy did not want to believe about Holt, but he had seen truth in the eyes of the men who had spoken of them.

The full weight of all those tall tales had eventually settled on the men who stood where Cassidy found him-self standing right now. Somewhere between the past and the present. Between life and death.

Which was why Cassidy's shoulders sagged before he walked away from the table and went to the back of the saloon.

"Don't forget about that coffee," Holt called after him.

Cassidy stopped midway up the bar, before continuing his retreat.

Mayor Chapman brought a hand to his face to hide his

smile. "Good God, Mr. Holt. I heard you're a hard man, but you do take chances, sir."

Holt went back to digging into his eggs. "If I can't handle a whoremonger, you wouldn't have sent for me in the first place." He glanced at Chapman. "You get the package I sent you?"

Chapman cleared his throat again and dug an envelope from inside his coat. "I did indeed, sir. I wanted to discuss a few of the terms you laid out in your document before I sign it."

"No need for discussion," Holt said between bites. "Either you sign it as is, or you don't. That's it."

The mayor unfolded the document and placed it between them on the table. "I wouldn't exactly say I'm a lawyer, Mr. Holt, but I know something of legal matters and every document between two parties is always subject to negotiation."

Holt glanced at the document. "Not that one. Says so in the letter I sent along with it. The terms are nonnegotiable, binding, and final for everyone involved. And if you read my section of the document, it's not just a contract, it's an oath to protect this town to the best of my ability."

"According to how you see fit," Chapman said. "You're asking me to cede full authority to you without oversight."

"For the duration of the contract, which is for two years and subject to extension," Holt said. "If we part ways before then, you pay me the balance of the contract and I'll be on my way."

"That part is more than fair," the mayor said. "In fact, I expected a man of your caliber to charge much more. But this document is hardly democratic. Why, I doubt Napoleon had such terms when he became emperor of France."

"I'm not Napoleon, Mr. Chapman, and Devil's Gulch is a long way from France." He finished the last of the eggs and wiped his mouth with a clean part of Mullen's napkin. "You've got a nice, growing town here in need of some tough rules. Your bank got robbed last night and it's thanks to me that you got your money back."

"And we're grateful to you for that," the mayor started.

But Holt kept talking. "I brought the men who robbed the bank into town across their saddles and the last of them is lying on the floor over there like a dead roach."

The young Turnbull boy cut loose with a string of curses, which Holt ignored. "That's not the first time that bank's been hit, and it won't be the last, either. Devil's Gulch is getting a reputation among the wrong people as an easy touch. You hire me, you hire my way of doing things. My way will make sure word spreads far and wide that this town is a place that men like the one squirming on the floor over there should avoid. Things being how they are, it'll take a good two years for that word to spread. So, either you sign that document right now, or I get on my horse and ride out to a town that'll agree to my terms with no questions asked. I've got a saddlebag full of letters just like yours and I'll be happy to show them to you if you need convincing."

Holt looked around for a waiter to bring him more coffee while the mayor started and stopped himself from saying something half a dozen times.

Holt was about to get up and see where Cassidy was with the coffee, when the mayor finally managed to work out what he was trying to say. "If I were to sign a document of this scope, there'd be questions raised. Questions that would be difficult to answer."

"Send them my way if you want." Holt watched a large, surly-looking man he took to be the bartender come out from the back with a pot of coffee. "All the answers they need can be found on the backs of those horses out there.

Along with the money they lost. In my experience, people are awfully forgiving when their money's returned to them, especially when it doesn't cost them anything."

The bartender lumbered over to the table and plunked the coffeepot down on top of the document. "There's your coffee."

As he walked away, Holt said, "Pour it for me."

The bartender turned around slowly. "What did you just say to me?"

"You heard me. Do it. Now."

The bartender looked toward the back of the saloon where Cassidy had gone but saw no sign of his boss. He stomped back over to the table, took hold of the cup and poured some into Holt's mug before setting the pot back down and walking away.

Holt stopped him by saying, "Now drink it."

The bartender turned quickly only to find himself face-to-face with Holt. He knew the barman had not heard him get up, much less know he was standing there. He took a step back when Holt held the mug out to him. "I said drink."

The bartender's eyes flickered. "I don't drink coffee."

"You do today." The coffee mug did not move. "I want to make sure it's fresh. That you didn't put anything in it, like maybe a dead rat or something."

Holt heard the mayor's chair creak as the man sat farther back in it, watching intently.

The bartender looked at the mug, then at Holt before taking the mug from him. He leaned over and took the pot too. "Come to think of it, the pot's been sitting there for a while. I'll go brew up something fresh."

Holt smiled. "You do that. Awfully kind of you."

He waited until the bartender went back in the kitchen

before he resumed his seat at the table. He took Dr. Klassen's mug and frowned when he saw it was only half full. He drank from it anyway. "Never met a doctor who didn't live on coffee and tobacco."

Mayor Chapman was still ruffled by what had just transpired with the bartender. "You don't actually think he put anything in the coffee, do you?"

Holt shrugged. "The pot hit the table kind of heavy. And I heard something slosh around inside of it that I doubt was sugar."

The mayor closed his eyes and held his napkin to his mouth. "Good Lord. I heard it too."

Holt suppressed a laugh. Chapman was obviously a delicate man. It could be fun to make him uneasy every so often.

The mayor swallowed down whatever had risen in his throat. "That's a man you should be mindful of, Mr. Holt. Bobby Simpson doesn't just work here. He runs the place for Cassidy. You don't want to cross him."

Holt set his mug aside. If Simpson was what passed for a hard case in this town, it would be the easiest job he'd ever had. "I'll keep that in mind." He tapped on the document. "Speaking of crossing things, you've got some t's to cross and i's to dot on your signature here. Sign it, Mr. Chapman. We both know you don't have much of a choice."

The mayor dabbed at his forehead with his napkin. "I can't say that I like it, but I'll sign it. I don't have a pen with me now, but if you'll come with me, I'll sign the copies over at County Hall."

Holt was glad that much was settled. He did not like the idea of getting back on the trail so soon after what had happened the previous night. "For now, a handshake will suffice."

Holt held out his hand to him and the mayor shook it. "Please don't make me regret this, Mr. Holt. I'm putting quite a bit of faith in your abilities and your judgment."

"Your faith is well-placed," Holt said. "Now sit back and relax. We've got some coffee coming."

The mayor sat up in his seat and looked down at the young Turnbull boy who was still on the floor. "What about him?"

Holt did not have to turn around to hear him squirming on the floor. "Don't worry about him. He'll keep."

CHAPTER 3

After they had signed both copies of the agreement in the mayor's office at County Hall, Holt reluctantly agreed to let the mayor walk with him downstairs to the crowd that awaited them on the street.

"I told you I'm not one for grand speeches or public gestures," Holt reminded him. "I prefer to let my actions do my talking for me."

"I don't blame you," Mayor Chapman chuckled, "but politicians live by them. Mayors most of all. And, as Devil's Gulch also happens to be the county seat, you'll be serving as both the town marshal and the county sheriff. I'd say that requires some manner of ceremony, don't you?"

Holt did not think so but kept his opinion to himself. Riding into Devil's Gulch with three dead men, a prisoner, and bags of stolen money had not exactly been a subtle entrance. Besides, going along with Chapman's request was a small price to pay to remain on the man's good side. Holt did not care about being popular among the townsfolk, but the mayor was the only one who could void his contract and release him from his oath.

That made him the one man in town Holt had to please.

He did not plan on deferring to him much—if at all—in the future, but there would be a time to make a stand. This was not it.

Chapman said as they descended the stairs, "I'm afraid I'll also have to ask you to set aside some time for our local reporter from *The Devil's Gulch Daily.*" Mayor Chapman added, "His name is Bill Cook and he's a good sort as far as newspaper men go. Tries to be fair when he can, like most men who have ink in their veins, he's never been one to allow the truth to get in the way of a good story."

Holt had never met a newspaper man he didn't want to shoot. They had been the fools who had saddled him with nicknames like "The Moses of Missouri" and "Gunner Holt." Monikers that put a target on a man's back whether he wanted it or not. Names Holt had been forced to defend in hopes of living.

Mayor Chapman spoke over Holt's concerns. "All of this sounds far more onerous than it really is. All you need to do is stand there and smile and be on your way after I hand you the keys to the jail. Leave all the questions to me. In fact, I think we'd both prefer it that way."

He would get no argument from Holt on that score. But Holt knew it was never that simple. "And what about the questions this reporter of yours asks me later on?"

Chapman patted his arm. "I'll not restrain your range of expression. All I ask is that you make every attempt to be civil to him. And if you can't be civil, then I ask you to be silent."

Holt had been expecting Chapman to force the issue and was pleasantly surprised he did not. Perhaps there was more grit to this soft man with the ready smile than he thought.

"However," the mayor added as they reached the bottom of the staircase, "I hope you won't be offended if I make a suggestion. And it *is* a suggestion, not a request."

Holt braced himself for disappointment. "Go ahead."

"Your choice in clothing is rather bland," the mayor said. "I was hoping you might be willing to entertain the idea of dressing in a more formal fashion."

Holt had not been expecting a conversation about his clothing. He looked down at his brown boots and brown pants and brown jacket and brown duster and caught the mayor's meaning. They were all the same—faded and dusty—including his weather-beaten hat. Only his holster was a darker shade of brown from all the use it had received since the war.

Holt realized he had never paid much attention to his clothing before. "I've never been a dandy. Always seemed to have more important things to spend my money on."

"Well, I happen to know of a good haberdasher in town that'll be more than willing to give you a generous discount on any items you purchase."

Holt was beginning to catch on. "That place wouldn't be called Chapman's Haberdashery, would it?"

The mayor's booming laugh was all the answer he needed as he linked his arm and led him to the front door of County Hall. "Yes, Mr. Holt, I think we'll get along just fine."

The boardwalk and the street were filled with people crowded around the entrance of the county hall.

Holt did his best not to frown, but as a frown happened to be his natural expression, he was sure he did a poor job of it.

Mayor Chapman held up his hands and asked the crowd to be quiet. "Ladies and gentlemen of Devil's Gulch, I have the honor of introducing you to a man who needs no introduction. You've undoubtedly heard of John Holt's reputation as a man who has tamed some of the wildest towns and has restored order to the most lawless places. We are fortunate to have been able to hire him to bring peace and prosperity to our humble hamlet here on the frontier."

As Chapman went on with his speech, Holt looked over the crowd that had assembled around them. The jail was directly across the street from the county hall, and he saw his horse was still hitched to the rail. The other horses he had used to bring in the dead Turnbull boys were gone.

Up in his office, Chapman had told him Joe Mullen and a member of the Devil's Gulch Vigilance Committee, had seen to that. They had also taken the Turnbull boy to the jail while Holt and the mayor made their agreement official.

The townspeople who looked up at him now resembled all the other people he had seen in many other towns after the war. Young and old alike with tired, drawn expressions from years spent trying to carve a living from the wilderness. Life was just as hard for these people in town as it was for the men working in the mines or clearing timber in the hills. The railroad was coming to the territory and the hope of riches that it would bring was evident on the faces of the people looking at him now. People who were counting on him to bring law and order to their town once the world discovered it was there.

Holt knew the same law and order he would bring to their lives would ultimately cause them to hate him. People liked the idea of discipline until it began to affect them.

That was when they convinced themselves that Holt had solved their troubles and it was time for him to move on. He hoped Mayor Chapman would back him when the time came or be willing to pay his handsome sum should they decide to cut him loose.

A sum he would exact in full, one way or the other.

Holt was snapped back into the present when Chapman laid a heavy hand on his shoulder as he said, "And without further ado, I present Sheriff John Holt with the keys to the jail and, by God, the keys to our fair town."

He thrust a ring of iron keys at him and pumped his right hand enthusiastically while the crowd applauded and cheered. Holt even managed to force a smile for their benefit.

"Speech!" some in the crowd began to shout. "Speech!"

The mayor stepped back and gestured for him to say something.

Holt had never considered himself much of an orator but saw no way to escape it. He cleared his throat and said, "You people have brought me here to enforce the law. I intend to do that to the best of my ability. I signed an oath to bring order to this town. I'm not here to make friends or run for office or be popular. Some of you are probably thinking you can win me over to your side. To make me see things your way. Maybe bend a little to your way of thinking. Don't waste your time. There's only one side I'm on." He pointed toward the county hall. "The law's side. I don't expect you to always like the way I do my job. Just know that I'll always do it as fairly and effectively as I see fit."

He felt a spark of pleasure as he watched the smiles fade from their faces. It meant they had heard him. "And many of you will hate me for it before long. That's to be expected. It won't stop me, and it won't change me. It'll just prove that I'm doing what you're paying me to do. Comply and we'll get along just fine. And know that anyone who gets in my way won't be there long."

The people started grumbling among themselves and he knew it was time to go. He nodded toward the jail across the street. "Now, if you'll excuse me, I've got a job to do. Any questions, you know where to find me."

The stunned crowd parted as he walked down the steps and went across the street to the jail. The time for talking had passed. It was time to get to work.

Holt found Mullen waiting for him in the jail. The chair of the Vigilance Committee was leaning against the largest of the two desks in the front office, enjoying a smoke. He smiled when he saw Holt walk through the door.

"Fine speech," Mullen said. "Won't make you very popular here in town, but I don't think you're looking to be popular."

"I said what needed to be said."

He walked past Mullen to the back of the jail where he imagined the cells were. He opened the iron door and found two rows of iron bars on either side of a wide aisle.

The Turnbull boy was on a cot in the last cell on the left side. His nose only bruised, not broken. He would not need Dr. Klassen's services while he awaited trial.

The young man sneered out at Holt as way of greeting as the sheriff walked to his cell and shook the door to make certain it was locked.

"Don't worry," Turnbull said. "I'm not going anywhere."

"No, you're not. Behave yourself and you'll be treated well. You've already seen what'll happen if you don't."

Turnbull cut loose with another stream of curses that was impressive for a man of such tender years. Holt walked back out into the jail and locked the iron door behind him. He knew he would never get used to the sound of the lock sliding home. It was the loneliest sound in the world and had sounded the same in every town he had worked. He hung the iron ring of keys on a peg beside the door.

"Yes, sir." Mullen grinned. "You certainly do come as advertised. I like it when a man lives up to his billing."

Holt hung his coat and hat on a peg on the wall beside the desk. "You've obviously got something on your mind, Mr. Mullen. Best come right out and say it. I'm anxious to get myself situated."

Mullen pushed himself off the desk as Holt took his seat and began going through the drawers of his desk. "You'll find your sheriff star in the top drawer. Had a fresh one struck out of silver from one of my very own mines. Figured we should start fresh, given as how the last sheriff we had tarnished it some."

Holt found it and took it in hand. It was gleaming silver and had *Sheriff—Devil's Gulch* engraved on it. He pinned it on his vest and resumed looking through the drawers.

"Not much for ceremony, are you, Sheriff?" Mullen observed.

"Not much of a dancer either," Holt told him. "Say what you've come to say or get out."

"So much for polite conversation." Mullen dropped his cigarette to the floor and crushed it under his boot. "I don't know how much Chapman told you up in his office just now, but I wanted to make sure you were clear on some things from the start. Devil's Gulch has all the promise of being a respectable town one day, but we've got plenty of rough edges that need to be hammered out."

"You already told me that in our correspondence," Holt reminded him. "Contrary to popular belief, I know how to read."

"I expect you do," Mullen said, "what with you having been a colonel in the Union Army and all."

Holt looked up at him. "That was a field command. Lost it after the surrender. Mustered out as a major, which is better than I came in." Holt saw something in Mullen's face he did not like. "You a Southerner, Mullen?"

"I'm a businessman," he said. "Managed to find a way to ride out the war right here in Devil's Gulch. We had our share of trouble from blue and gray alike. As far as loyalties go, I'm a Gulcher to the core."

"That what y'all call yourselves?" Holt asked. "Gulchers? I like it."

"There it is again," Mullen observed. "That accent. It slips through every once in a while. Sounds Virginian to my ears."

"It is." Holt went back to searching his desk drawers. "And to answer your next question, yes, I fought for the Union against Virginia. I'd taken an oath to uphold the Constitution of the United States. Didn't see fit to break it just because my neighbors decided to do so."

He shut the last drawer on the left side and moved over to the right. "Same kind of oath I signed just now up in the mayor's office. And I intend to stick to it now just like I did back then. You and the rest of the Gulchers would do well to remember that in the days ahead."

"I have a feeling you won't let us forget it if we tried," Mullen said. "Mayor Chapman's a good man. A simple man who doesn't appreciate some of the eccentricities of town life."

"Meaning?"

"Meaning that Devil's Gulch is a complicated place, Sheriff. In all your remembering, you'd do well to remember that. It'll make your time here easier, especially for you."

Holt found a sheaf of papers in a drawer and hefted them out. "My predecessor wasn't big on paperwork, was he?"

"No need for it," Mullens said. "This town is the kind of place best governed by feel rather than formality. The quickest way between two points isn't always a straight line. It tends to wind a bit, like the road that'll lead you up to the top of one of those mountains out yonder."

"I like straight lines," Holt told him as he thumbed through the pile of papers. "I like paperwork too. Records give everything an official shine to it. Makes it easier to tell what happened in court. Guess the army taught me that."

"Some folks around here won't take kindly to that way of thinking, Sheriff. Folks like the McAdam widow, for instance. She runs the Railhead Saloon on the other end of town."

Holt did not recall reading about the McAdam widow in any of his correspondence from Chapman or Mullen. "Trying to poison the well on her already?"

"Don't let her feminine nature fool you," Mullen said. "She's as much of a stone-cold killer as any of the boys she's got working for her. Will slit your throat and take your boots faster than any road agent you ever saw. And she'll do it with a smile too. You won't even know you're dead until you're shaking hands with the devil."

Holt set the papers aside. "Friend of yours?"

"Hardly. As chairman of the Vigilance Committee, it won't do me much good by counting the town's least desirable citizen among my many friends. But you could say that I've managed to strike something of an agreement between us over the years."

Holt figured it had been something like that. "How so?"

"She keeps things to a dull roar and my men turn a blind eye to some of her more unsavory activities." He offered a modest shrug. "It's not perfect, but it's worked so far."

Holt scratched his chin. "Got you on the dole, has she?"

Mullen demurred. "Like I said, we have an understanding. Same kind of understanding we've got with all the other shopkeepers and saloons in town. My committee performs a valuable service to this town, Sheriff. We keep the peace and keep the wild horses on a short tether. It's an arrangement I'd like to see continue."

Holt sat back in his chair and crossed his legs. He had not formed an opinion of Mullen when he had read the letters that he and Mayor Chapman had sent him, asking him to come to Devil's Gulch. He had not had time to form an opinion of the man before he raced out of the Blue Bottle Saloon earlier that morning.

But he had begun to form an opinion of him now. And the more Mullen talked, the less Holt liked him. "My predecessor in on this agreement of yours? Frank Peters, I believe his name was."

"It still is," Mullen said. "I'm sure you'll be making his acquaintance soon enough. He's the top man in the McAdam woman's stable. He went to work for her after we ran him out of office."

Holt caught that. "Got too greedy for you, did he? Asked for too large a slice of the pie for your liking."

"That was part of it," Mullen allowed, "but not all of it. He's a disreputable man and as crooked as that mountain trail I mentioned earlier. The man has no honor, and I won't trust a man without honor."

Holt swiped at a spot of dust on his leg. "I've seen honorable men do some mighty dishonorable things in my time. And I've seen wretches do the most honorable, selfless deeds imaginable. It all depends on how you look at it. And the circumstances."

"There's only one way to look at a man like Frank Peters, Sheriff. And that's constantly. Never take your eyes off him. He's every bit as dangerous as that old hag who pays him."

Holt had not paid much attention to mentions of Peters in their correspondence. But Mullen had made him curious. Not only about Peters or the McAdam widow, but about other things.

"To hear you tell it, you've got this town tamped down pretty tight. Why'd you agree to hire me in the first place? Sounds like you're paying me a lot to do very little."

"You're good at what you do," Mullen said. "Having you in town will be good for business and, like I said, I'm first and foremost a businessman. Got myself a good ranch started and a stake in some of the mines hereabouts. Copper and silver mostly. A man of your caliber might add a little class to the place and, hopefully, some investment in the future."

Holt was beginning to see things clearly. "If I didn't know better, I'd think you're telling me to sit easy and not make any waves in the tub."

"Nonsense. We're paying you good money to do an important job. We want you to do exactly that, just within certain boundaries."

"Boundaries you set."

Mullen's grin broadened. "Boundaries set by time and tradition."

Holt winked. "Never been too good at boundaries. Never been too good at understanding what some might call the subtilties of polite society either."

He slowly stood up and Mullen's grin faded. It was not a challenge, just claiming the area around him.

The two men both stood a shade over six feet tall, virtually the same height.

Holt said, "Want to know something else I've never been fond of?"

"Can't wait to hear it."

"Vigilance committees. Yours is disbanded, as of right now. Enforcing the law in Devil's Gulch is my job, Mullen. Not yours or anyone else's. If I need a posse, I'll raise one. If I need help, I'll ask for it. You and your men have served their purpose. I'm sure your fellow Gulchers are grateful. I'll even recommend to the mayor that he throws a parade in your honor. But the law's my stock-in-trade. Mine and mine alone. Here in Devil's Gulch and in the rest of the county. You'd do well to remember that when you walk out of here today."

Mullen slowly shook his head. "Real sorry to hear that, Sheriff. The Gulch can be a friendly place if you let it, but it can be a mighty lonely place too. You're about to find that out if we leave things this way."

"Then the sooner you leave, the sooner I'll begin my education."

Mullen touched the brim of his hat and turned to leave. Holt expected him to stop, maybe say something before he left.

But he did not stop, and the two men had already said what needed to be said. Holt was glad Mullen had not stopped to ruin the moment.

He enjoyed making a new enemy and it would have been a shame to spoil it.

CHAPTER 4

After Mayor Chapman stopped by to check on him, Holt gave him a list of things he needed. The first was to remove the second desk and replace it with a cot he'd need to guard the prisoner during the night. The next was for someone to arrange for his horse to be stabled at the livery once he had taken his saddlebags and rifle from its back.

He asked after the horses he had brought in with him and requested that they not be sold until he had a chance to look them over. He wanted to take a closer look at the spirited animal that had given the Turnbull boy so much trouble. His mare had seen a good bit of the war and too much of the trail in the years since. She had been a good animal and deserved as good a life as Holt could secure for her. He would see to it once he handed off the Turnbull boy to the territorial sheriff when he next swung through town.

His next request of the mayor was to find another place besides the Blue Bottle Saloon that could send over three meals a day for both him and his prisoner. The mayor said

Le Café had the best food in town and would arrange for meals to be sent over with the owner, one Gene Roche.

Once the mayor left, Holt went about fixing the jailhouse to his liking. He took down the moth-eaten shade from the small window and threw it out back on the scrap pile. He moved the remaining heavy desk to the center of the room so that he not only faced the door but barred the way back to the cells. The mayor had insisted on having a bed brought over from the Greenwood Hotel, which fit perfectly in the corner and stopped well shy of the doors to the cells.

Holt decided the desk and its placement would come in handy if someone tried to rush the jail. Bitter experience had taught him the benefit of having ready cover in a crisis, especially while he slept.

He looked up when he heard a light rapping on the front door. He did not go for his gun but was glad it was still on his hip. "Who is it?"

He heard a delicate female voice through the door. "Dinner's here."

Holt unbolted the door and opened it a crack to see who was on the other side. He found a slender Negro woman standing there with a basket hanging on her arm.

He opened the door all the way and allowed the young woman to enter. "You from Gene's place?"

"I am Jean," she told him as she entered and set her basket on the desk. "I own the café."

Holt had been expecting a "Gene" as in "Eugene." The presence of a woman took him completely by surprise. "My apologizes, ma'am. I was under the impression you'd be a man."

She looked at him and placed a hand on her hip. She

had bright brown eyes under her white bonnet. "You still under that impression?"

He shook his head. "Hardly."

She went back to her basket and opened it. "Just like I'm hardly a *ma'am*. I'm only twenty and near enough in age to be your daughter, I reckon."

Holt had always looked older than he was. It had been that way when he had enlisted. And four years of constant blood and violence had not served to make him appear any younger. "I'm only about ten years older than you, so that's doubtful."

She took a loaf of fresh-baked bread from the basket and Holt's mouth began to water. He had not smelled anything so appealing, much less had anything but hardtack and bacon since hitting the trail to Devil's Gulch.

She took out two plates and set them on the table. She then removed a small pot and began to divide chicken and rice on both plates. "You want more for yourself than the prisoner or you want it split even?"

"Even's fine with me." Holt had found well-fed prisoners were more likely to cooperate.

She began to divide the portions appropriately. She had an elegant, yet efficient way about her that Holt found appealing. "You the new sheriff around here? The one they call John Holt?"

"I am," he admitted. "Let me guess. You haven't heard good things about me."

She shook her head. "Gulchers don't have a good word for anyone who's not a Gulcher. Why, they'd speak ill of the good Lord himself if he showed up in town one day, not that there's much chance in that. This is a godless town, John Holt. Always has been and I was born here.

Wasn't much more than a mining camp back then. In some ways, I guess it still is."

He folded his arms and leaned against the wall. "You're the third person today to give me a completely different version of this place." He was careful about mentioning names. Jean might own Le Café, but, in his experience, eating places were notorious dens of gossip. "One man told me this was a decent town. Another told me it's got its problems. Now you're telling me it's something straight out of the Old Testament."

Jean shrugged slender shoulders. "Guess all that means is that this town is a lot like life. It's what you make of it."

She finished putting her pan back in the basket and placed her dishtowels on top of it. "I can bring you a pail of beer if you want later, but I've been told it's not very good. I can talk to the owner of the Railhead to bring some over for you if you want."

But Holt made it a practice to stay away from drink, even beer, while guarding a prisoner. "Thanks, but we'll stick to coffee tonight."

She slid the empty basket on her arm and looked at him closely as she turned around. "You a southern man, John Holt?"

He nodded. "I was born in Virginia but fought for the Union if it means anything to you."

"Don't mean much to me one way or the other," she said. "Southern men have to eat, same as Northerners. Don't have too many customers from the South in my place, though." The Negro woman smiled. "Must have something to do with my cooking."

Holt found himself smiling—really smiling—for the first time all day. "From what I can see, it's their loss."

He thought she might be close to smiling herself, but

she tossed her head back as she swept toward the jailhouse door. "I'll be back in the morning with breakfast at nine o'clock. Best answer when I knock because, if you don't, I'll just leave the basket out front. I won't be responsible for what happens if some scoundrel comes along and takes it. The town's paying for three meals a day and three meals is what you'll get. Whoever eats it doesn't matter to me."

"Don't worry," he said as he went to the door and opened it for her. "I'll be here. Looking forward to it too."

She looked at him a final time as she walked out the door. "Hope you don't expect me to treat you like I owe you something, John Holt. Like I said, I was born here and born free. Your war didn't do me any favors."

"Your fine cooking will be favor enough," he said. "And thank you."

He stood in the doorway and watched her walk along the boardwalk back toward her café. It was already going on full dark by then and he quickly lost track of her among the lights spilling out onto the street from the few businesses that were still open.

Holt stood alone in the doorway and looked over the town that was now under his care. The street was much too dark for his liking. He'd talk to Mayor Chapman about putting up torches or oil lamps to cast some light in the evening hours. People tended to be more mindful of their actions when they risked being seen.

He would also make it his business to get to know Jean Roche from Le Café. He not only liked the way she cooked, but the way she thought. The fact she was easy on the eyes might make the task before him even more enjoyable.

For despite all his bluster about independence, John Holt

knew he would need allies in town to give him information from time to time. To help him make up his mind about who was who and what was happening in Devil's Gulch. One man could only see so much, even if that one man was John Holt. He had never been shy about admitting his limitations, even if only to himself.

He was about to go back inside to feed his prisoner when he heard a single gunshot echo from somewhere on the street. Not on the street itself. It had been too dull for that. More likely from one of the buildings across the thoroughfare. His eyes fixed on the dull light of a saloon in the direction of where he had seen Jean walking.

He shut the jailhouse door as he drew his Remington and ran toward the saloon. Dinner would have to wait.

As Holt got closer to the place, he saw the sign out front read *Railhead Saloon*. It was the same place Jean had mentioned only a few moments before. He heard a commotion inside and pushed his way through the batwing doors.

The saloon was packed with men at the tables and standing at the bar. Everyone was looking up the stairs, but none of them seemed curious enough to go up there.

Holt spoke to a gambler seated closest to the door. "That shot come from upstairs?"

The man did not look up from his cards. "Appears so, mister. Sounds like one of the girls got themselves in some trouble."

Holt pushed his way through the crowd of men who were standing around doing nothing. He took the stairs two at a time; his head up and his pistol leading the way. When he reached the top, he found all the doors open and the hall filled with sporting ladies in various stages of undress. Whatever modesty they still had was forgotten as they clamored around a single room in the middle of the hall.

"Make way," Holt called out, not bothering to announce himself as the sheriff. The star pinned on his vest was plain enough for them to see and the ladies complied.

He pushed his way into the room and found a sobbing, half-naked woman cringing in the corner being tended to by an older woman with a shawl around her shoulders.

The crying woman had a smoking pistol in her hand.

"There, there, Cassie," the woman soothed her. "You ain't in no kind of trouble at all. We'll see to that."

Holt stepped around the woman in the shawl and took the pistol from the sobbing woman before either knew he was there.

The older woman in the shawl stood and put herself between Holt and the woman as she attempted to push him away. "Who the hell do you think you are?" she seethed. "Get out of here!"

Holt ignored her as he looked at the man who had been shot. His body was slumped on the floor. A large hole in his chest where his heart used to be. His eyes vacant in death. Holt followed the dead man's eyes. The last thing he had seen in this world was a chamber pot on the floor of a sporting house. . He knew death was not particular about where and when it visited.

He noted the man had a belt wrapped around his right hand.

The matron stopped yelling at Holt when she saw the star on his vest. He looked down and saw the bruises and swelling beginning to rise beneath the frightened woman's tears.

He spoke to her when he said, "Besides the bruises, are you hurt?"

The woman sobbed as the matron spoke for her. "What kind of fool question is that? Can't you see what he did to her?"

Holt kept looking at the murderess as he said, "I care about the wounds I can't see. Did he knock her around? Bust a rib. Break her arm?"

The crying woman cradled her midsection. "He stomped me some, but I don't know if anything's broken."

Holt looked at the women clustered around the doorway. "One of you get the doctor and bring him here. This lady needs attention."

The women looked at the matron, who nodded her approval. Only then did one of them break away to get the doctor.

Holt figured this must be the McAdam widow Mullen had warned him about.

He heard another commotion out in the hall and the women scattered like birds when a large brute of a man stumbled into the doorway. Holt judged him to be a shade shorter than himself, but much thicker and wider. His shirt had been white at one time but had been sweated through and dried again many times since he had first put it on.

Tufts of coarse dark hair showed where it was open, and on his arms where the sleeves had been rolled up. He had a full head of equally dark hair that had not seen a comb in ages. His face had once born strong features, but drink had given him a feral, porcine look. His reddened eyes and uneasy stature told Holt he was drunk now.

If the matron was the McAdam widow, he imagined this must be Frank Peters, his predecessor and the widow's lackey.

"What's going on in here?" he slurred. He squinted at Holt. "And just who the hell are you."

"I'm the new sheriff," he said. "Stay out there and don't let anyone in."

The brute ignored him and came into the room.

He froze when Holt aimed his pistol at him.

The women in the hall gasped.

Neither man said a word. The sight of the Remington spoke volumes.

As drunk as Peters was, the sight of the pistol had a sobering effect.

The matron said, "Do as he says, Frank. We've had enough blood for one night. Get the girls back to their rooms and get those men down there back to drinking. I ain't losing any more business on account of a lousy drover."

Peters kept his eyes on Holt as he uneasily backed out of the room. He wheeled on the girls and took his embarrassment out on them, screaming at them to clear the hall before heading downstairs.

Holt lowered his gun but did not holster it. He watched the matron pull the terrified woman toward her and stroke her head.

"You the McAdam widow?" Holt asked.

When she looked up at him, he saw hard blue eyes and roundish face that sported too much rouge. He judged her to be about forty, though the powder she wore covered a variety of sins. "I see you've been talking to Mullen. Only he calls me that. Most folks around here call me Ma."

Holt did not care what she was called or what she called herself. He only cared about the woman she was cradling. "Here's what's gonna happen next. The doc will look her over and tend to her wounds. Then we're gonna take her to another room where she can rest and feel safe."

Ma held the sobbing woman tightly to her bosom. "You're not taking her to that rotten, stinking jail, Sheriff."

"I was thinking your room would be better," Holt said. "After she's had time to calm down, I'll come back and ask her what happened here, though it's plain enough to see." He glanced back at the dead man on the floor. "He a regular of yours?"

"Maybe," Ma said. "Could've been. We get a lot of his kind in here."

Holt remembered something she had said earlier. "You called him a drover."

"Drover, miner, carpetbagger, card sharp, snake oil hawker," she said. "He'll still be just as dead no matter what he did in life. What difference does it make?"

"It'll help me figure out who he is."

Ma held the crying woman tightly. "He was an animal who got what he deserved."

"Might have friends who won't take kindly to his demise," Holt went on. "Might come to town looking for trouble. Trouble for you." He looked at the bruised young woman. "Trouble for her too. I like to know when trouble's coming. Makes it easier to head off when I do."

The young woman began to sob and buried her face in Ma's willing bosom. "Protecting this place is Frank's job. Anyone comes looking for trouble, he'll polish them off right quick."

Holt figured the only thing Frank would polish off is the whiskey jug in his room but decided not to add to their discomfort.

His gun hand tensed when he heard more footsteps in the hall, but relaxed when he saw it was only Doc Klassen. He was lugging a large black medical bag with him but stopped short when he saw Holt. "May I come in?"

Holt beckoned him to enter. "Look her over and if she's fit to move, help her get to Ma's room."

Doc Klassen glanced at the dead man as he took a knee beside the woman and gently eased her arms away from her stomach to begin his examination of her ribs. To Holt, he said, "I take it that fella is beyond my assistance?"

"He is." Holt looked at the dead man again. It was as clear-cut a case of self-defense as he had ever seen. There would have to be an inquest, of course, but he had no doubt the outcome would be in Cassie's favor. He did not know how quickly such things took in Devil's Gulch, but he would use any influence he had to make it happen in a day or so. Her bruises would still be fresh and would convince a jury she'd had no choice but to kill that man.

He watched Klassen move a strand of hair from Cassie's face and he got his first good look at her bruises. The low-down hyena had broken her nose and her right eye was swollen shut. Her left arm was already spotted with bruises.

He felt his anger rise. He hated flesh peddlers but held woman-beaters in a much lower regard. He did not know a word that fully described what he felt for them. For all bullies of any sort.

Klassen placed his hands under her shoulders and said, "Nothing feels broken, but I know you're hurting, Cassie. Why don't you let us help you up and bring you into Ma's room where you'll be more comfortable?"

Cassie nodded weakly and Ma helped Klassen lift her to her feet. Holt noticed she was a bit unsteady, but Ma had a firm grip around her waist and bore most of her weight. "Come on, honey. Let's get you cleaned up and warm. It's cold as ice in here."

Doc let the madam take her from the room as he closed

his medical bag. "Poor thing took an awful beating. She's lucky to have grabbed hold of his gun when she did."

That made Holt think of something. He walked over to the dead man and saw him slumped where he had found him. On his left side. He placed the tip of his boot against his shoulder and pushed him over onto his back.

His gun was still holstered on his right hip.

He was glad he did not have to spell it out for the doctor. "That's interesting," Klassen said.

"Yeah." Holt hated interesting dead bodies.

"She could've had the gun for protection," Klassen offered.

Holt held up the .44 he had taken from Cassie. "A woman her size would likely go for a smaller pistol."

He did not like the conclusions he was beginning to make.

A billowing curtain drew his eye. So did the shade that was pulled down behind it. The slat of wood sewn into the base of it was cracked and part of the wood was poking through the fabric.

Not inside the room, but toward the outside. Toward the open window.

Holt gestured for the doctor to move to the other side of the bed as he used his pistol to raise the broken shade. He ducked his head and peered out the window into the darkness. He could not see the ground but saw the plank-wood roof of the back porch of the saloon only a few feet below. An easy drop, especially for someone in a hurry.

Two men had attacked Cassie. One of them was dead. The other was on the run.

"I know what you're thinking, Sheriff," Klassen said.

"That shade could've been broken tonight or a year ago. It doesn't prove anything. Neither does an open window."

Holt let the shade drop and holstered his Remington. "You've got an easy way with her, Doc. When she calms down a bit, ask her if she had two customers up here tonight. Try to do it when Ma's not around."

"Easier said than done," Klassen said. "Ma McAdam is true to her name. She watches over her girls like a mother hen. Wish more of the houses in town took such care of their ladies, considering the lives they lead."

Maybe, Holt thought. But in his experience, women like Ma McAdam usually looked out for themselves first. He hoped Cassie had not suffered for her madam's sins.

Holt nodded toward the dead man on the floor. "Do you cart him off or do you have a man who handles that?"

A man from the hall said, "That sacred task falls to me, sir."

Holt saw a tall, gaunt man with long, stringy dark hair that fell to his shoulders. He held a black stovepipe hat to his chest in reverence for the dead. "My name is Earl Sibert and I take it you're Sheriff Holt. I'm the undertaker in these parts. Got the concession for the whole county, as a matter of fact."

"Bully for you." Holt stepped aside and beckoned Sibert to enter along with two equally disheveled helpers bearing a stretcher.

Doc Klassen took this as a good time to leave. "I'd best look in on Cassie. I'll stop by the jail later and let you know how she's faring."

Holt understood his meaning. "I'd appreciate it."

Klassen left to go about his business while Sibert went about his. He knelt next to the corpse and examined the body. "He died quickly, Sheriff. I imagine his was an easy passing."

"Too easy to suit me. You ever see him before?"

The mortician shook his head. "Can't say that I have, though the nature of my business does not exactly make me a welcomed guest in most of our town's establishments. People shun reminders of the fate that awaits us all."

Holt could tell he would have quite a time getting Sibert to tell him anything straightforwardly. "Go through his pockets. See if you can find anything to help me figure out who he is."

"I assure you a thorough examination of his person will be made when we bring him back to my mortuary."

Holt looked at him until he understood he wanted it done now and searched the dead man's pockets. He came up with two gold pieces and a black button.

"That's all he had on him," Sibert said as he began to slip the coins into his vest pocket. "Not much to show for a man's life."

"Those coin pieces will do nicely." Holt held out his hand. "Give them to me. Needs to be part of my report."

Sibert looked as though he was about to protest, but quickly thought better of it and handed them up to Holt.

"You can keep the button," the sheriff told him. "Send word around to the jail when you've got him stripped. I'll want to see if he's got any marks that might identify him, in case someone comes to claim the body."

The mortician bowed his head as he stood. "It shall be done as you ask, Sheriff. And thank you."

That struck Holt as strange, even for a mortician. "What're you thanking me for?"

"Not even one full day on the job and you've already got a dead body to report." He bore a smile of yellow teeth.

"It's a promising omen that you'll be quite good for my business."

Holt walked out of the room. He hoped Sibert was wrong but had a sneaking suspicion he would be proven right before long.

CHAPTER 5

Holt was halfway down the stairs when he saw four men with rifles pulling men out of chairs and shoving them toward the bar. He was about to go for his pistol but saw Joe Mullen directing the riflemen. A bright blue ribbon was pinned to the lapel of his coat.

Holt had seen similar ribbons in other towns before. They usually represented members of a committee of some kind.

In Mullen's case, it was the Devil's Gulch Vigilance Committee. The same committee Holt had ordered him to disband earlier that day.

An order Mullen had defied.

Holt had a good head of steam by the time he reached the bottom of the stairs and started straight for Mullen.

The committeeman saw him coming. "Got them all cleaned up and ready for questioning, just like you asked, Sheriff. Made sure no one left the premises by either the front or the back door."

Holt stopped short. He knew questioning the men in the saloon would be the next logical step, but he had intended on doing it on his own.

"What is this nonsense anyway?" Frank Peters slurred

as he pushed past one of the committee men. "I run the Railhead, Sheriff, not this puffed-up vigilante. Everyone knows what happened. No need to go ruining my business over it."

Holt told Peters, "Get back in line before you fall down." To Mullen, he said, "A word outside."

Mullen followed Holt out into the street where a crowd had formed around the front of the saloon.

Holt had never seen a town that liked to form a crowd so much. "Get back to your homes. There's nothing to see here. Go on. Move."

As the people began to disburse, Holt turned his attention back to Mullen, who already had both hands raised in surrender. "Before you set to yelling at me, Sheriff, I'm not defying your orders. My men and I are only here to keep people from leaving until you've had a chance to ask some questions. That's all."

Holt pointed at the silver star on his vest. "I told you that the law's my job, Mullen. Not yours or your men."

"But this town's our home," Mullen argued. "We live here and have a right to see that it's a fit place to raise a family and run our businesses. I know you're a tough man, Sheriff. I'm the one who convinced the mayor to hire you, but you're only one man. This town's too big for one man to handle on his own without a little help from time to time. So, while you were upstairs doing your job, my men were doing their job by keeping anyone who might know something from leaving. You want to turn them loose, go right ahead. I'll be the last one to stop you. But don't start barking at me because your pride's hurt. This ain't about pride. It's about doing what needs doing. And you know I'm right."

Holt wanted to be angry with him. He wanted to belt

him for disobeying him, so Mullen remembered who the real lawman was in town.

But Mullen's words had struck home with him, and he took a step back. He looked back at the jail and remembered the Turnbull boy. In all the excitement, he had left him alone and unguarded.

Mullen said, "Don't worry about the jail. Two of my men are over there right now watching him. Even managed to give him supper. They've done it before and know what they're doing. You can trust them."

Holt placed his hands on his hips as he faced Mullen. "And what about you? Can I trust you?"

"As far as it goes," Mullen admitted, "in helping you defend this town, you can. As for the rest of it, the part we talked about in the jail, well, that's different and has nothing to do with you. Won't matter much anyway once you're settled and in charge of things. But like it or not, that'll take time. You know that and so do I. Until then, me and my boys are here to help you."

Mullen looked around to make sure none of the civilians were within earshot. "And you need my help, John. I'm offering it willingly."

Holt continued to look away as he thought it over. He had remembered an old saying from Sun Tzu that General Nathaniel Banks was fond of quoting when in control of New Orleans at the end of the war. "Keep your friends close, but your enemies closer. Provided you don't have many enemies, of course."

The general's prudence had proven wise in the closing days of the war and after peace was declared. It was not always clear who was a friend and who was an enemy, especially in a city as complicated as New Orleans. Devil's Gulch was a good distance from Louisiana, but the general's wisdom had not escaped him.

He may not trust Mullen, but he did not have much of a choice. "A girl named Cassie shot a customer dead up there. She got banged up some, but she'll live."

Mullen shook his head. "She's a sweetheart. Who'd want to harm her?"

"That's what we're going back in there to find out," Holt told him. "We'll put the question to them if they knew who went upstairs with her. Then, if you and your boys really want to help, I want two men posted in the back of the saloon until morning. No one's to walk back there and no one's to go out the back door. You can change them around if you like, but I want that area kept clear until sunrise when I can get a better look around. Understand?"

"Of course," Mullen said. "I have enough men to post two there for an hour at a time. Can I ask why it's important?"

But Holt did not trust him that far yet. "That's a question I hope I can answer in the morning." He flicked Mullen's ridiculous blue ribbon. "Now, come on. We've got some drunks to question."

As Holt expected, he had not been able to learn much from the customers of the Railhead Saloon. Those who weren't too drunk to speak had been too preoccupied by their card games or with the women gliding around the gaming tables to be of much use. Holt had always found questioning men in a group to be a worthless endeavor. They either used the fact of their numbers to blend into the background or feared speaking up in public. But the questions had to be asked and the effort for answers made. It was not a complete waste of time. Frequently a man would step forward later in private with some nugget of information that might be helpful in uncovering the truth.

But as he had watched the last of the Railhead's

customers filter back to their tables and their bottle, he doubted the next day would uncover anything more than hangovers, empty pockets, and tall tales about what they had seen and heard at the saloon the previous night. There would be no shortage of witnesses then, bragging about being there when it happened.

Holt was back in the jail, writing his report, when he saw the first hint of sunrise appear in the eastern window. He had not only made it through his first day in Devil's Gulch, but he had also managed to avoid sleeping.

He set his report aside and decided he would finish it later. The sky was gradually brightening, and he wanted to get a good look at the back of the saloon as soon as possible. He only hoped Mullen's men had not gotten bored or tired and gone home.

Holt locked the jailhouse door behind him and walked over to the Railhead Saloon. He avoided the alleys on either side of the building out of concern of what he might find there, much less walk through. He took the alley of the dry goods store next to the saloon instead as a shortcut.

He was happy to see two committeemen in place and alert at their posts. Both men greeted him with the informality of volunteers. "Thank you, boys. Best get on home and grab as much sleep as you can. I'm grateful to you."

Both men went their separate ways, avoiding stepping in the area Holt had asked them to guard throughout the night.

The sky began to brighten more by the second, which helped him get a better look at the ground behind the saloon. Even if none of Mullen's volunteers had stepped through the area, the ground was as muddled as the thoroughfare on Main Street. The ground was deeply rutted by delivery wagons that stopped to drop off goods. Some Railhead customers apparently liked to hitch their horses at the back entrance instead of using the front entrance. They did not want news of their visits upstairs to reach their wives and friends.

The ground may not have been easy to read, but Holt knew it could still tell him much.

He walked around the area and onto the rough moss and weeds that grew beyond the mud. He saw the window of Cassie's room and, in his mind, traced the route a second man might have taken once he jumped from her window. There were several fresher marks on the ground where a pair of boots might have landed.

He squatted down and took a closer look at the marks. From there, he could see where the mud had been pressed down by two sets of four hooves. One set was deeper in the mud than the other as the two horses disappeared into the muddle of marks on the back road.

One horse had belonged to the dead man. One had carried the second away from the saloon, hence the deeper hoofprints.

Holt took a closer look at the fresher droppings he judged to be from both animals. They were perhaps only a few hours old.

He slowly stood up and looked north, in the direction the rider had headed with the two horses. *Who are you? Why did you hurt Cassie?*

He walked in the grass as he followed the muddy trail north, but after a block or so, decided it was useless. The back road was used by all the buildings and houses on Main Street as a place to dump the scraps and their chamber pots. The entire area was filled with tracks from wild dogs and other animals who lived on such leavings. He knew he would find no trace of the fleeing man there.

But his search had not been a total loss. He had left the

jail with nothing but questions. At least he knew there was
a good chance there had been two men in Cassie's room.
One of them had gotten away and ridden north. *What was
north?*

He did not know the town well enough yet to answer
that question on his own but knew someone who might.
He only hoped she was still awake. He would hate to dis-
turb her sleep after such an ordeal, but justice waited for
no man.

Or woman.

CHAPTER 6

Given the early hour, Holt could not tell if the Railhead Saloon had not yet closed or never closed at all. A card game was breaking up at one of the tables and the bartender yawned as he wiped at a spot on the bar. Frank Peters was nowhere to be found. He was probably up in his room sleeping it off.

Holt went over to the bartender and asked about Ma McAdam's room.

The bartender did not look up from his towel. "Ma's not taking customers this morning, mister. She's busy."

"I look like a customer to you, boy?"

The bartender looked up from his bar rag at the silver star on Holt's chest, then went back to his cleaning. "That star don't make you any less human. And it don't change the fact that she's still not seeing visitors of any kind."

Holt snatched the barman's cleaning arm, causing the man to cry out when he pulled him across the bar. He used the mirror behind the bar to watch the gamblers back away from their table. None of them was armed, nor did they seem inclined to interfere.

Holt twisted the bartender's arm a little. "Tell me where Ma's room is, or I break it."

"Upstairs and take a left," the barman yelled. "The one at the end of the hall. Biggest room in the place."

Holt let go of his arm and let the bartender slide back behind the bar. He felt the eyes of the few remaining gamblers on him.

The oldest of the bunch, a tattered dandy with a thick white mustache spoke for the group. "You got a real mean way with you, mister. Hoppy was just doin' his job. He ain't hurtin' anyone."

Holt had never liked busybodies or gossips. Or people who told him how to do his job. He took the steps upstairs quietly and said, "You'd best keep your concerns to cards, old-timer. This is law business, not gambling, and has nothing to do with you."

He found Ma McAdam's room at the end of the darkened hallway, exactly where the bartender had said he would find it. Candles still burned in holders on the wall, but the approaching light of day had caused them to lose some of their luster. Holt imagined that not even a den of inequity could keep the sun away for long.

He knocked lightly on Ma's door before turning the knob and finding it unlocked. Knowing a woman in her profession was not given to conventional modesty, he slowly opened the door.

He found Ma McAdam glaring at him from a chair beside her bed as she slowly stroked Cassie's soft brown hair. Cassie's eyes were dark and almost swollen shut by her bruises, but he could tell she was not asleep. She was facing the window. Her eyes as open as they could be given her condition. He had been in her position before and knew the pain kept sleep from coming as easily as one might expect.

Ma put her hand across Cassie's stomach as if to protect her. "What are you doing here?"

"I need to talk to her. Alone."

"No chance, mister. You don't talk to any of my girls without me standing right beside them. Now, get going or I'll call to have Frank throw you out."

"He's still sleeping it off," Holt told her. "And if you bring him in, he'll be carried out. That'll be on your head, not mine." He gestured toward the door. "Now, do as I told you and get out."

Ma was about to say something, but Cassie took her hand. "Please, Ma. He's only trying to help. Let me talk to him alone. Guess I'll have to talk to lots of folks now. Might as well start with him."

Ma reluctantly stood up and kissed her on the forehead before pulling her shawl around her again. She stopped beside Holt before she left. "You and I have some talking to do, mister. I'll be down at the bar waiting when you're done."

"Put on a pot of coffee. It'll be an interesting conversation."

Ma quietly closed the door behind her, leaving him alone with Cassie.

"Doc Klassen stopped by the jail last night," Holt said. "He told me nothing's broken. I suppose that's the best news we could've hoped for, considering."

"There's no *we* here, Sheriff," Cassie said without looking away from the window. "*We* didn't get beaten up and *we* didn't kill a man. I did." He watched a single tear streak down her ruined face, but her voice remained steady. "What happens now? You take me to jail?"

"No cause for that," Holt told her. "There'll be an inquest, of course, but it's clear you were defending yourself. A blind man could see it."

She looked neither relieved nor sad. She simply nodded once as another tear followed the first.

"You've got nothing to fear from the court or from me," Holt said. "But I need to know what happened in your room last night, Cassie. What really happened. Not the story Ma wants you to tell me."

She turned to look at him and he saw the full horror of her face. Her right eye was far more swollen than her left, though both were black and ugly. A long cut ran down the right side of her face that Holt doubted was a fist or from the dead man's belt. A man had taken a blade to her. The man she had killed did not have a knife. Not even an empty scabbard on his belt. And Holt had not found a knife in her room.

Her voice remained flat as she asked him, "What makes you so different from the others? Why should I tell you anything I won't tell a judge or jury?"

"Because I think you're in trouble, Cassie. And I know I'm the only one who can help." He realized he did not know the town well enough to know if that was true, so he added, "I'm the only one who wants to help because it's my job. I'd wager you don't place much stock in Frank's abilities to keep you safe. And he works for Ma, not you. Me? I work for you and everyone else in this town."

"Including Ma," she said, sharply.

Holt shook his head. "No. For you."

He felt guilty when her lower lip began to quiver as the defenses that she had built up since the beating began to weaken. She was beginning to trust him, though she did not want to.

He decided to help her get to the truth a little faster. "Ma told you to say there was only one man in the room last night, but there were two, weren't there? Two men who weren't customers but came to hurt you."

Her swollen eyes opened as large as they could in their condition. "How'd you know that?"

He offered a smile. "I've been doing this kind of work a long time. These things are easy to spot if you know how to look." He wanted to spare her all the details, so he only shared two to show his sincerity. "You've got marks on the right side of your face and the man you killed had his belt wrapped around his right hand. I'd expect the left side of your face to have more damage if he'd hit you. There's also the gun. It was too big for you to keep stashed, so I figured you'd taken it from someone else. The fella that did that to you. The left-handed one who escaped."

There were other details, of course. The lack of blood on the dead man's belt. Given the extent of her wounds, if he had hit her, Holt would have expected to find some blood on it.

It was circumstantial evidence, of course. The prosecutor would be well within his rights to ignore it if he chose to.

But there was evidence that would stand up in a court of law, and evidence of another kind. The tears that now flowed freely from the poor young woman in the bed was all the evidence Holt needed to tell him he had been right.

He spoke over her quiet sobbing. "Who were they, Cassie? Why were they after you?"

She wiped away her tears with reddened hands. "If I tell you, you can't go tell Ma. Not yet. She won't be happy about it."

Her fear of Ma McAdam caused the fire of his temper to spark in his belly. For her sake, he kept it under control. "I promise anything you tell me will stay between us. I can't promise it'll always be that way, but I won't say a word until I tell you first. No matter what happens, you won't have anything to fear from Ma or anyone else. That much I *can* promise you."

She looked up at the ceiling and swept more tears away. "The ones who did this to me are the Bostrom Boys. Hank and Em. It's short for Emil. He's the dead one."

Holt had heard of the Bostrom Boys, but he wanted Cassie to tell him. "Who are they?"

"Robbers, rustlers, hired men and thieves," she told him. "They'll do just about anything for anyone willing to pay or if they've got something they want. There's about ten men who ride with them off and on, depending on what they need them for, but the three brothers do everything together."

"Who's the third brother?"

Her lips trembled again and her voice finally broke. "Bob Bostrom. He was the oldest and their leader. I was a favorite of his and he was a regular customer whenever he and the boys were in town. He wasn't like the other two. He was rough in front of the others, but that was just for show. He used to pay Ma to take me out for a week at a time after he made a score. Last time we were together, he even took me to Golden City. Treated me real nice. Bought me things. Took me to the best restaurants. The finest hotels. First time in my life I felt like a real lady."

But Holt was focused on something else. "He must've hit a pretty big score."

"The biggest of his life," Cassie told him. "A bank wagon full of cash and gold. But he'd hid it from his brothers. Told me he didn't trust them not to go out and spend it all at once. Said he wanted to keep it from them until they were ready to go their separate ways and make lives for themselves. Said he wanted to take me to California."

She winced as she managed to sit up a little straighter. "Promised to take me to San Francisco and make an honest woman out of me. I've had a lot of men promise me a lot of things, mister, but Bob was different. He didn't have to say those things to me, and he never made a promise he didn't keep." Her ruined face soured. "He would've done it, too, if he hadn't gone and done something stupid."

"Which was?" Holt asked.

"His brothers wanted them to make one last score together," she said. "They told him about an army payroll troop that was set to make its first stop at Fort Collingwood from back east. Said that, along with the money they'd taken from the bank wagon, would set them up for life and could go their separate ways. Bob was a hard man, but he always had a weak spot for his brothers, so he went ahead with the job. Promised me that we'd go out to California soon after."

Holt imagined he knew how the story ended. "How long ago was that?"

She ignored him and continued with her story. "I was all packed and everything when I got word he'd been killed during the robbery. The payroll story was a lie. There was nothing in those wagons except soldiers and a Gatling gun."

She blinked hard and more tears came. "Em and Hank and the rest of the gang just rode off like scared dogs. Not the way they tell it, mind you, but that's what they did. Said when they went back to find Bob that there wasn't enough left of him to bury." She shook her head and looked out the window. "I don't believe that, though. I doubt they ever went back for him at all."

Holt could tell how much telling the story pained her, and he tried to ease her suffering. "So, his brothers came to you last night, figuring you knew where Bob had buried the money from the bank wagon."

She slowly nodded. "They were after me for weeks to tell them where it was. I told them I didn't know and that was the truth. I even told them I'd go out and dig up the money myself if I knew where it was. But they didn't believe that. They thought I was just waiting them out to make my move. They'd already searched all the places where they'd stashed money before and came up empty. They burned through the small amount Bob had given them and, with the army payroll being a bust, they started getting desperate. I didn't know how desperate until I came up to my room last night to get ready for a special customer Ma said wanted to see me. I found them waiting for me instead. Must've climbed up the back way because I was in the saloon all night and didn't see them come in the front. And I would've noticed them. Especially those two."

But Holt was stuck on something. "So, it was Ma who told you about this special customer. Who was he? Don't worry about him getting in trouble. I said I wouldn't say anything to anyone, remember?"

"That's just it," she said. "I don't know. Ma said he was a new client. A real high roller who had requested me. Said he was willing to pay top dollar for my services, twice the going rate." She frowned. "Guess he must've been scared off when he heard the ruckus in my room."

Holt's jaw tightened. He did not think it was that easy.

But Cassie was too deep in her story to see his reaction. "Hank was the one who got rough with me. Em was always the scarier of the two, but he didn't touch me. My face was all Hank's doing. He grabbed hold of me after he worked me over some, and I snatched the gun he always kept tucked in his belt for show. Thought it made him look like a dangerous man. I fell back against the wall with the gun and pulled the trigger blind. I wasn't even trying to hit anyone, not even Hank. But I guess I missed him and hit Em instead. That's when Hank dove out the window before

Ma came in after hearing the shot." She swallowed with great effort but did not look away from the window. "You know the rest."

Holt, indeed, knew the rest. He knew more than this poor broken girl even knew. All she knew was pain. He knew the reason for it. And who had caused it too.

He would not let that stand.

Holt did not know if she could hear him, but he spoke anyway. "The town attorney will want to talk to you. I'll be up here with him when he does. Stick to the story you told me last night. No one needs to know there were two of them except you and me."

"And Ma," she said. "I told her everything. I'm sorry, but I was upset and needed to tell someone."

"Don't worry about Ma." Holt had special plans for her. "Just stick to your story, and everything will be over in a few days except for the healing."

She nodded but did not take her eyes from the window. "What are you going to do in the meantime? About Hank and his boys, I mean."

"You don't have to worry about them," Holt told her. "Just worry about getting better."

When she looked away from the window, her expression almost broke his heart. "You'd better be careful with Hank, mister. He might not look like much, but he's crazy. So are all the men who ride with him. I don't know their names, but I've heard what they can do. You've never gone up against the likes of them."

Holt rested his hand on her foot beneath the blanket. *They have not gone against the likes of me.* "You just get better. I'll try to send word when the lawyer wants to speak with you."

He turned to leave but stole a quick look at Cassie as he closed the door. She was back to looking out the window again and he wondered what she saw. Was she thinking about what had happened? What could have been? Maybe, but not what would be. The future held no value for her.

As he closed the door, he made a vow that he would give her the future Bob Bostrom had promised her. He would fulfill the outlaw's promise.

And that future would start with a conversation with Ma McAdam downstairs.

CHAPTER 7

When he got to the bottom of the stairs, Holt found the saloon was empty. The front doors had since been closed and the bartender he had roughed up was nowhere in sight.

He found Ma McAdam sitting alone at a table beside the bar, sipping coffee from a cup. In another setting, she might've looked like an elegant older woman enjoying a cup of coffee at the beginning of a new day.

But here in the Railhead Saloon, Holt saw her for what she was. An evil old hag who had set up Cassie to take a beating from the Bostrom brothers.

She did not offer him a chair as he approached her table, and he did not look for one.

She did not move, save for holding up a finger to caution him as he drew closer. "Speak kindly, or I'll have you thrown out of here on your backside."

"Not before I throw you in jail for what you've done to Cassie."

She slowly placed the cup on its saucer. "I haven't harmed a hair on that girl's head."

"But you sure allowed it to happen, didn't you?"

She pulled the shawl tighter around her shoulders. "I don't know what you're talking about and neither do you."

"That special customer you told her about last night," Holt said. "The reason why she'd gone up to her room alone instead of working the floor. There was no special customer. It was Em and Hank Bostrom, wasn't it?"

The madam looked away. "I didn't know that at the time. The request came through a special arrangement that assured privacy for everyone involved."

"You've already betrayed her once. Don't do it again by lying now."

Her eyes shifted back to him. "You want the truth? Fine. How was I supposed to know they'd hurt her? They were friends. They'd spent hours together at the bar down here and at the tables."

Holt did not know if that was true. It did not matter, even if it was. "They offered to cut you in on the money if Cassie told them where to find it, didn't they?"

"They never said anything about hurting her and that's the truth," Ma told him. "And if you ask me, the one who got himself shot for his trouble had it coming. He's no loss."

Holt slowly shook his head. "Em's dead. You've got nothing to fear from him anymore. Hank's a whole other story. He got away. And by what Cassie says, I think he got shot, too, before he ducked out that window."

The McAdam widow looked up at him slowly. "What are you talking about?"

"Cassie thinks she missed him and shot Em," Holt said. "Hearing the way she tells it, I think she winged Hank and the bullet would've kept going straight through until it hit Em standing behind him." He saw doubt in her eyes. "At that range, and with a bullet that powerful, it's more than possible. It's likely."

Whatever flash of acknowledgment that had appeared in her eyes quickly died away. "Even if that's true, what does that have to do with me?"

"Just this." Holt leaned on the table with both hands. "You made a deal with a dangerous man and didn't live up to your end of the bargain. His brother is dead, and he's likely injured. He's no closer to finding the money now than he was yesterday. He's down two brothers and he's running out of both money and options. Just how long do you think he'll be patient, waiting for Cassie to tell him where that money's buried?"

"But she doesn't know," Ma implored. "Believe me, I've tried to get her to tell me where it is plenty of times. The poor girl has no idea where they could even begin to look."

Holt put more weight on the table. "But you know where I can look, don't you, Ma? For Hank, I mean. I'll even give you some help. When he rode out of here last night, he headed north. I lost his track about halfway up through town. If you tell me where he is, I'll go get him and we can put this whole thing to bed once and for all."

"And if I don't?"

"Then he comes back here as soon as he heals up. And since he's all out of brothers, he won't be alone. He'll be with some mighty desperate characters who'll be looking for their share of that stolen money. He won't take no for an answer this time and he'll be coming for blood."

Ma laughed as she looked him up and down. "You sound like you know him. You've never even set eyes on him. You've barely been in town for a day. What makes you think you know so much?"

"You're right. I don't know Hank Bostrom. I've never met him and don't know what he looks like. But I've known plenty of men like him. I know what they're capable of when they're desperate and Hank's about as desperate as a man can get. Tell me where I can find him and I can stop him before even more people get hurt, including you and your business."

Ma ran her finger over the edge of the faded felt of the card table. "Could just cut my losses and send Cassie packing. Let her take her chances on her own."

"That won't do any good," Holt said. "Because if Hank can't find her, he'll come looking for you. You won't like it when he finds you."

Ma's eyes turned dark. "If that brushpopper comes my way, he'll regret it. I'm not as young as I once was, but I've still got plenty of teeth in my head."

"Hope you're not counting on Frank Peters for much help," Holt said. "He won't stand a chance against Bostrom if it comes down to it."

Holt bristled as he felt the cold steel of two shotgun barrels pressed against the back of his neck.

Ma McAdams smiled. "What was it you were saying about Frank just now, Sheriff?"

In a single motion, Holt turned, snatched the shotgun out of Peters's hand and flipped the weapon so both barrels were under Peters's chin.

He had not reacted to Holt's movement until he felt the gunmetal under his throat.

He could smell the alcohol coming through Peters's pores and from his breath. The presence of gun barrels under his chin did not make him smell any better.

Holt shoved Peters backward and he fell across a chair. Holt opened the shotgun, dumped both shells on the floor and dropped the unloaded weapon on McAdam's table, causing some of her coffee to spill from its cup and onto her saucer. "I'll be back in a couple of hours to check on

Cassie. Use the time to think about whether or not you should tell me where Hank is holed up."

"I don't know!" she yelled after him as he left the saloon.

"Then you best start finding out some likely locations," Holt said as he opened the door. "For all of our sakes."

CHAPTER 8

H olt looked up to check the large clock in the tower of the bank building as he crossed the thoroughfare and saw it was already past seven o'clock. Still two hours before Jean brought breakfast. He was already getting hungry and thought about heading over to Le Café to get an early meal. Turnbull could wait for his breakfast.

Holt realized he did not have anyone to watch the prisoner. He had left him alone long enough as it was. The chances of him escaping or anyone getting into the jail were remote, but not impossible. And if anything happened to him while he was in Holt's custody, the judge would likely throw Holt in a cell. He decided not to risk it. He ignored his growling stomach and headed back to the jail.

He slowed his pace a bit when he saw a man with pure white hair and a gray suit pacing back and forth in front of the jail. The man was unarmed, save for a thick beard that flowed from his face, but no mustache. His build made Holt take him for a farmer and his look for a Quaker. Neither of which explained why he was stalking his jail so early in the morning.

"Who are you?" Holt asked as he got closer to the jail.

The man stopped pacing and looked at the silver star pinned to Holt's vest. "Ah, you're the new sheriff, I take it. John Holt."

"Still haven't told me who you are, old-timer."

"Old-timer?" the stranger repeated. "One more insult like that and I'll have you in the territorial prison breaking rocks until you're my age!"

Holt immediately knew who the man must be as the man told him, "I'm Judge William Cook, young man. I'd expect you to know such things."

Holt had never met the jurist before but, from his correspondence with Mayor Chapman, knew of his prickly and peculiar disposition. Chapman had written that Cook was a firebrand judge given to frequent outbursts and varying sentences depending on his humor at the time of judgment. He was known to have those he believed to have offended him locked up on a whim without any questions asked. The legality of this was questionable, but a question few were likely to ask of the domineering Cook.

"I'm sorry, Your Honor," Holt apologized. "Things have been a bit thick around here since I got into town. Just had a killing last night. I haven't had a chance to meet everyone yet."

The judge pulled his coat closer around his shoulders. "All will be forgiven, sir, as soon as you open this door and get me out of this infernal cold. I feel as though I have been standing on the street for ages. Simply ages."

Holt quickly opened the door and the judge barged in. He swept off his coat and laid it across one of the chairs facing his desk.

Judge Cook looked around the jail. "I see you've rearranged the place some. It's good for a man to make a place his own after he takes over. I certainly wouldn't feel comfortable leaving things the same after Peters. A low man, sir. Very low indeed."

Holt was not in the mood to discuss Frank Peters or his previous role as sheriff. But he was glad he had finished most of his report on the Cassie incident from the previous night. He would have to make a few changes to it now that he knew the man Cassie had killed was Emil Bostrom, but it was fit enough for the judge to read.

Holt picked up the report from his desk and held it out to him. "Here's my preliminary report on the incident that took place at the Railhead last night. I—"

Judge Cook surprised him by waving it down. "I've already heard all about it, Sheriff. This town is infected with gossips and Mrs. Cook is far from immune. If anything, she's a carrier of the disease. She's almost as bad as Mayor Chapman's wife. I don't need to read a preliminary report. Your final report will be sufficient. I understand it seems to be a clear-cut case of self-defense."

Holt was about to explain, but the judge waved him down again. "That's all well and good, but there'll be time enough for that. I didn't come here to discuss that case. I come bearing bad news for you."

Holt did not like the sound of that. "How bad?"

"Bad enough that I suggest you sit down before I tell it to you."

Holt sat down and braced himself for whatever the judge had to say.

Cook pointed to the back where the cells were. "I take it you still have the young Turnbull man back there?"

"Of course. You haven't even arraigned him yet."

"Nor will I be arraigning him." The judge frowned.

Holt had not found himself speechless often, but he found himself that way now.

Judge Cook spoke over his confusion. "Mayor Chapman didn't tell you the details of the bank robbery, did he? Neither did Mullen, I suppose. No, of course not. They were both undoubtedly too taken with your apprehension of the robbers and the return of the money to get into particulars. They're both good men in their own way but have a habit of forgetting details when excited."

Holt told Cook what he knew, hoping it would change his mind about the arraignment. "I heard the Turnbull Gang was planning to rob a bank here in Devil's Gulch as I rode out here. I wired the mayor from every town I stopped in, but never got a response. I tried to catch the gang, but never got closer than a day's ride. Since I knew they usually hit at night, I camped outside of town, hoping my campfire would draw them in. I was right, but that's all I know about what happened."

The judge frowned. "This is the first I'm hearing of any telegram. The service is still irregular out here, so I'm not surprised they didn't get it. I'm even less surprised neither Mullen nor Chapman explained what happened once you arrived in town, so let me amend that oversight now. The Turnbull bunch slugged two guards rather hard in the hopes of rendering them unconscious during the robbery. Both lived, thank goodness, but only one of them saw the robbers as they rode away. He swears there were only three of them, not four."

"Three of them?" Holt repeated.

Cook nodded. "It gets worse. None of the men he described resembled the young lad you're holding back there. I had the guards visit Sibert's mortuary last night to view the bodies. Both men testified that those were the three who robbed them. The only three. Your prisoner doesn't fit their description and I see no reason why they would lie about such a thing. One of them has double vision and Doc Klassen fears the damage may be permanent. Without a witness willing to swear young Turnbull was not at the bank when it was robbed, I'm afraid you'll have to cut loose of him."

Holt could not believe what the judge was telling him. "He was still an accomplice after the fact. He aided and abetted them after—"

This time, Judge Cook held up both hands to silence him. "I don't know you personally, Holt, but I know you by reputation. You've seen men walk out of courtrooms on stronger cases than we have against Turnbull. All he needs is one attorney to tell him those older boys forced him into helping them. Held him at gunpoint. Given his age and the fact that both guards are willing to testify he wasn't there, we can't charge him with anything, so there's no point in holding him any longer."

Holt did not like this. He had brought the thieves back to town over their saddles. He wanted to use young Turnbull's trial as a good way to make an impression on his new town. Freeing one of them now would be dangerous for his reputation and the prisoner.

Of all the questions that filled his mind, he only asked one. "How will the town take the news?"

"Poorly, to say the least," Cook said. "The unfortunate shooting in the Railhead will keep them preoccupied, but they won't react well to a bank robber's accomplice being allowed to go free. You'll need to let the boy go tonight. Put him on a fast horse. Hopefully, he'll get away before some of our more vigilant citizens take it upon themselves to dole out some good old-fashioned frontier justice beneath the nearest stout branch."

Holt ran his hands through his hair. He knew Turnbull

would not get far. Mullen and his men would raise a posse to track down young Turnbull. "I'll figure out a way to help him leave town."

"I was hoping you'd agree," Cook said. "Give him two days' worth of rations and some ammunition and send him on his way. You can put it on the town account at the general store." The judge winced as he said, "Your reputation may suffer for this, Mr. Holt, but it's early enough in your tenure for you to overcome it. From what I understand, you're not a man who's affected by the ill opinion of others."

"You understand correctly, sir." Since Holt had the judge's attention, he decided to share some of his own bad news. "I've begun my initial investigation into the Railhead shooting. It's going to be a much more complicated case than I thought."

Judge Cook closed his eyes. "I came to this town in the hopes it would be a quiet place from which I could administer the law. I don't like complicated matters, Mr. Holt. I like the cases that appear before me to be as straightforward as possible. The people of this town are an uncomplicated lot, but vengeful."

Holt thought that might be the case. Towns that formed vigilance committees often only had a limited respect for the rule of law. When they believed the courts failed them, they took justice into their own hands. He imagined the people of Devil's Gulch would be the same way.

Holt had found himself in the middle of such groups before, but it would be helpful if he had the court on his side. "I'd like to send you reports of my progress in the Railhead shooting, Your Honor. I'd like to have your perspective on the matter as I go along."

Judge Cook frowned as he mulled it over. "That could raise some difficult questions when the case comes before me. Show it to Lester Patrick instead. He's the town attorney and serves as our prosecutor when the need arises. He's a sharp young man and you can trust him. He'll undoubtedly make a good judge someday when I retire. I'll defer my role in the matter to him until you're ready to go to trial."

He cleared his throat and adjusted himself in the seat. "But I promise to keep you informed of anything I learn from Mrs. Cook. My wife is not only tapped into the town grapevine, but drinks heartily from it. I hope it will help you in your quest to bring this matter to a rapid and judicious end."

Holt did not know if gossip would help him against Hank Bostrom and his gang, but he was in no position to be picky when it came to information. "I'll do that, sir. Thank you for the suggestion."

Judge Cook stood up and shrugged into his coat, buttoning it up tight against the morning chill, before extending his hand to Holt. "I'm glad to say you've lived up to your billing so far, Mr. Holt. Never be afraid to seek me out for advice. It often helps to have a fresh perspective on matters. I promise to make myself available to you whenever you need me."

The two men shook hands. Holt was glad he had an ally besides Mayor Chapman. He imagined he would need all the allies he could get in the days ahead.

He walked the jurist to the door and opened it for him. Cook said, "I understand you're a West Point man. Served as a colonel in the late war."

Holt had heard that too. "My rank of colonel was a field command. I was only a captain, but they let me leave as a major after the war. Never went to West Point, either, but I've studied war a fair amount."

Cook grunted his approval. "Such studies will serve you

well here in Devil's Gulch, Mr. Holt." He doffed his hat to him before moving along. "Good day to you."

Holt watched him walk across the street to the county hall and spotted Jean coming toward the jail with a basket over her arm. She was wearing a simple brown dress, an apron, and a cook's bonnet, but he still found something striking about her. It was not that she was pretty, but that she had a certain pride in the way she walked. She may only be the owner of a café in a town in the middle of nowhere, but it was her café. Her business and she was clearly proud of it. Not everyone could change where they had been planted in this world, but she had chosen to sink her roots deep in town and flourish.

Staying put took a certain amount of grit that Holt did not seem to have.

"Morning, John Holt," Jean said as she swept past him and into the jail. "What's the matter? Didn't think I'd be here on time?"

He glanced up at the bank's clock tower and saw it was nine o'clock on the nose. She was nothing, if not punctual.

"The thought of you being late had never crossed my mind," he said as he followed her into the jail and closed the door.

She set the basket on his desk. "I'm gonna need you to fetch those plates I gave you for dinner last night. The fork too. Utensils don't grow on trees, you know?"

He took down the keys from the peg on the wall, opened the door and went back to the cells. He found young Turnbull sitting on his cot. His arms folded in defiance. Holt was surprised to see the plate and the silverware were already in the aisle in front of his cell.

Holt stooped to pick them up. "Breakfast's coming."

Turnbull continued to sulk. "Sound carries in this place. I heard what you said to the judge out there just now."

Holt had not counted on that. "Then why the long face. You're gonna be a free man this time tomorrow."

"Ain't nothing free in this world, Major. You ought to know that by now."

"Heard that part of the conversation, too, did you?"

But the young man ignored him. "Don't go thinking you'll be doing me any favors by letting me go. I won't last two days out there before your friends run me down. I've heard what Mullen and his men do to thieves."

Holt wanted to hear more but decided it could wait. Turnbull wasn't going anywhere, and neither was he. "We'll talk after you eat. I don't like making decisions on an empty stomach if I can help it."

The prisoner continued to sulk as Holt brought his plates out to Jean, who had already laid a plate of biscuits, gravy, and scrambled eggs on the desk. The aroma reminded him that he hadn't eaten since the day before. The committee men that Mullen had sent to guard Turnbull had helped themselves to his supper.

"I didn't bring coffee," she reminded him. "Lugging this stuff over here is hard enough without bringing a heavy pot of hot coffee to make it worse."

"Wasn't part of the agreement," he said as he brought the plate to Turnbull. "I remember."

When he walked back into the jail, Jean had already packed up the dirty dishes in her basket and was already leaving when he called out to her, "Can't you wait a moment?"

She opened the door and stood impatiently on the boardwalk. "I've got a café to run, John Holt. I don't have time for pleasantries."

He did not have anything to say to her and did not know why he had called out to her to wait. He just knew he liked her company and did not want to see her leave so soon. He thought of something to ask. "What's on the menu for lunch?"

"Don't know yet," she said, "and I don't take special requests either. Not based on what the town's paying me to keep you fed, anyway. You'll get whatever I have and whatever I have will be good."

He smiled, admiring the young Black woman's confidence. "I'm sure it will."

She did not return the smile. "Now, if there's nothing else, I've got to get back to work."

She turned and walked back to the café. *Her* café, she would have corrected him had she paid any mind to him. But she had not paid any mind to him, which might be the reason why Holt found her intriguing. Most people shied away from him or ignored him altogether. They did not like crossing paths with him and they sought to avoid his company at any cost. A working gal in New Orleans had told him it was due to the air of danger about him. She had said it seeped through his pores like whiskey off a drunk.

He knew the effect he had on people and had made a career of using it to his advantage. He had built a reputation of standing alone against overwhelming odds where such a disposition came in handy.

But neither his reputation nor his disposition seemed to bother Miss Jean Roche one way or the other. Like him, she had a job to do and was intent on doing it. Nothing could distract her from it, not even the presence of a new sheriff. Perhaps it was her indifference to him that made her more appealing? Perhaps that was why he decided he would try to win her affections, though he did not know how.

The smell of breakfast reached him again and he remembered what he had said to Turnbull. Decisions should not be made on an empty stomach. He bolted the jailhouse door shut and ate his breakfast.

CHAPTER 9

Hank Bostrom's wail of pain echoed throughout the abandoned mine.

"Now, just hold still," Cal Abel told him as Charlie and Ted did their best to hold him down. "Squirming around won't help me get a look at that wound any better."

"It went through and through," Hank said through gritted teeth. His voice was already raspy from all the yelling he had done. "Just close it up. We need to get back there to find Em."

"You're not going anywhere until I clean out this wound." Cal Abel knew Hank Bostrom was a hardheaded man, but even the most stubborn men were susceptible to bleeding to death.

He held a rag to the bullet hole that had punched through his right side. The bleeding had let up some, telling Cal that there did not seem to be much damage to Hank's innards. He was no doctor but had seen enough gunshot wounds to know a good one from a bad one by sight.

Cal gestured to Duke March to hand him a bottle of whiskey on a crate beside him. The outlaw reluctantly agreed, and Cal snatched it from him before he changed his mind. They were running low on supplies. Whiskey most of all. In some ways, the men prized it as much as Bob Bostrom's hidden gold.

Cal pulled out the cork with his teeth and spat it out. He struggled to hold Hank still as he told him, "I've got to sterilize the wound, Hank. I'm gonna pour some whiskey on it and it's going to hurt, but it needs to be done. You can holler all you like. Nobody'll hear you."

Hank began to protest but screamed when the alcohol washed over the hole in his side.

Cal dabbed the wound dry and cast the bloody rag aside. "The bleeding's stopped for now." He grabbed a shirt from behind him, tore it along the seams and packed the wound before he wrapped it around Hank's middle. It was a good thing the outlaw was skinny, Cal thought, or the shirt would not have covered much.

Hank demanded to be set free, but Charlie and Ted looked to Cal for guidance. "You're gonna have to stay still for a while, Hank. That wound's still gonna leak if you move. Best sit still for the night."

Hank ordered Charlie and Ted away from him and Cal nodded his approval, though he stayed to keep the gang's leader in place. "You boys tend to his mount. Make sure there's no blood on the saddle or the animal that could give us away. See to it that she's well-fed. He put in some mighty hard riding to get here tonight."

The two men moved out of the mine while Duke looked longingly at the whiskey bottle Cal was holding. There was still a small amount left inside and Cal tossed it over to him. "Go drink it somewhere else. Me and the boss have some important things to talk over."

Like a dog with a stick, Duke was happy enough to oblige, leaving Cal and Hank alone in that section of the old mine.

"Damn it, Cal," Hank said. "Why didn't you just heat up a knife and burn it shut."

"On account of you could still be bleeding inside," Cal said. "I want to keep an eye on it in case you get a fever. But it looks like you were right. The bullet went clean through and didn't hit anything vital."

"How would you know?" Hank spat. "You ain't a doctor."

"On account of you still being alive," Cal said.

Hank lay flat on his side. "Bullet went right through me and hit Em. Send some men to go back and get him."

Cal didn't blame him for forgetting. "Art Somers and Ed Volk rode into town with you and Em. Art helped you get back up here while Ed hung back to watch your trail. Kept an eye on the Railhead. Em never came out the window, so he took Em's horse."

Cal tightened his grip on Hank's shoulder as he delivered the bad news. "But Ed did see Earl Sibert's wagon pull up in front of the place. They carried out Em's body soon after."

Hank's handsome features twisted into an ugly mask of sadness and pain as Cal held on to him tightly. He did not want him moving around and getting that wound bleeding again.

That did not keep Hank from pounding the dirt beside him. "Not Em. He was the last of us. It can't be him. Not shot by a fallen woman."

"It was a lucky shot, Hank," Cal reminded him. "Em just happened to be standing in the wrong place at the wrong time. Nothing anyone could've done about it. Nothing anyone can do about it now. Just a bad break all around."

Hank bit off his tears and his pain. Cal had been there when Bob had been cut down by the Federals and knew how hard he'd taken it. He had heard the rumors in Devil's

Gulch about how Hank and Em had set Bob up for a bullet or might have shot him themselves in the panic once the Gatling gun started firing. He could understand the gossip. Bob had hidden the money from his brothers and men had been killed for less.

But Cal had been riding with the brothers since their wilder days in Mexico before the war. He'd ridden with them during the war, too, when they had hit supply wagons on both sides of the Mason-Dixon Line. He knew how close they were. He knew they would never turn on each other over any amount of money.

And even if Cal had any lingering doubts, the sight of Bob and his horse after the robbery removed them from his mind. Both had been hit fewer than twenty-five yards from the wagon. There was not enough left of old Bob to bury.

Hank and Em had run the gang since then and had focused on trying to find where Bob had stashed the bank money. They had dug up every favorite hiding spot since then and got only holes in the ground for their trouble. Given Bob's affection for Cassie, the girl was their last resort. Bob had always been fond of her, so it stood to reason that she might know where he had hidden the money.

Cal knew Hank had not expected to lose another brother in pursuit of the treasure, at least not that way, but he had. And it was up to Cal to keep the man sane. He still had a gang to keep together if they had any hopes of finding that money.

"I'll kill her!" Hank yelled through clenched teeth. "I swear to God I'll burn her alive for this!"

"You'll do no such thing." Cal shook some sense into him. "It was an accident and that's all. The whole town knows why you were there, and they'll be looking to put a bullet in you if you show your face. Besides, they've gone and hired themselves a new lawman who's got a real nasty reputation."

The information seemed to take Hank's mind off his grief. "Who?"

"John Holt."

Hank's features relaxed as he looked up at Cal. "From New Orleans?"

"The very same. Worked a lot of other places since, from what I've heard."

Hank slowly laid his head back down on his arm. "That boy gave us a time in New Orleans. Think he'll remember us?"

"I doubt it. We never exchanged pleasantries, only shots when he caught us in front of that bank."

"Killed Sancho and Old Whiskey in that scrape," Hank remembered. "All with a pistol too. What's a man like that doing in the Gulch?"

"Earning a pretty penny, I'd imagine." Cal was glad to keep him talking about Holt. It kept his mind off other things. "We've been hitting the area hard for the past year or so. Mayor Chapman probably brought him in out of fear we might hit the town next. Another gang took the bank the night before last. The Turnbull outfit, from what I heard."

Hank spat. "The Turnbulls ain't no gang. Just a bunch of kids with too many guns and not enough sense."

"Had enough sense to rob the bank at night," Cal offered. "But didn't have enough sense to keep on riding. Heard they ambushed Holt on their way out of town, or he ambushed them. Depends on who you ask. From what Ed heard, Holt rode into town with three of them across the saddle and one upright."

Cal knew Hank had heard him, but he was beginning to

drift off to sleep. The pain and the hurt and the hard riding had taken their toll on him. "John Holt," he said as exhaustion and pain took him. "A bad man."

Cal stayed with him until his breathing slowed and he began to snore. He pulled a blanket over him before going outside to speak to the others. He had seen other gangs break apart before when their leader was down. Men who lived on the other side of the law were not known for their loyalty and were quick to bolt for greener pastures.

Cal knew they could not afford to lose a single man now. Not if they had any hope of finding the money Bob had hidden somewhere in these hills.

He found them huddled around a fire at the bend just after the mouth of the abandoned mine. There were eight of them now and each of them had ridden a tough road before joining up with the Bostrom outfit. Every one of them had spent his time in irons. Each of them had killed their share of men in their time. Cal might have questioned their loyalty, but not their grit, nor their greed.

He was counting on that greed now to keep them together.

"How's Hank?" Stew Adams asked. He'd ridden with the Red Legs during the war and became a Bostrom man soon after.

"He'll be fine after a few days of rest," Cal said as he took a seat at the fire and helped himself to a mug of coffee. "Em's dead, though I'm sure you boys already knew that."

"Yeah," Adams said. "We heard. A good man, Em. Hate to lose him."

The outlaws hung their heads in their version of a moment of silence. Cal sipped his coffee. Such sympathy was for the living, for he knew the dead were far beyond it now.

It was Ted Graham who broke the silence. "What does that mean for the rest of us? As far as the money, I mean."

"We don't mean *the* money, mind," Charlie Gardiner said. The Cajun outlaw had joined up with the outfit right before they planned to hit that bank in New Orleans. The same bank where Holt had killed two of their men. "We're talking about just plain old money now. The type we can use to buy supplies and such. I hope you enjoy that coffee, Cal, because that's the last of what we have on hand."

"Could steal it," Roger Jenkins offered. He was an easterner and normally the quietest in the bunch. "Miners up in these parts aren't wanting for coffee."

"We're not paupers," Cal said. "Stealing from banks and the army is one thing. Holding up a storekeeper or a miner for provisions is just low. We've got enough left for coffee and bacon and biscuits through the morning. I'll head into town tomorrow to fetch some more."

Cy Wentworth added, "But there is *the* money to talk about. We all had high hopes that Bob's woman would've told Hank where he buried it. But I suppose he didn't have time to wait around for an answer once the lead started flying."

Cal fixed the man with a hard glare. "Hank was lucky to get out of there with his life, boys. He and his brothers have seen us through hard times before and we've come out all right. Hank might've been the youngest, but he learned plenty from Bob and Em before they passed on. We'll find Bob's stash and split it up proper just like we promised. That much is as certain as the rising of the sun. Until then, we stay here, wait for Hank to get better and decide our next move."

He tried to put a shine on it for them. "Might even try to stretch the money to see if I can't get us a case of whiskey for you boys come tomorrow."

The men of the Bostrom Gang smiled but did not laugh as he had hoped.

Duke March seemed to speak for them as he said, "We've been patient about the money, Cal. We'll take the whiskey and the vittles gladly, but it won't make us think about the money any less."

Cal drank his coffee rather than argue with the man. He knew there were cracks beginning to form in the gang's foundation. Duke had only given voice to it. It did not make it any easier to hear, but he could not allow him to have the last word either.

"No one's forgetting about anything. Especially me."

CHAPTER 10

Up at the Blue Bottle Saloon, Joseph Mullen waited until Mayor Chapman and Doc Klassen left to go about their day before speaking to Tony Cassidy in private.

"What do you make of our new friend the sheriff?"

Cassidy poured himself another mug of coffee from the pot. "He's no friend of mine. He's an uppity one to be sure. Nasty too."

"Agreed," Mullen said. "I was hoping that business about him being tough was just a lot of hot air, but I don't think it is."

Cassidy drank his coffee. "Took a piece out of you and your outfit from what I heard. Disbanded the Vigilance Committee. You boys have gotten mighty fond of the money you were able to scrounge up from that angle."

"He did," Mullen admitted, "but I'm working on it. That shooting up at the Railhead showed him how helpful me and my men can be. He's a tough man but he's still only one man. He saw that for himself last night."

Cassidy set his mug back down on the stained green felt of the table. "The Bostrom Boys will give him more trouble than he bargained for. They won't rest until they know where Bob buried that money."

Mullen knew the lost money was an open secret in town. Not everyone had heard about it, but only because those that knew about it hoped to find the stash for themselves. He knew none of the men in the saloon the previous night would tell Holt about it. There was nothing to be gained by letting the lawman know about the lost treasure.

But there was one person who may have told him. "Cassie probably said something to him. I hear he was talking to her this morning."

Cassidy groaned. "I heard that too. Was hoping it was just a rumor."

"Hoping won't make it so," Mullen observed. "Holt's found himself on the wrong side of Ma, which puts him on the wrong side of a lot of people in this town."

"Only the kind of people Holt's liable to go up against anyway," Cassidy said. "Their poor opinion of him won't hurt him much. You heard how Chapman gushed about him just now here at breakfast. To hear him tell it, Holt can walk on water and cure lepers."

Mullen found himself smiling at the memory. The mayor gushed like a schoolboy. "It's only been a day, Tony. Right now, Holt's a shiny new toy to play with. I expect the varnish will wear off him soon enough once Holt starts doing things his way. He's nobody's puppet and he's bound to ruffle some feathers. Give it time."

Cassidy looked down into his mug. "I've never been a patient man, Joe. You know that. I know it's only been a day, but every day that passes lets Holt dig his claws into Chapman a little deeper and we can't have that, you and I."

Mullen had never thought much of Cassidy or his chosen profession. Like Holt, he had never held flesh peddlers in high regard, but he never discounted the man's capacity for ruthlessness.

"You're chewing something over, Tony. Best spit it out right here and now before it chokes you."

The skinny man leaned closer to Mullen. "Him visiting Cassie ain't the only rumor I heard today. I also hear old Judge Cook's going to kick the Turnbull boy loose."

Mullen moved his hand away from his mug. "He's what?"

"You heard me," Cassidy went on. "I hear those bank guards told him they saw only three men robbing the bank. They were in here last night talking all about it afterward. Said the boy Holt brought back was nowhere in sight. The judge did everything he could to get them to say that he was, but they only saw the three dead men Holt brought into town. They've even put it in writing. Signed it and everything."

Mullen slowly ran his right hand over the arm of his chair. "But Holt found him with the others. That means he's as guilty as the dead men, even if he wasn't there." He was not sure of the legal term, but he knew something of the law. "Accomplice, I think is the word."

"I don't care what you call it," Cassidy said. "I just know the judge thinks he has no choice but to cut the Turnbull boy loose. Can't see as how that'll sit well with a man of Holt's beliefs."

"No." Mullen gripped the arm of his chair. "Neither do I. And even if he'll abide it, me and my men won't."

Cassidy's eyebrows rose as he twisted his mouth like he was giving thought to something. "Could be a way we can make something good come out of this. Something that's good for your interests and mine. Maybe even for the town too."

Mullen looked at Cassidy. "And Holt?"

Cassidy smiled. "That'll depend on him." He poured

more coffee into Mullen's mug. "Hear me out. You might like what I have to say."

Holt watched Turnbull closely as he lugged the heavy chamber buckets out of the jail and brought them around to the back, where he dumped them down the hill that ran behind the jail.

The young man stood up and pulled his face away from the stench. "Almost makes a man want to give up eating."

"Only if you're the one dumping the buckets." Holt had his hand on his pistol, but kept it holstered. Turnbull was still his prisoner, but not for much longer. Running now would be stupid and the young man did not strike him as stupid. "Pick up those buckets and bring them back inside."

Turnbull did as he was told with Holt trailing close behind him.

"Guess you'll have to find someone else to do this for you tomorrow," Turnbull said. "The way my luck's running, you'll probably find me at the bottom of this hill come sunrise."

"Don't worry about tomorrow," Holt told him. "Worry about now. Keep going."

He watched Turnbull lug the buckets inside the jail. He placed one in the far corner of the office and brought the other back to his cell. He looked surprised when Holt said, "Now come out here and sit down. We've got some talking to do."

Turnbull held on to the bars. "Talking? You mean out there?"

Holt pulled one of the chairs out as he rounded the desk. "That's what I said."

But the prisoner was in no hurry to move. "You're not

trying to set me up for a bullet, are you? Shoot me saying I was trying to escape?"

"It's not that kind of conversation." Holt pointed to the empty chair. "Sit there. Now."

Turnbull quickly moved around Holt and took his seat. He looked younger in the chair than he had out on the trail or in the cell. He supposed the trappings of civilization had a way of showing the true nature of a man.

"How old are you, boy?" Holt asked as he sat down.

"Old enough," Turnbull answered.

"Mind that smart tongue of yours or it'll cost you some teeth. Answer the question."

"I'm sixteen, near as I can figure. Pa wasn't much on particulars."

"Got a name? Can't go around calling you Turnbull all the time."

"Why not? Ain't like you're gonna be calling me anything after tonight."

Holt began to get up.

The young man flinched. "Jack Turnbull's my name."

Holt settled back in his seat. "No, it's not. I can tell. What's your real name?"

He blushed and looked away. "My given name's Jack Pusie. French, to hear my old man tell it. Pronounced, 'Pew-say.'"

Holt understood why Jack had blushed. "Oh."

"Yeah, 'oh.' That name caused me no shortage of trouble for a lot of reasons, so I'd just as soon be known as Jack Turnbull from now on if it's all the same to you."

Holt saw no reason why it mattered. "Jack Turnbull it is. Preferably Turnbull."

The prisoner sneered. "It'll look great on my gravestone when those committee men catch me. Keep people from giggling when they step over me."

"What makes you think you're getting a tombstone?"

Turnbull cut loose with a nervous laugh. "You sure know how to make a fella feel better about his impending death, Sheriff. You learn that delicate touch from the blue bellies in the war?"

Holt had not meant it like that, but understood why Turnbull had, so he let the sarcasm go. "I meant you might not die tomorrow."

Turnbull leaned forward in his chair. "Mister, I wouldn't give a penny for my chances once you cut loose of me tonight. I'm fair enough on a horse as it goes, but not with a posse on my tail. And Mullen's committee men or thugs or whatever else you want to call them will ride me down and string me up no matter how fast I ride. I've heard about those boys and what they do to the men they catch. While you were busy tending to that business over at the Railhead, Mullen's men were all too happy to tell me what they'd do to me if I tried to escape. They even unlocked my cell door and offered me a running start."

Holt was not surprised by that. Mullen and his men were the type to toy with a prisoner. They were bullies and Holt hated bullies.

Holt examined his nails as he asked, "What else have you heard about Mullen and his men?"

"Enough to know they'll send a man to hell on a lark if they're of a mind to. Devil's Gulch is their own personal slice of Heaven, and they don't take kindly to anyone who gets in their way. They've killed men who looked at them funny, rustled their cattle or ran down their brand after drinking too much whiskey. They don't care much about what happens outside this county, but they have this county pretty locked up. Always ride out with at least ten men, often more than that. And they like to have fun with a boy before they get around to stringing them up. So don't think you'll be doing me any favors when you let me go tonight because you're not. I'd almost prefer to have that old judge hang me instead. At least it'd be proper."

Holt switched his examination to the nails on his left hand. "You deserve to swing, Turnbull? I've got two witnesses that say you weren't at the bank when it was robbed."

The young man shifted uncomfortably in his seat. "I was minding the camp while they were gone. They wouldn't let me come along with them. Said I wasn't fit for much except keeping the campfire lit and safe for their return. When they were done, I helped them break camp and hit the trail. That's when we found you."

"Sounds like they didn't treat you very well," Holt observed. "Why stay with them?"

"On account of I had nowhere to go," Turnbull said. "And Cleat got me away from my pa, so I kind of owed him. They weren't a bad sort, mister. Just took the wrong trails after the war is all."

Holt had known many men who had done the same thing after the surrender. They had not been born crooked, but four years of blood and horror had a way of changing a man. Take away any hope he had for a decent job or land to work, and he had little choice but to fall back on the only thing he was good at. Finding a way to survive. One way or the other.

Holt knew that, had he taken a few wrong turns along the way, he might have found himself riding with men like the Turnbulls instead of riding into town with them lashed across their saddles.

Holt stopped examining his nails. "You really believe what you just said. About how taking the wrong trail can make a man good or bad?"

"I guess so." Turnbull shrugged. "Not that I've seen enough of life to know much."

"I'd wager you've already seen enough to know a fair amount. What trail do you think you're on right now, Jack? The right trail or the wrong one?"

"The one that leads to a long drop at the end of a short rope beneath a big tree."

Holt's eyebrows rose. "Doesn't have to end that way."

"That so?" Turnbull's sneer grew bigger. "You aim to keep Mullen and his men at bay while I make a run for it, Major?"

"You don't get to call me that, boy," Holt told him. "I'm not in uniform anymore and neither are you. I'm offering you what's called an alternative."

"Big words are wasted on me, Sheriff. Pa never put much stock in schooling either. This alternative the same thing as a choice?"

"It is in this instance."

He saw a spark of hope in the young man's eyes. "What kind of alternative do you have in mind?"

"You don't leave Devil's Gulch tonight or any other night. You stay here and work the town. With me."

Turnbull let loose with a laugh. "Oh, that'll win you lots of friends in town. Hiring a thief as your—what? Your deputy?"

Holt did not laugh. "Of a fashion. You'll do odd jobs in the jail, mostly. Guard prisoners. Clean up the place. In time, maybe even go on patrols with me. Who knows? You might even turn yourself into a respectable man in ten or twenty years. I can't promise you much, except that if you agree to it, neither Joe Mullen nor anyone else will be able to lay a finger on you, much less hang you."

Turnbull looked as if he was waiting for Holt to say more. To tell him it was all just a joke at his expense. But Holt did not say that. He did not say anything while he sat and watched the young man mull over his prospects.

"You mean it, don't you?"

"It's an offer, not a demand," Holt went on. "You've got your freedom as of now. You can get up, walk out that door, get yourself a horse, and ride off. Take your chances on the trail. Or you can stay here with me. I can teach you how to be a lawman and how to handle yourself when you have to."

"I already know how to shoot," Turnbull said. "My pa taught me that much."

"Any fool can shoot, boy. And if you do this job the way I teach you, chances are you won't have to use your gun at all."

"And if I do?"

Holt grew still. "Then I'll teach you how to kill a man before he kills you. How does that sound?"

Turnbull shook his head. "Sounds like the mayor and Mullen will never go for it."

"You won't be working for them," Holt told him. "You'll be working for me. I'll be paying you out of my own pocket, not the town's. And when I pin that star on your shirt, you won't be swearing an oath to the town. You'll be swearing one to me. Personally."

Turnbull's sneer softened as he grew to become accustomed to the idea. "Mullen has his committee men, and you'll have me. Is that how it works?"

"For starters," Holt said. "I aim to add to our ranks as we go along, providing I can find the right sort to join us."

"What makes you think it'll be that easy?" Turnbull asked. "Mullen and his boys have had their way for a long time. I don't see them letting you get away with much."

Holt had always kept his own counsel and saw no reason to explain himself to a young thief less than a day's ride from a hanging party. "I'll worry about Mullen. You worry about you. Do you want the job or not?"

Turnbull shrugged. "Can't see as I've got much of a choice, so yeah, I guess I accept."

Turnbull flinched again when Holt stood. "We've all got a choice, boy. Some are just easier to make than others. You've made the right one. Now on your feet and let me swear you in."

Jack Turnbull slowly stood but did not raise his hand. "I'd like to see the star you'll pin on me first. See if it's to my liking."

Holt admired the young man's gall. "Son, when word gets out you're working for me, you won't need one. But I'll see what I can do. Now put up your hand and take the oath."

Turnbull slowly raised his hand and swore allegiance to John Holt.

CHAPTER 11

Lester Patrick was not as young as Judge Cook had described, but Holt figured anyone south of seventy was young to the aged jurist. Holt had him pegged to be about forty. Despite spending most of his day in an office, he had maintained a lean build. The streaks of gray in his hair gave him the look of a competent man that people expected their authority figures to have. The spectacles perched on the end of his nose gave him a studious appearance.

The town attorney looked up at the sheriff across his desk after he finished reading the report. "You have remarkable penmanship, Sheriff. West Point, I take it?"

"No. My mother was a schoolteacher." Holt cared more about what the report contained than how it looked. "Tell me how you want to handle Cassie and Hank Bostrom."

Lester Patrick took off his spectacles and laid them atop the report. "You're certain she won't swear out a complaint against Hank Bostrom?"

"I barely got her to agree to speak to you," Holt said. "And you can bet that Ma McAdam will be in the room with her when you take down her statement. I don't want

that girl's death on my conscience, and I don't think you
do either."

"Need I remind you that there's the law to consider,
Sheriff Holt? One could say you and I would be suborning
perjury. The whole truth and nothing but the truth still
applies."

"I've read the wanted posters in my office," Holt said.
"Most of them are members of the Bostrom Gang. We
already have enough to charge Hank Bostrom with to hang
him ten times over. There's no reason to put Cassie at risk.
There's the law and the unwritten law. Both can be satisfied if you take her testimony her way. Hank is my concern. He doesn't need to be Cassie's. He's already hurt
her enough."

He watched the lawyer wrestle with the idea. "If I question her only on facts currently in evidence, I suppose we
could keep Hank's name out of it, especially because we
don't know where he is at present."

"About that," Holt said. "You've been in this town a
long time. Any idea where he might be holed up?"

Les Patrick nodded toward the window. His office had
a view of the Blue Bottle Saloon's balcony that over-
looked Main Street. Majestic, snow-covered mountains
rose beyond it in the distance. "Take a look around you,
Sheriff Holt. There are any number of gullies, caves,
abandoned mines and holes in the ground where a man
like Bostrom could hide. You could send an army out to
find him and they could ride within fifty yards of him
without even knowing it. And I wouldn't count on the
good people of this town to tell you much either. The
same people who might know where to find him wouldn't
dare tell you. Besides, they have designs on finding that
buried money and wouldn't want you finding it before
they did."

Holt knew Hank did not know where the missing money was, so how could they? But he decided to let that point go. "I told you Hank's my concern. Just make sure you give Cassie a free pass at the inquest. She's had it rough."

Holt had meant it as more of an order than a suggestion and Patrick took it as such. He looked as though he was about to say something about it when a great cry went up from the street. Both men stood and went to the window to see what the fuss was about.

Holt watched the undertaker, Earl Sibert, stop a wagon in front of the Blue Bottle Saloon. Men on the street pulled a canvas tarp aside, revealing three corpses in lidless coffins. Their faces sported too much rouge to hide their deathly pallor. Their hands had been folded across their laps and they wore the same clothes they had been wearing when Holt had killed them.

He watched a group of men clamor to pull the coffins from the back of the wagon and pitch them at an angle against the wall of the saloon. Holt noticed the bodies remained upright, probably due to planks of wood Sibert had placed behind them.

"Ghastly, isn't it?" Lester Patrick said. "They do that every time they get their hands on a criminal. It was Mullen's idea. Says it serves as a deterrent to anyone who thinks about breaking the law in Devil's Gulch."

Holt had seen the practice in other towns but had never grown accustomed to the sight. "They didn't even kill them. I did."

"A point of fact which does not appear to have been lost on them." He pointed down at a large, hand-painted sign they were lifting from the wagon bed. "They seem to have given you all the credit."

Holt squinted as he read what they had painted on the wood.

SEE WHAT HAPPENS TO OUTLAWS
IN DEVIL'S GULCH.
GOD BLESS JOHN HOLT,
SHERIFF AND PROTECTOR

Holt's jaw tightened. "I didn't tell them to write that. I didn't have anything to do with any of this."

"You didn't have to," Patrick said. "They're always quite generous when giving credit where credit is due. The irony of it all is that they'll all be drunk and disorderly tonight. Old Cassidy's place always does a great business when the men celebrate dead outlaws. They'll be out on the street, shooting at the moon and telling themselves how brave they are for making spectacles of the men you killed."

The attorney let out a heavy sigh. "Earl Sibert won't be able to buy a drink for himself tonight. It's customary to let the undertaker have his fill, simply because he's allowed Cassidy to post dead men in front of his saloon. As I said, a ghastly practice."

The sight of the carnage disgusted him, but Holt could not look away. A thick crowd had already surrounded the corpses. Cursing at them. Spitting at them. Someone had even placed a torch in iron holders affixed to the wall so they could be seen in the encroaching night.

"Mayor Chapman and Judge Cook allow this?" Holt asked aloud.

Lester Patrick shrugged. "There's not much to be done about it. They've spoken out against it, of course, but this town clings to its traditions, especially the more distasteful ones."

"Well, if they won't do something about it, I will."

Holt began to leave when the attorney took firm hold of his arm. "I'd advise against that, Sheriff Holt. You're a brave man, but you're only one man against a drunken mob. If you go down there and try to break up their fun, they're liable to turn on you. A riot will be the least of your problems."

Holt looked down at Patrick's hand on his arm until the lawyer let him go.

But Patrick was undeterred. "If you make trouble, it might be you being propped up in front of the Blue Bottle tomorrow. And I'd hate to see that happen."

But John Holt had never allowed overwhelming odds to deter him before. "Get over to Cassie's place and get her statement. I want her clear of this Bostrom mess as soon as possible."

The attorney called after Holt as he walked out the door. "It's been nice working with you, Sheriff. However briefly."

Holt pushed through the crowd that had formed in the thoroughfare. Wagons loaded with goods on both sides of the crowd were blocked. Their horses growing unsettled amid all the commotion.

Holt began pushing the crowd aside. Hard, at first, then easier once people saw it was him. When they parted enough, Holt began waving the wagons through. When the knot of human and horseflesh was undone, he headed straight for the spectacle of death in front of the Blue Bottle Saloon.

Mullen spotted him in the crowd and bellowed, "Make

way for this man! Make way! The hero of the hour has come to take his bows."

Judging by the stench of whiskey Holt caught from the leader of the Vigilance Committee, he had started his celebration early.

"Let him by, I say," Mullen continued to yell at the crowd. "Let us thank him properly for what he has done to protect our fair town."

Those who had not moved out of Holt's way were pushed aside by the sheriff as he made a straight line for Mullen.

"How do you like it, Holt?" Mullen asked when he stepped up to the boardwalk. "Oh, it's not a pretty sight, I know, but a little death and blood now and then keeps the flock in order."

Holt ignored the smell of whiskey as he drew even with Mullen. "I didn't give permission for this."

Mullen looked at him with boozy indignance. "Your permission isn't required, sir. This is tradition."

"Not anymore." Holt pointed at Sibert, who was already halfway into the saloon. "Put them back in the wagon. Now."

Those who had heard him grew quiet, but most of the crowd was too caught up in the celebration to notice.

Sibert began to turn slowly toward Holt. "I beg your pardon?"

"You heard me, Earl. Load these bodies back in the wagon and get them out of here. I don't care if it's back to your shop or in the ground. I want these bodies out of here and I want them out of here now."

Sibert looked around as if someone might help him, perhaps even Mullen. But no one did. They just looked at the angry lawman as if he had appeared out of thin air.

Holt stepped over to the undertaker and loomed over

him. "I gave you an order, boy. Best get to doing what I said before you get hurt."

Quiet descended over the crowd. An uneasy silence quickly spread to both sides of the thoroughfare and to the boardwalk in front of County Hall.

Mullen tried to angle his way in between Holt and Sibert. "Sheriff Holt, you're new to town, so I guess you don't understand how we do things around here. We've been putting outlaws and criminals on display like this since as long as I can remember. We—"

Holt turned his attention to Mullen. "And get this crowd out of here. You say you want to help, that's how you do it. By sending these people on their way and letting Sibert take down this spectacle."

Holt heard the grumbling behind him and knew the crowd was beginning to turn on him. He did not care about that. Only about the two men in front of him and what they would do next.

He looked at Sibert. "If you don't get about your business right now, I'll throw you in jail for a week."

"On what charge?" one of the men shouted out at him.

"For disturbing the peace, inciting a riot, and anything else I can think of."

As Sibert began to reluctantly make his way toward the coffins, Mullen rested a hand on Holt's shoulder and lowered his voice. "Sheriff, if a riot breaks out, the only one inciting it will be you."

But Mullen had not noticed that Holt had already pulled his Remington until he felt it pressed against his stomach. "You'll be beyond caring by then, Mullen. You'll already be dead." He thumbed back the hammer. "I already told you what to do. I won't say it again."

Mullen looked down at the pistol, then back at Holt. "You pull that trigger and these people will tear you apart."

Holt dug the pistol deep into Mullen's belly until the man moved aside. "You willing to bet your life on that, boy? Because I am."

Sibert wriggled out from behind Mullen and beckoned his assistants up to the boardwalk to help place the coffins back in the wagon. The men grumbled but quickly complied.

"Your turn, Mullen." Holt used the barrel of his pistol to shove the committeeman forward.

Mullen rubbed his sore belly as he said, "Sorry, everyone, but Sheriff Holt has asked us to refrain from this manner of celebration. And seeing as how he's the one who killed these boys, I suppose he has a right. Best if we all go about our business, whether that's home or here at the Bottle, where the first round of drinks will still be on the Devil's Gulch Vigilance Committee."

Some of the crowd remained on the street, clustered together as they watched Sibert and his men load the Turnbull boys back into the wagon.

A fair number of the spectators filed past Holt and Mullen as they entered the saloon for the free drinks they had been promised.

Mullen turned and smiled at Holt. "Can't arrest a man for offering free drinks, now can you, Sheriff?"

Holt slid his Remington back into its holster. "That's the one thing you don't understand, Mullen. In this town, I can arrest a man for just about anything. The quicker you realize that the better it'll be for all concerned."

Mullen looked Holt up and down. "You've made yourself a lot of enemies tonight, Holt."

"Same amount as those who came rushing to your rescue just now, I'd expect."

Mullen's smile disappeared. "You've made an enemy out of me."

"That was going to happen anyway. All I did was hurry things along a little." He snatched the thin signboard that had been hung above the coffins and easily broke it over his knee before tossing it into Sibert's wagon. "At least we both know where we stand."

Mullen slowly backed up toward the saloon. "But only one of us knows the hellfire that'll come because of it." He touched the brim of his hat. "A good evening to you, Sheriff Holt."

Holt waited until Mullen and his men were inside the Blue Bottle before turning his attention to the undertaker, who was already up in the wagon's box. "I want those men buried immediately."

Sibert looked at the sky. "But, Sheriff, it's already going on dark. We won't be able to dig three graves before nightfall."

Holt grabbed one of the torches they had set up for the coffins and threw it up to Sibert, who surprised him by catching it. "Good thing you boys brought torches. Now get going."

Sibert sagged as he released the hand brake and got the wagon moving toward the cemetery.

Holt looked at the people who had hung around to discuss what they had just seen. None of them returned his gaze and eventually moved on. Anywhere was better than standing around the sheriff. They had obviously decided it was dangerous to be found around such a man.

CHAPTER 12

Joe Mullen strode through the crowd of men lined up at the bar of the Blue Bottle Saloon, tamping down his rage by backslapping and joining his neighbors in toasts to Lady Justice. The crowd was less than half of what he had promised Tony Cassidy it would be. That would mean he and the committee would get less of a payoff at the end of the evening.

What's more, he would have to endure Cassidy's gloating for he had predicted something like this might happen earlier that day.

And as he clinked glasses of whiskey with the men of Devil's Gulch, Mullen could see a change in them. In the way they looked at him. Some of the reverence they had held for him had been lost. Their faith in his ability to make committee men above their fellow citizens was now in doubt. He could not blame them. After all, Holt had forced him to call off their celebration in public. Many of them had not seen the gun Holt had to his belly. Even if they had, they would have blamed him for not asking for help. Holt was only one man, even if he was John Holt, and they were many.

When he made his way to the end of the bar, he found

Tony Cassidy lurking in the corner. A glass of beer in his hand. The saloon owner had never developed a taste for whiskey.

Cassidy inclined his head back toward his office at the rear of the saloon. It was a subtle invitation for Mullen to follow him. An invitation Joe Mullen was in no position to refuse given his recent public defeat at the hands of Holt.

He finished a round of forced laughter at bad jokes with the last group at the bar before he slipped away to Cassidy's office. The fact that none of them seemed to notice he was leaving bothered him to no end. Could his hold on the town have been so fragile? Could his authority be shaken by one bad run-in with the sheriff?

He grabbed a bottle from the end of the bar and brought it with him into Cassidy's office.

To call it an office would have been generous. It was little more than a storage room with a desk and chairs inside. The decor was always changing, depending on how many cases of whiskey or beer were needed out front. On delivery days, the office was filled from floor to ceiling with crates. On busy nights, the walls were bare and cracked. The lighting perpetually dim thanks to the oil lamp that sat on Cassidy's desk. The space always reminded Mullen more of one of the mines he owned rather than a proper office.

He elbowed the door shut and dropped into a seat.

Cassidy sat with his hands folded across his flat stomach. Mullen had always been amazed that a man who lived on beer could manage to remain so thin.

"Bad night, Joe," Cassidy said.

Mullen thumbed the cork out of the bottle and refilled his glass. "I've had worse."

"Not in this town, you haven't. Why'd you let Holt treat you that way?"

Mullen did not want to talk about it. "He had a gun in my belly."

"You could've had fifty pointed at his head. All you had to do was say the word."

Mullen downed the drink in one swallow and poured himself another. He hoped it would dull the pain of the memory. The look he had seen in Holt's eyes. A look that told him his life was about to end. "He would've killed me, Tony. I firmly believe he would've shot me dead on the spot had I so much as looked like I was going to ask for help."

The saloon owner frowned. "He's got you turned, doesn't he? You're as meek as a lamb now."

Mullen lost his appetite for whiskey and set the glass and bottle on his desk. "It's not like that. One bad night doesn't tell the tale. I cooperated with him. I'll get him back on our side."

"You think it'll be that easy?" Cassidy asked from the edge of the lamplight. "You count the crowd out there? I did. We were expecting twice that number, easy. We've got less than half than we normally do for a showing. The rest are either over at the Railhead or at home with their wives. I was counting on that money, Joe. You made me a promise, remember."

"I was counting on it, too, remember?" Mullen had taken the stick from Holt, but he was not inclined to take it from a skinny whoremaster , even if it was Cassidy. "You can forget about my share of tonight's take if you want."

"Oh, I've already forgotten about it. I'll be lucky to break even after the free drinks you promised them. But this isn't about the money."

"It's always about the money with you."

"It's always been about who really runs this town,"

Cassidy corrected him. "Money's just the way we've kept score up until now. We worked together to keep this town under our thumb and out of Ma's control. Chapman only thinks he runs this town."

"He knows that," Mullen said. "He still comes here every morning to kiss our rings, remember? He's not likely to grow a backbone just because Holt's around."

"We'll see if he comes tomorrow," Cassidy said. "The doc too. Maybe they'll start having breakfast somewhere else. At the Railhead, for instance."

Mullen had not thought of that. "They wouldn't dare. Besides, the Railhead doesn't serve breakfast."

"They'll start if it looks like there's something in it for them." Cassidy reached over, took the bottle from the desk, and set it on the floor beside him. "I think this stuff is starting to become a habit with you, Joe. It's beginning to cloud your thinking just when I need you sharp."

Mullen grabbed his glass and drank it down before defiantly slamming it on the desk. "I reckon I've always been as sharp as I need to be."

"You have," Cassidy allowed, "but Holt's presence changes things. The man has barely been in town for more than a day and he's already got the mayor eating out of his hand. You heard him babble on about how impressive he is over breakfast this morning. Holt's even got Ma McAdam under his thumb on account of him going easy on Cassie after the shooting last night. And tonight, he ran us off without firing a shot. The crowd out there would've torn Frank Peters to pieces if he'd ever pulled a stunt like that. But Holt? They just shied away and disappeared like smoke in the wind." Cassidy slowly shook his head. "We can't have that, Joe."

Mullen did not like hearing Cassidy give voice to the same concerns that had been rattling around in his head all day. It was like a smoldering fire he dared not allow to breathe. "Like I told you this morning, Holt's new. His luster will dim after what he pulled tonight. You can always rely on the people of Devil's Gulch to want a good time."

Cassidy surprised him by bringing a thin fist down on his desk. "But they're not having it here. Now. Tonight. Out there in my saloon. We're not the only place in town, Joe. There are plenty of other places they can go to drink and eat and gamble. They come here because they think it buys them some influence with you and me. If they stop thinking that influence matters anymore, Ma McAdam will greet them with open arms."

He pointed a thin finger at Mullen. "We worked too hard to take this town away from that greedy old hag just to have her snatch it back now."

Mullen had not considered that. "I think you're getting worked up over nothing."

"And I don't think you're worked up enough. We staged that show out there tonight to give you a chance to show Holt what you're made of, and instead of anteing up, you folded. Why, my people tell me the mayor is over at the jail right now, talking to Holt instead of being here where he belongs."

Mullen wanted to argue but could not. Cassidy's words stung him deeply. He was sorry he had drunk down all the whiskey in one swallow. He could use some now.

Cassidy sat back in his chair and folded his hands across his stomach again. "Well, you may have lost the hand but I'm making sure you're still in the game."

Mullen did not like the sound of that. They usually worked well together, with Cassidy making suggestions and Mullen deciding what to do and how to do it. He felt a shift in their arrangement where Cassidy may begin to make decisions on his own, leaving Mullen no choice but to follow. He had not liked backing down to Holt, but he could not allow Cassidy to forget his place.

"Careful, Tony. It's best if you leave the rough stuff to me."

"It doesn't need to be rough," Cassidy said. "It just needs to happen. Tonight, before word of your weakness spreads more than it already has. Lucky for us, I know exactly what to do."

CHAPTER 13

"I was wondering if you might consider a different approach next time," Mayor Chapman said as he sat across from Holt in the jail later that evening.

"No other way to approach something like that except head-on." Holt sipped his coffee and cursed his luck. He either put in too many grinds, making it mud, or too little, which made it taste like dark water. He was glad the mayor had turned down his offer of a cup. It had saved him considerable embarrassment.

Holt did not know Jack Turnbull was standing behind him until the young man said, "They really did that, Sheriff? Prop up my kin outside a saloon like that?"

"Only for a time, boy," Holt told him. "Best get back in there and let me and the mayor have our discussion."

After Jack did as he was told, Mayor Chapman said, "I know Joe Mullen isn't an easy man to get along with, but I'm afraid he's a man you will have to work with eventually. He and his committee provide an invaluable service to this town. A service that can benefit you if you allow it. Just because he and your predecessor didn't get along doesn't mean you have to be enemies."

"Frank Peters was bought and paid for by Ma McAdam

years ago," Holt reminded him. "Mullen's either in Cassidy's pocket or it's the other way around. That's why they didn't get along. Me? I'm in nobody's pocket except the law, so their arrangements, traditions, and whatever other troubles they have don't matter to me."

Holt did not give the mayor a chance to argue. "A band of outlaws beat up a lady of the evening last night, sir, and I think they're bound to take another run at her. I can't afford to let Mullen have a drunken mob under his thumb in the bargain. They're liable to do anything in that condition and you're paying me good money to stop that from happening. I couldn't do much to keep Cassie safe from the Bostrom Boys because I didn't know enough to do it, but I sure know enough now. I can't defend her and fight a mob at the same time. I've seen how quickly a bunch like the men I saw at the Bottle can turn when they get enough whiskey in their bellies and hot air in their lungs over being brave men. I won't stand for it, and neither should you. With me around, you won't have to."

The mayor pawed at his face, obviously distressed by the course the conversation was taking. He had clearly come to the jail in the hopes of being able to talk some sense into the new sheriff. To find middle ground. He had not expected a debate.

Holt had no sympathy for him. He was a politician. He should have known that everything in life was a debate, especially where John Holt was involved.

"Things could've gotten ugly back there," Chapman offered.

"They got ugly enough."

"There could've been a riot, sir."

"But there wasn't and there won't be as long as you keep backing me up," Holt told him. "And one way you can do that is to pass a law against unlawful assemblies."

Chapman's mouth went slack. "A what?"

"You heard me," Holt said. "I've had it done in a few towns I've worked. Anyone who wants to have a large gathering like that needs a permit. You can justify it by the fact that there were no fewer than five wagons bottled up because of their nonsense. A team of horses almost bucked and ran wild. People could've been hurt. Your people, Mr. Mayor. If they complain, tell them it's with their best interest at heart." Holt smiled. "It even has the virtue of being true."

"People around here don't like too many laws, Holt." The more the mayor thought of it, the less he liked it. "I don't think such a law will be received well."

"But they'll obey it," Holt told him. "They might not like it at first, but they'll comply with your law, your rules, not Mullen's. And right now, he's the one I'm concerned about."

Holt could tell he was quickly losing the mayor when he said, "I don't know about that, Sheriff. Joe Mullen is a friend of mine. Why, I have breakfast with the man almost every day. He and I haven't always agreed on everything, but he's always had the best interest of the town at heart. You might not like the man and maybe you have your reasons, but you don't know him well enough to accuse him of undermining me."

Holt knew he had to choose his next words carefully. He had to give him evidence, not opinion, if he hoped to secure his support. "Did you see what happened in front of the Blue Bottle tonight? From your office, I mean. I know you weren't on the street."

"I saw it when it started and again when they fell silent," the mayor admitted. "Why?"

"Then you saw a crowd that was entirely under Mullen's control, not mine. They were putting those bodies on display because neither you nor Judge Cook told them otherwise."

"Now, stop right there," Chapman said. "I've never supported the practice and have always denounced it in public."

"Maybe, but that's all you've done," Holt pointed out. "If you make it a law, you're taking the tradition away from Mullen and putting it where it belongs. With the people elected to run this town, not those who run it at gunpoint. He's got them on a rope, sir. They'll do whatever he says. That's great for him but bad for you."

Mayor Blair Chapman may have been a soft, amiable man, but he was no fool. "Sounds to me like any law I pass takes power away from Mullen and gives it to you."

"To the town," Holt corrected him. "Not to me."

"Semantics," Chapman said. "You've been spending too much time with Lester Patrick. I swear that man could find a way to debate the merits of chicken soup." He looked at Holt. "You know I'm an elected official, John, and not an entirely popular one at that. If Mullen were to run against me, he'd win in a landslide. If I push him too hard, that's exactly what he'll do."

"You just got reelected to a new term," Holt reminded him. "And people have short memories. Now's the time for a law like this. A law I can use to curtail Mullen's power. You'll look stronger and people around here will start remembering that he's just a man bound by the law, just like the rest of them."

"That includes you, John," Chapman said. "You not only have to enforce the law but obey it as well."

No, the mayor was not a fool after all. "Give me a law to obey and I'll enforce it."

Mayor Chapman closed his eyes. "I think you may prove to be as antagonistic as Lester Patrick."

Holt decided to try to put an end to it by trying a personal approach. "You know a law like this is right, Blair. And I promise I'll make it work to your benefit."

Mayor Chapman nodded. "Fine, John. You've made your case. I'll bring the matter before the town council in our next session. The day after tomorrow. I don't know how they'll vote, but I'll put the matter to them."

Holt imagined that was as good as he could hope for.

He looked at the door as he began to hear voices grow louder out in the street. The mayor turned in his seat and looked that way too. "What's going on?"

"I don't know," Holt admitted as he got to his feet. He took his Remington from the top drawer and slid it into his holster. "But I'm going to find out."

As he walked to the door, Holt heard the crowd begin to chant, "May-or Chap-man. Come out now! May-or Chap-man. Come out now!"

The rhythmic chant only grew louder as more people joined in.

"Good God," the mayor said as he slowly rose to his feet. "That must be the drunken rabble from the Blue Bottle Saloon."

Holt pulled a blanket out from under his bed and unwrapped it, revealing a Henry rifle. He levered a cartridge into the chamber and told the mayor, "Get back in the cells with Jack. You'll be safer there."

But the mayor surprised him by walking toward the door. "This is still my town, Sheriff, and those are my people. They're calling for me and I intend to face them." He swallowed and his bravery dipped a little as he added, "Though I'd appreciate it if you'd agree to stand by my side."

Holt hefted the rifle until the barrel was across his shoulder. "Henry and I'll be proud to stand by you, sir. Lead the way."

Chapman unbolted the jail door and walked out to meet the people calling his name.

Holt stood in the open doorway of the jail while Chapman raised his hands in a bid to calm the angry crowd. Holt judged there to be about fifty men. All of them drunk. Some had torches. Others had brought their whiskey bottles with them.

Mullen was in the back of the crowd, weaving as he smiled at the torment he had brought.

"My friends," Mayor Chapman shouted over them. "What troubles you this fine evening?"

A townsman Holt had never seen before stepped to the front of the crowd. He had a miner's stoop and skin that was permanently darkened from years of toil below ground. A grit that had seeped into his soul that no amount of scrubbing could wash away, not that Holt imagined he would want to be cleansed of it anyway.

Holt kept his rifle across his shoulder. The crowd had seen it. He would only bring it level if he had to.

"We've got concerns, Chapman," the miner said. "What's this business we hear about you turning the Turnbull boy loose? The very same man who robbed us."

The crowd cheered their approval as Chapman beckoned them to be silent again. "It's good to see you up and about, Ott." Chapman looked back at Holt. "This here is Ott Heller. Been living in town since the beginning. Been sick as of late. An ailment of the lungs." He looked again at the miner. "How are you fairing, Ott?"

Holt thought it was a good trick on the mayor's part. Talking about the man made it personal. Ott Heller was less part of a faceless mob and now an individual. Maybe Chapman was not as hapless as Holt had first thought.

"Good to be seen, Mayor," Heller said. "Now, what's this we've heard about the Turnbull boy?"

"The decision to keep young Turnbull in jail or to set him free is beyond my control. Only Judge Cook has the power to jail or free him, not me."

The crowd booed and hissed as Heller began to speak for them. "But he's a town judge and you're the town mayor. Ain't you gonna do something about it?"

"We're a nation of laws, Ott," the mayor said. "It's not a matter of who's mayor, but of what the court decides. I know we're only a territory, but we must still abide by the law of the land."

Some of the southerners in the crowd cursed the memory of Lincoln while others shouted that Chapman was a liar.

Heller continued to speak for the crowd. "We elected you, not Judge Cook. If you can't do anything to stop him, what good are you?"

Chapman held up his hands again to quell the crowd. "You've elected me as your mayor to administer to the town's needs. I know I'm only in the middle of my term, but from what I've heard from most of you, you seem to be pleased by what I've been doing in that regard. If you decide I'm not worthy of the office, you can always vote against me in the next election."

The drunken crowd rose again, saying that's what they would do, demanding an election immediately.

And from the back of the mob, Joe Mullen stepped forward and shouted over them. "I don't know about you, boys, but I'd like to hear Sheriff Holt's opinion on the subject."

The crowd voiced their approval and all eyes fell on Holt.

He kept the rifle barrel on his shoulder. "I'm an officer of the law. Not a judge. Not a jury. I take my orders from

Judge Cook. If he tells me to release him, I'll release him. If he tells me to keep him locked up, he stays locked up."

Mullen played to the crowd. "There you have it, boys. Sounds like we can't count on the mayor or the sheriff for much. Sounds to me like if we want some justice around here, we'll have to get it for ourselves."

The mob yelped and cheered. One cut loose with a rebel yell that was echoed by others.

Holt spoke over them. "No one in this town is above the law, Mullen. That goes for me and you and everyone out here tonight. Any man who thinks otherwise will answer to me."

"We make the laws." Heller swayed as he yelled. The liquor seemed to be hitting home now. "Our town, our laws."

The crowd picked up the chant and spoke as one. *Our Town. Our Laws.*

And while they chanted, Heller said, "You got the Turnbull boy in there, don't you? If you're not man enough to do what needs doing, stand aside and let us have at him."

The crowd cheered, but Holt did not move from the doorway. "No."

Heller stepped forward and spat, striking Holt's right boot.

Holt hit the miner under the chin, sending him sprawling backward into the crowd.

The men began to surge forward until Holt leveled the Henry at them. "Come ahead if you're coming."

The crowd froze where they stood as Chapman stepped between the sheriff and the mob. "Gentlemen, please. There's no reason for this. The Turnbull boy is still in jail. Judge Cook hasn't ordered his release yet. You're just getting yourselves all lathered up over something that might not even happen. Remain calm, please. There's a proper way to address your concerns."

Holt watched some of the men up front help Heller to his feet. He thought he was pulling up his pants but did not see the gun until it was already in his hand.

"Talk," Heller said as he raised the pistol. "All you do is talk."

Holt fired two shots in the miner's chest just as Heller pulled the trigger. The mayor spun from the impact and cried out as Heller fell to the thoroughfare.

The crowd began to scatter as Holt waded into them. He rammed his rifle butt hard into the face of a man in front and across the jaw of another. A backswing caught another man in the temple before the rest managed to scatter into the darkness.

He looked around for Mullen, but the man was nowhere to be found.

Chapman's moans from the boardwalk snapped Holt out of his hunt for Mullen and he leaped up onto the boardwalk to tend to the wounded mayor.

He was glad to see Doc Klassen running toward him with his medical bag in hand.

"He's been shot," Holt said as he knelt beside Chapman. "Looks like the belly."

Klassen dropped beside him and began to examine him. "Cover the street. There might be more trouble yet."

Holt got to his feet and yelled into the jail, "Jack, get out here."

He heard the young man come out from the cells and stand in the doorway. "They're looking to kill me, and I don't even have a gun."

"I do," Holt reminded him as he watched the street. "Get out here and help the doc get the mayor inside."

Chapman cried out again as Turnbull helped Klassen haul the mayor into the jail. Holt stole a quick glance down at the blood on the boardwalk and knew Chapman was in a bad way. He saw a large gouge in the wall where the bullet had stopped. He had seen too many such wounds in the war to have much hope for the mayor's chances of survival.

The sound of shattering glass from behind him caused Holt to wheel around in time to see flames begin to shoot out from a storefront. It was Mayor Chapman's haberdashery. Flames were flickering in the window as they found ready fuel among the fabric within it.

Instinct told him to rush to the store and try to tamp down the flames, but he remained where he was. Doing so would leave the mayor, the doctor, and Turnbull exposed. Even with the bar across the door, it would not take long for a determined mob to break in if they wanted.

Holt had no choice but to remain where he was and watch the fire burn.

Other citizens of Devil's Gulch began to fill the street. Not the mob, but men in nightshirts and robes cast on hurriedly in the darkness as they scrambled to fight the fire that not only threatened Chapman's shop, but every other wooden building in town. They used blankets to try to stomp out the flames they could reach while a line quickly formed passing buckets of water from one man to another to douse the flames.

These were the real people of Devil's Gulch. The people Holt had sworn to serve and protect.

One of the three men Holt had struck during the melee began to sit up, holding his shattered nose. "You broke it, you idiot."

Holt brought down the butt of his rifle on the back of the man's head, rendering him unconscious. He snatched the man by the collar and dragged him into the jail, around the bed where the doctor was tending to Chapman and into the cells.

He told Turnbull, "Bring in the other two. Drag them if you have to. Put them each in separate cells. No sense in crowding them in there unless it comes to that."

The young man was too taken by the sight of Chapman's blood to argue. He looked relieved to be given another task away from the blood.

Holt dumped the unconscious prisoner into Turnbull's old cell and shut the door. He would worry about locking it later.

He looked outside and saw Jack leading the two wounded prisoners into the jail. He hoped his new deputy was not shy around blood.

Because there was a good chance he would be seeing plenty more of it before all of this was over.

CHAPTER 14

Later, Holt was not surprised when Doc Klassen joined him out on the boardwalk. He quietly closed the door behind him, which cut the sound of Mrs. Chapman's plaintive wails from inside the jail. He was careful to avoid the blood still congealing on the boardwalk.

Holt stood watch while Turnbull sat on the edge of the boardwalk. His head was between his legs. The combination of acrid smoke that filled Main Street and the sight of blood inside the jail had done a number on the boy's stomach. He had gotten sick several times since the townsmen had managed to put the fire out about an hour before.

Klassen pulled a cigar out of his bag and offered one to Holt, who declined. He did not think the smell would do Turnbull any favors, but the boy was in no position to make requests.

"They put the fire out?" Klassen asked as he bit off the end of it and thumbed a match alive.

"Looks like it," Holt said. "Don't think it spread. No wind tonight." He had never been one to avoid difficult subjects, so he asked, "Chapman's not going to make it, is he?"

Klassen took a few deep draws on the cigar until the flame took before tossing the dead match into Main Street. He exhaled a long plume of smoke as he looked toward the sky. "I'm amazed he's lasted this long. Bullet tore right through the middle of him. Couldn't even save him if I had an operating theater at my disposal, which I don't. I doubt he'll last until morning."

Both men looked down at Heller's corpse, which still laid flat in the thoroughfare. The mob had trampled him underfoot as they fled, which did not make him a pretty sight to behold. Holt had decided to leave him where he was until Earl Sibert got around to noticing him.

The doctor gestured at Heller's body with his cigar. "He was sick you know. Cancer of the lungs. Spread throughout his body near as I can figure. Damned fool must have coughed up half a pint of blood each morning before he could get out of bed and go back to the same mine that killed him." Klassen caught himself. "That's an exaggeration, of course, but you get the idea."

Yes, Holt got the idea, but not the one Klassen had expected. "Anyone else know his condition."

"It wasn't exactly a secret," Klassen said. "He didn't walk around with a sign or anything, but people knew. Saloon talk. Town gossip. That kind of thing. Sometimes I think miners are bigger gossips than washer women."

Holt looked at the pistol that had been trampled into the thoroughfare by dozens of feet looking to get away. "I wonder."

"Wonder what?" Klassen asked as he followed Holt's eyes to the pistol.

"How much of that mess did you see?" Holt asked. "Of the crowd bunched up in front of here, I mean."

"I heard them when they started shouting and figured I should get over here in case things got out of hand," the doctor told him. "I stayed back when it looked like you had them stopped but came running when I heard the shots. Why?"

Holt could not take his eyes from the corpse. "Heller was a miner, wasn't he?"

"Yes, he was. Worked there for years."

"You ever know him to carry a gun?"

Klassen removed the cigar from his mouth as he gave it some thought. "No. Can't say that I did come to think of it."

"See anyone else in the crowd sporting pistols or rifles as they ran away?"

The doctor shook his head. "Other than Mullen, who always goes armed, no. And good thing they weren't. You would've had a bloodbath on your hands."

But Holt was not concerned about that. "All those drunks and only one of them thought to pull a gun. The same one they'd elected to speak for them. The only one in the bunch who happened to have a pistol tucked away. A man who wasn't given to walking around heeled."

Klassen lowered his cigar to his side. "John, I don't like the sound of that."

Neither did Holt. But it was hard to deny the facts. "Let me guess. Heller has family, doesn't he?"

"A wife and five kids," the doctor told him. "He's much older than Rita, but they kept having them just the same. They live in a shack up at Mullen's Sarabelle Mine."

Holt looked down at the corpse. "Isn't that a coincidence."

"I don't think you'll have to worry about having a grieving widow on your hands," Klassen said. "I got the impression that she didn't like him very much. Heller was a hellion when he got drink in him. Why'd you ask?"

"Because I'm gonna need you to keep your ear to the

ground for me. I need to know if they suddenly come into some money. Buy fancy clothes or such." He nodded down at the body. "Because Heller was a dead man walking. And I don't think it would've taken too much effort to talk him into shooting the mayor if it came down to getting a proper payday for his family."

Klassen thought it over as he brought the cigar up to his lips and smoked. "It'd be impossible to prove. All the miners will kick in something to help them out now that Ott's gone. And you can bet Mullen and his committee men will be more than generous."

"Not that generous," Holt cautioned. "And if they are, you'll let me know." He looked at the doctor. "Don't believe everything you've heard about me, Ralph. I don't enjoy this kind of thing as much as I'm supposed to. Just because I don't run from it doesn't mean I like it."

Another wail from Mrs. Chapman cut through the night, causing Holt and Klassen to cringe.

"Sounds like you'd better get back in there," Holt told him.

"Not much I can do but try to keep her calm." He rested a hand on Holt's arm. "She's liable to be angry with you when she comes out of there. I'm asking you to take it, no matter what she says. She's a difficult woman, but she loved old Blair something deep."

Holt nodded and the doctor walked back inside the jail to tend to his patients.

He looked over at his young deputy, who was still sitting on the edge of the boardwalk. It was tough to tell in the weak light from the jail, but the boy appeared to look better.

"How're you faring, Jack?"

Turnbull picked up his head. "You mean what you said just now. About that old fella there being put up to shoot the mayor?"

Holt had forgotten he had heard that. "It's possible."

The boy ran a hand across his mouth. "I don't know what's worse. The notion that it's possible or that you can think that way."

Holt envied Turnbull his youth. "When it comes to figuring folks, it's best to aim low so you don't get disappointed."

"Or shot."

Holt nodded. "That too."

CHAPTER 15

Mullen had made it back to the Sarabelle Mine just before sunrise. It was closer than his ranch. He had not wanted to leave town. He did not want it to look like he was running from Holt or his responsibilities in town. But Cassidy had convinced him otherwise. He knew that once word reached his men about what had happened to Ott Heller, there was no telling what they might do next. At least if he was at the mine, he could corral their more basic instincts of revenge.

That was, of course, until the time was right to use it for his own advantage.

Being at the mine also allowed him the opportunity to console Heller's grieving widow, Rita.

Unfortunately, she had already decided to take her consolation from a jug. She had already downed a fair amount of moonshine by the time he had reached the camp and Mullen's presence did not stop her.

"Good for John Holt," she said, sloshing her glass as she raised it to the disgust of the miner's wives who had come to be with her. "I'm glad Ott's dead."

Mullen could hardly blame her. Her eye was still swollen from the last beating her late husband had given her and her split lip was still mending from the beating before that.

"Keep your voice down," Mullen said. "He was mighty popular with the men, and they won't take kindly to anyone running him down. Not even you."

"Let them hear," she said as she drained her glass, then pointed at the other women with her. "They're no better than he was. Just look at all their womenfolk here. We've taken our lumps thanks to our men digging rock out of the ground for you. And what do we have to show for it? Bruises and sore arms and marks on our throats from the chokings and such. Why, Old Missy there's jaw still ain't set proper. She'll never talk right again, not that she ever could. That Kentucky accent of hers is thicker than molasses."

Missy lunged at her, but the other wives caught her in time and eased her back onto her stool.

Mullen's own wife, Sarabelle, for whom the mine was named, tried to ease the glass from Rita's hand. "You've had enough for now, honey. Why don't you get some rest? We'll tend to the children for you."

But Rita would not relinquish her hold on the glass and even managed to grab the jug of lightning water. "Don't worry about my boys. They'll be happier than I am when they find out the old fool went and got himself shot. I only wish he'd had the decency to have gotten himself shot sooner."

She pulled her arm free of Sarabelle's grip and poured herself another drink. "Do you know what he put us through? Coughing and spitting all the time. Couldn't get a good night's sleep with all his rattling and dying. Only good thing to come of it was that it kept him off me. No more mouths to feed." She smiled at a thought. "And now we've got one fewer. Just so happens it was the biggest one of all."

Mullen heard the men begin to gather outside, anxious for their employer to tell them what had happened to Ott Heller. Their foreman and friend. The man who had been killed in town by the low-down murdering Sheriff John Holt.

But he had to get Rita under control first, if that was even possible.

He spoke to the other ladies gathered around the shack. "I'd be obliged to you all if you'd head back to your homes and tend to your families. Sarabelle and I'll look after Rita for you. Maybe a couple of you could come back later when she's feeling better."

"I'm feeling just fine," she bellowed as the women began to leave. "I haven't been happier since before I laid eyes on that no-good yellow-belly."

Mullen smiled at the ladies as they filed out and quickly closed the crooked door behind them.

Now that it was just Rita and his wife, he no longer had to keep up appearances. "You'd better learn to control that mouth of yours before you go and say too much."

"Like what?" she slurred. "Like about all them dirty secrets you and Ott shared? Like how you've bilked men just like them out of their claims?" Her eyes grew narrow and nasty. "Or are you afraid I might talk about all that money Bob Bostrom stashed with you for safekeeping."

Sarabelle surprised him by smacking Rita hard enough across the face to knock her off the stool. She dropped the bottle of moonshine when she fell, and it rolled along the dirt floor of the shack.

Mullen knew his wife might be slight and pretty, but

she was a pioneer woman and much stronger than she looked.

"You mind how you speak to my husband, now. If you can't keep a civil tongue in your head, I'll have to rip it out of you."

Rita picked herself off the floor and grabbed the rolling jug. "You two don't scare me. Ain't much you can do to me anyway. I'm the grieving widow, remember. My beloved husband gunned down in the streets of Devil's Gulch. I'm what you might call an institution now."

She attempted a curtsey before dropping onto the bed she had shared with her husband. "So, you'd do well to treat me kindly, or maybe I'll start speaking my mind more freely. Maybe I'll start off slow by telling them that it was you who tipped off the Federals about the robbery where Bob went and got himself killed."

Sarabelle went to hit her again, but Mullen grabbed her arm and pulled her behind him. "You'll be treated more than fairly," he said. "I can assure you of that."

"Good," Rita slurred, "because I know what comes next."

Mullen grinned as he folded his arms across his chest. A drunk's logic always entertained him. "Tell me."

"You want me to keep my mouth shut about the Bostrom Boys. About how you set them up for an ambush. About the stolen money you're holding. You'll want me to talk you up as the only man who can bring order to that flea-bitten town you love so much. You want me to wail and moan about poor old Ott and how my children will grow up without a father." She pointed the jug at him. "You want me to build you up so you can tear John Holt down."

Mullen was impressed. Perhaps she was not as drunk as she let on. In his experience, what miner's wives lacked in elegance, they more than made up for with common sense. "Does any of that sound unreasonable to you?"

"Not especially," she said. "As long as I'm provided for."

"I already said—"

But Rita kept talking. "Because I can still cause a whole lot of trouble for you without ever mentioning the Bostrom money." She looked for her glass, which had rolled under the bed, and decided to take a swig straight from the jug. "Won't have to make up any of it either. For instance, I could talk about how you just stood there while John Holt shot my husband in cold blood. And how you were one of the first to run away when the shooting started."

She winked lazily at him. "Don't think all those fine, upstanding men on the Vigilance Committee would look too kindly on their fearless leader scampering off like a scared deer at the first sound of gunfire."

Mullen's temper spiked. "You weren't there. You don't know what happened."

"I know you're alive and Ott's dead doing what you probably put him up to doing," she sneered. "And don't go telling me different because that man never had an original thought in his life. He didn't even like shooting rabbits for our supper, so I know, if anyone put a gun in his hand, it was you."

Mullen had always known Rita Heller was a difficult woman and life with Ott Heller had only made her more so. But her knowledge of his arrangement with Bob Bostrom and his ultimate betrayal of him made her dangerous. Under different circumstances, he might have killed her, or asked Sarabelle to do it for him. Rita was known to often drink too much, and few would raise an eyebrow were she to be found at the bottom of a mineshaft one evening. They would say she must have wandered around and fell.

Mullen might have considered it if it were not for her children. It was not her motherhood that gave him pause, but the idea of taking that pack of feral brats under his roof. For that was what would be expected of him, if anything happened to Rita.

She summoned up a smug smile as he and Sarabelle stepped toward her.

"What's this?" she asked as she struggled to stay upright. "You two trying to bully me?"

"No," Mullen said. "No one's going to lay a finger on you, I promise. But we must come to an agreement and soon, Rita, for your sake and the sake of your children."

"Best choose wisely and quickly," Sarabelle told her. "Our patience is wearing thin."

Despite her drunken state, Rita Heller seemed to know she had pushed her luck for as far as it would go. She drew herself up and sat tall on the bed. "I want a good life for me and my young ones. Someplace nice. Civilized. Let's say California. Maybe even San Francisco. And a monthly payment so I can raise up my boys right."

Mullen had been to San Francisco several times. The bustling city would be too much for a miner's wife. It would chew her up and spit her out. He imagined she would burn through whatever money he gave her and be dead in a month. Her children would be forced to run wild through the city, looking for ways to survive. But that did not matter to him. At least they would no longer be in Devil's Gulch. That would be a blessing.

"We can work out all of the details in the coming days," he assured her.

As Rita began to weave, Mullen nodded to Sarabelle to take the jug from her before she dropped it.

He heard his miners beginning to gather outside the shack and knew they would be expecting news about Ott

Heller's death. He intended on getting them worked up just enough to do his bidding when the time came. For now, he needed them to work his mine and wait.

To his wife, he said, "I'll go take care of the men while you take care of her."

But Rita had already fallen over on the pillow and was snoring.

Sarabelle was not so easily dismissed. "We both know we can't rely on her to keep quiet about the Bostrom business, Joe."

Mullen gestured for her to be quiet. The walls of the shack were thin, and the men were just outside. "Keep your voice down."

He immediately regretted it. His wife was not a woman given to blind obedience. "I'll speak my mind whenever I please and however I please, Joseph Mullen." She pointed down at Rita, now snoring against her pillow. "That woman is going to be nothing but trouble for us. We can't have that drunk holding a knife to our throats for the rest of our lives. She'll bleed us dry if we let her. You know I'm right."

Mullen had grown tired of people talking back to him. Cassidy had become more unbearable than normal. Chapman had been insufferable, but he had paid the price. He might even be dead by now for all he knew. And Holt, with his dead eyes and lethal calm. He could not be run off or cowed. He would never be brought to heel because Mullen had no leverage against him.

And now his own wife was giving him sass. His only consolation was that he knew it was for his own good. Rita's big mouth could cost them dearly. Not only the missing Bostrom fortune, but with the law too.

"Sounds like you've got something on your mind, Sara," Mullen said. "What is it?"

"Giving her money is like throwing it in the wind. She's in an agitated state. We've got a room full of people who can testify to that when the time comes. Maybe it's best if we stop her now before she goes too far."

Mullen never forgot that his wife was every bit as ruthless as he was. He imagined that was why they had been attracted to each other in the first place. They never grew angry at the same thing at the same time. While one raved, the other always managed to remain calm. This balance had not only benefited their marriage, but also Mullen's growing business interests.

He had not been surprised by Sarabelle's discussion of murder, though he was concerned about the timing of it. "Stopping her is possible, but only if it's done properly."

Her blue eyes sparkled. "I take it you agree?"

"Take it any way you'd like, provided you can make it look convincing." He left the matter to her, knowing she would do it whether he gave his permission or not. "Now, I have to go talk to my men. Get them ready for the battle that's ahead."

She popped up on her tiptoes and gave him a kiss. "Work well, darling. I'll take care of everything here."

He stepped out of the shack and gathered his men around, knowing that she would.

CHAPTER 16

It was going on eight o'clock in the morning when Holt watched Earl Sibert bring his funeral wagon to a halt in front of the jail. He was there to take Mayor Chapman's body back to his mortuary.

It was not the common buckboard he had used to bring the Turnbull boys to the Blue Bottle Saloon the previous evening. Nor was it the same wagon he had used to haul away Ott Heller after sunrise.

It was a black, polished affair with brass fittings and beveled glass panels that showed the body it carried. Even the dark, four-horse team had been done up with black feathered plumes perched atop the headpiece of their browbands.

The four men lumbering behind it were clad in black coats and wore white gloves. The undertaker's ability to conceive of such dignity surprised Holt.

He watched Sibert step down from the wagon and remove his stovepipe hat as he approached Holt. "I understand the mayor's remains are ready to be removed, Sheriff?"

Holt had little patience for the man after the events of

the previous evening. "I sent for you, didn't I? He's in the jail on a bed behind my desk."

Sibert bowed his head. "I shall ask my men to attend to him immediately." He looked at his pallbearers and motioned for them to go inside. "Please inform Mrs. Chapman that she has my deepest condolences. Mayor Chapman was a fine man."

But Holt was not interested in the gravedigger's condolences. "You get those Turnbull boys planted like I told you?"

Sibert nodded solemnly. "As evidenced by the dark circles under my eyes. The ground was almost frozen, and my men had a difficult time digging one grave." His Adam's apple bobbed as he swallowed. "The conditions forced us to take some extraordinary steps." He closed his eyes as if preparing himself for a blow. "We had to bury all three of them in one grave. This is not a common practice, you understand, but—"

Holt did not care about that either. "They're planted. That's all that counts."

Sibert opened one eye, then another when he realized he would not be struck. "I'm glad you concur, Sheriff Holt. And I assure you that I will use all of my skill to ensure the mayor is presentable for his public viewing."

After the shooting from the previous night, Holt had objected to the idea of having Mayor Chapman's body lie in state inside the county hall. But Mrs. Chapman insisted, and he was not inclined to argue with the widow.

Although she had spent most of the night wailing over her husband, she was surprisingly poised after his passing fewer than thirty minutes before. He and Doc Klassen had escorted her across the street to her husband's office in the county hall, as her home had been destroyed in the fire that burned down her husband's store.

Sibert asked, "May I inquire as to Mrs. Chapman's condition?"

He did not trust the undertaker to keep his mouth shut, so he kept the details to a minimum. "She just lost her husband. How do you think she's doing? The doc is with her now."

Sibert looked around at the few people gathered on the boardwalks on both sides of Main Street. Men had their hats off. Women had handkerchiefs to their eyes and noses.

Sibert surprised him by saying, "I'm scared, Sheriff."

"Of what?"

"Of what will happen next. I've been in this town ten years and I've never seen it this ugly. You've succeeded in creating a great amount of turmoil in a short amount of time."

Holt would not give any more wind to keep that fire going. "As long as everyone obeys the law, they've got nothing to fear from me."

"The law, Sheriff? Or your law?"

"Same thing."

Sibert cast his eyes down toward his shoes. "May I offer a word of warning? Meant in friendship and as a citizen of this town. Not in a dangerous or threatening manner of course."

"No," Holt said. He already knew what Sibert would say. He would tell him that Mullen is a dangerous man. That his committee men will be looking to gun Holt down. That he has Holt outnumbered ten to one?

Holt did not want to hear it because he did not need to hear it. He already knew all that and hearing it would only give it life. It would be a waste of time and Holt did not have a moment to lose in preparing himself for the fight that surely lies ahead.

Sibert let out a heavy breath. "Well, at least you can't stop me from praying for you, Sheriff. You're a hard man to like, but I do admire your grit. And I sure hope I won't have to load you into my hearse someday."

Holt looked over the funerary rig. If he wound up getting killed, at least he would take his last ride in style.

"Everybody dies," Holt said. "It's what you do with the life you have that counts."

Both men turned when they heard the pallbearers shuffling out of the jail. Holt kept his rifle at his side as he swept his hat from his head out of respect for the dead mayor.

He never understood all the fancy ceremony that surrounded a death. He imagined that lack of understanding came from his time in the war, when the bodies of brave and cowardly men alike were strewn across the field of battle. When soldier and officer—whether they wore blue or gray—were food for crows and vultures and wolves looking for a meal. The carrion that lived off the dead had no regard for rank or uniform. Left outside for too long, the bodies became swollen and distorted and threatened to spread disease among the living.

Holt understood the ceremony of a soldier's death, of course. It gave those who witnessed it the promise of dignity in their passing should they die in battle. It served as a reminder to the living that they had survived to fight another day.

Yes, Holt decided. Death brought out strange emotions and creatures of all sorts. It gave birth to wild notions too. Notions of honor and revenge and regret.

Holt mourned the passing of Mayor Blair Chapman, but he did not regret how it had happened. He only resolved himself to avenging this good man in any way he could.

He looked over the gathering crowd as the pallbearers slid the mayor's body into the hearse. He looked for Mullen somewhere in the crowd. He wanted to throw the pecker-wood in a cell with the three others he already had locked up. But the head of the Vigilance Committee was nowhere to be found.

Holt did spot Anthony Cassidy standing in front of the Blue Bottle Saloon. A few of his working girls were wearing black dresses and matching veils.

He looked at the opposite end of the street toward the Railhead Saloon. Ma McAdam and some of her ladies were on the boardwalk, though none of them wore black. Frank Peters stood beside them and looked surprisingly sober.

As the pallbearers closed the gate of the hearse, Earl Sibert put on his stovepipe hat. "Please let Mrs. Chandler know that I will send word for her to view the body privately when I complete my preparations. You or the good doctor may wish to accompany her. It tends to be an emotional time for the surviving spouse."

"Just do your job, Sibert. I'll do mine."

The undertaker frowned as he climbed up into the box, released the hand brake and slowly set the two-horse team to walking.

He stood in front of the jail until the death wagon moved off Main Street toward Sibert's mortuary on the outskirts of town.

Holt pulled his hat back on and went inside the jail. He found Jack Turnbull sitting at his desk with his back turned to the blood-soaked bed. Even Holt had to admit that, without the mayor's body on top of it, it was a gory sight.

He tried to take the boy's mind off it. "How are the prisoners?"

"Hungover," Jack told him. "Heads hurting something awful. Don't know if it's from whiskey or those beatings you gave them, but they're all mighty sick. They want to know when you're gonna let them go."

"After we bring them before Judge Cook, but I've got a few things to do first. I'll send word to Jean over at the café that we'll be needing four breakfasts today. She'll be happy for the business."

Jack seemed to do the math in his head. "Four? Don't you mean five?"

"I'm not hungry," he said as he grabbed hold of the ruined mattress. "Besides, I don't have time to eat."

Holt dragged the bloody mattress and sheets behind him as he moved through the center of the thoroughfare. He ignored the gasps of fright and horror from the townspeople he passed. Most of the women averted their eyes at the sight of so much blood. Some of the men did too. Most looked on with gaping mouths and eager eyes, wondering what their new sheriff was going to do with his cursed bundle.

He dragged the mattress until he reached the front of the Blue Bottle Saloon. He left it in the middle of the street and went to the general store, which had not opened yet. An oil lamp still burned from the night before. He pulled the lamp off the hook and went back to the thoroughfare and walked back to the mattress.

By then, Cassidy had stepped out onto the boardwalk

with his bartender, Bobby Simpson, at his side. The man was standing halfway in the doorway. His right side was still in shadow. Holt could not see if Simpson was holding a firearm but given how he was standing, he was almost certain he was.

Holt kept his eyes on them as he shattered the burning oil lamp on the hard packed ground of the thoroughfare. The burning oil quickly spread to the bloody mattress and caught fire.

Holt stepped around the flames and stood between it and the saloon. Simpson began to push past his boss, but Cassidy eased him back.

"What's that supposed to mean, Sheriff? Don't you think this town has had enough fire already?"

"You and your customers got a good man killed, Cassidy." He pointed back at the mattress, which had become completely engulfed in flames. The heat from it began to singe his back. "You caused it. Now you get to clean it up."

Cassidy folded his skinny arms across his bony chest and leaned against the doorframe. "Now that's mighty funny, Sheriff, because I thought cleaning up messes was your job."

"It is," Holt replied. "And when I start, it'll start with you or that coward Mullen."

"I'd be careful about what you wish for, Sheriff. If it starts with us, it might end there too."

Holt took a couple of steps closer to the saloon. His hand against the holster on his hip. "Could start right now."

The saloon owner, bartender, and lawman stood looking at each other, each waiting for the other to make the first move.

It was Cassidy who made the first move, by pushing himself off the doorway with a grin and urging his bartender back inside the saloon.

Holt waited until he was sure they were not coming back out to go about his business. He walked down the middle of Main Street and entered the county hall.

He had just declared war on Cassidy and Mullen. Now he needed the firepower to back it up.

CHAPTER 17

Holt had not expected Judge Cook to be happy with his proposal, but he had not expected such a fierce response.

"Martial law?" His voice filled his chambers. "Are you out of your blessed mind?"

Holt looked to Lester Patrick for support, but the attorney continued to stare down at a law book on his lap. He would get no help from the town attorney.

Holt continued to lay out his case. "Last night, we came awfully close to having a riot on our hands. A riot that was caused by Joe Mullen and his band of rabble-rousers. He got them liquored up and had them march on the jail, calling for Mayor Chapman's head. Well, he got it. Mullen and Cassidy are dangerous men and should be handled that way. And not allowing them to gather after dark is the best way I know of keeping the streets clear and stopping something like that from happening again."

"Convicting the men who participated in the action is the surest way to ensure justice is done," the judge said. "I understand you have three of them in your custody at the moment."

Holt knew that would not be good enough. "I have

them, but they're not talking. Each of them was full of whiskey when they marched on the jail. It doesn't make them any less guilty, but they'd never testify against Mullen or Cassidy."

"Mullen was there, Your Honor," Patrick told him. "I saw him on the periphery of the mob. I can't swear that he was the leader, but his presence speaks for itself. His absence from town this morning also speaks volumes."

Cook focused his attention back on Holt. "The man who killed poor old Blair is dead. We have three men to hold accountable for the act. We'll make examples out of them, I assure you. But asking me to hand control of the town over to you is simply madness. The people would never stand for it. They certainly won't obey the curfew you propose, and you have no way of enforcing it. Besides, I'm not the mayor and we don't have one right now. Only he would have the power to order such a drastic measure."

"That's why I'm here," Holt said. "You're the only semblance of law we have. The town council's a joke and there's no mayor to bring them under control. If you find a way to pass martial law, I'll enforce it."

But Judge Cook clearly had his doubts. "Our menfolk like their drink, Sheriff. Even I've been known to imbibe from time to time."

"This isn't just about the drinking," Holt told him. "It's about maintaining order and saving lives. It's about setting up Mullen for him to do something I can arrest him for. Cassidy, too, if he defies the curfew by keeping the Blue Bottle open past the curfew."

Again, Patrick spoke up. "I think you've poked those bears hard enough for now, Sheriff. You can't enact restrictions that will punish everyone just to entrap two men.

You're bound to turn the entire town against you, and you have too few allies as it is."

"None in this room," Holt said. "That's for sure."

Cook's eyes narrowed as they bored into him. "The law's not on anyone's side, Mr. Holt. It is its own side. The only side that counts. The line where men find themselves on one side of it or the other. What you're suggesting straddles that line and perhaps even crosses it. There's also the matter of enforcing it. You're only one man. You don't have enough deputies to help you make sure people are obeying the curfew. And you certainly can't rely on Mullen's committee men to assist you. They're the biggest drinkers in town."

Holt ran his finger across his chin. The old jurist was focusing too much on the drinking aspect of the plan and not enough on the safety aspect of it. "I managed to turn them last night when they put the Turnbull boys on display. They're not as united as you think."

Lester Patrick added, "Some could argue that you caused the whole mess to begin with by breaking up their party, John. In fact, some already have."

Holt looked at him. "Like whom?"

"Ty Arbour for one," the attorney explained. "I doubt you've met him yet. He's an attorney here in town. Usually represents most clients who find themselves in jail. I suspect he's been in league with Mullen and Cassidy for years, though that's hardly a crime. But he always seems to represent the cases that involve their interests with far more enthusiasm than those that involve Ma McAdam."

Holt failed to see how any of that had anything to do with him. "So?"

"So, he's already petitioned the court to nullify your employment contract with the town. He filed it with the clerk first thing this morning."

He took several pages from the pile on his lap and handed them out to Holt. "It makes for some interesting reading. He argues that your employment was with Mayor Chapman, not the town. And, since he's dead, your contract died with him."

Holt ignored the papers, and Les Patrick took them back. He did not need to read them to know there was nothing to them. "He signed that agreement as the mayor of the town on behalf of the town."

"I didn't say it was a valid argument," Patrick reminded him, "but it is an argument that the court will have to rule on. Clamping down on the town at a time like this will do more harm than good. I'm afraid Judge Cook is right. Granting your request for martial law is impossible since the office of mayor is currently vacant."

That was part of Holt's argument in the first place. "Someone's got to be in charge. If not me, why not the judge here? Or you?"

"I've already sent a telegram to the territorial governor for a ruling on that," Cook said. "I should hear back in a day or two. In the meantime, your charge to do everything in your power to maintain law and order in Devil's Gulch remains the same. That means you're to tread lightly and not instigate any further violence. Your stunt with burning the mattress in front of the Blue Bottle just now is the end of it, Sheriff. This town will be busy mourning the loss of a good man for the next few days. I don't want you doing anything to antagonize the situation. Do I make myself abundantly clear, sir?"

Holt felt like a fool for raising the notion in the first place. He should have known Judge Cook did not have the stomach for a fight like this, especially now with tensions running so high in town.

He'd had his ears pinned back by other judges in other towns before. He saw no reason why Judge Cook would be any different. "I understand."

The judge sat back, satisfied. "Now that we've put that nonsense to bed, Mr. Patrick here spoke to Cassie last night and got her formal, sworn statement about the unfortunate shooting in her room a few days ago. We've decided to postpone the inquest until after the mayor's funeral, and I can all but promise you that she'll sail through without any further trouble from us."

Holt was glad to hear it but cursed himself for not having had the time to hunt down Hank Bostrom. He had promised Cassie he would, and he liked to keep his promises.

Something Cassidy and Mullen would find out soon enough.

"Now on to other business." Judge Cook cleared his throat as he held out a folded paper to Holt. "There's the release order for the Turnbull boy. He's free to go as of now, which should lighten your burden a little." He cleared his throat again. "Now, if there's nothing else, I have other matters that require my attention. I bid you gentlemen a good morning."

Les Patrick got to his feet before Holt and headed for the door.

Holt was slower to stand and paused to make one final point before the matter got swept under the proverbial rug. "Ott Heller was one of Mullen's miners."

Cook had been reaching for a pen and stopped in mid-motion. "I believe he was. Why?"

"How many men does he have working that mine?"

The judge looked to Les Patrick for an answer.

The attorney said, "Twenty or so last I heard. Could be more. Why?"

"No reason," Holt said as he began to leave. "Just wanted to know how much ammunition I should buy when they come down from the mountain looking for blood."

He ignored the stream of Judge Cook's curses that followed him out into the hall.

If Cook would not help him fight Mullen and Cassidy, he would need to find help elsewhere.

And he had no idea of where to start looking.

Holt decided he had spent too much time cooped up in the jail to head back there directly. He thought a walk around the town might do him some good. Let the people see him and know he was there.

The people he passed on the street were cordial enough. Men tipped their hats and women bowed politely to him. A couple stopped him on the street and thanked him for killing the man who had gunned down the mayor. A few even offered to pray for him. He thanked them, knowing he could use all the help he could get in this world or the next.

He stopped by the burnt shell of the Chapman haberdashery. The building still reeked of charred wood and burned clothing. His time in the army had made him fond of the smell of burning wood. It often meant the end of a long day's march or fighting. It meant a respite from the rigors of war and death.

Now it only reminded him of another death. The death of the good man who had come to this town to open a clothing store. A man who had gotten himself elected mayor to serve the town. A brave man in his own way, who refused to hide when Holt had given him the opportunity.

Holt regretted not forcing Blair Chapman into a cell,

but that was not Chapman's way. He had not known the man long enough to consider him a friend, but Holt liked to think they could have become friends if they had been given enough time to forge such a bond.

But Mullen had other plans. And he was undoubtedly forming another plan now, high among the mountains where his mines were. A plan that would be designed with his death in mind.

Holt had faced down men like Mullen before. Men who had sought to do him harm in other towns. But it had always been after he had been in a town for a while. Where he had made friends willing to either stand with him or stand aside. He had always had enough time to prepare for the eventual conflict that followed.

This time, things were different.

He had a boy deputy who got sick at the first sight of blood. A jail full of rioters. A Remington on his hip and a Henry rifle by his side. Half the town hated him, and the other half did not know him.

He began to feel like he might have bitten off more than he could chew here in Devil's Gulch, and he had no idea how it would turn out.

"There you are," said a woman from behind him. "I was beginning to think you never left that stuffy old jail."

He was glad to see it was Jean Roche. She had a basket over her arm and a smile he would have liked to think was for him.

"Had some business to attend to," he said. "Figured getting some morning air couldn't hurt."

"Same air morning, noon, or night around here," she said as he began walking with her. "I hear you've been having quite a time of it. I saw some of what happened last night. I guess us Gulchers haven't treated you too well since you've come to town."

Holt liked her, but not enough to trust her, so he remained guarded. "Nothing I can't handle. Wasn't expecting to get the mayor killed, though. That's a first for me."

She stopped and looked up at him. "That wasn't your fault, John Holt. You're a man of many faults. That's plain enough. But you didn't get the mayor killed. The only one who did that is already dead and answering for his sin before the Lord. As it should be."

He smiled. "I hope most people in town think the same way. But I've got a feeling you'd get a fair amount to disagree with you."

The Black woman shrugged. "Never bothered to care much about what people thought of me one way or the other. Got too much living to do. Too much that needs to get done. Running a café is a lot harder than it looks."

They resumed walking again, only at a slower pace this time. "I guess you've had it rough here too. Considering."

"Can't control what other people do," she said. "Only what I do. Something tells me you learned that the hard way a long time ago."

Holt liked the way she thought. "For a woman who hardly paid me any mind for the past couple of days, you see a lot."

"That's on account that I've seen a lot," she said. "Seen enough to know good when I see it. And bad too."

"And what do you see when you look at me."

Jean gave the question some thought as they walked. "A bit of both, I suppose, though more good than bad. I don't make any judgments, though. I leave that business to the Lord. I'm too busy with the café." She nudged him with her arm. "These folks might not invite me to sit at their dinner table, but they sure like sitting at mine."

Holt laughed and it made him feel better. "An army marches on its stomach. Good food and the people who prepare it are usually popular. Especially if it's good."

"I just keep doing what I do and hope it'll work out for the best." She nodded up at the bank's clock tower. "Business was off a few months ago and I had to go in there and ask for a loan. I figured that man was gonna laugh me right out of his office. Know what he did? He not only gave me everything I asked for, but some from his own pocket too. Turns out he enjoys my cooking so much that he didn't want to see me go out of business."

"Good for you," he said, meaning it.

"Taught me that, sometimes, someone you least expect to help can do good for you when you need it. Doesn't make you friends. Just means you're useful to each other. And sometimes being useful is more important than being friends."

This time, it was Holt who stopped walking. "Why do I have a feeling we're talking about more than your café?"

She placed her free hand on her hip. "Why, John Holt. Whatever could you mean? I just run a café for hungry people is all. A café that happens to be just up the street from a saloon filled with folks who don't like some of the same people you don't like."

He looked beyond her and watched the wooden sign with the rail spike carved on it sway in the wind. The Railhead Saloon.

This time, he was sure her smile was for him. "You're pretty dense for a lawman, John Holt."

"And you're pretty smart by any measure." He surprised himself by kissing her softly on the forehead. "Thank you."

They continued walking together until they reached her café. "Just don't go getting yourself killed now. I'm counting on you to keep that jail filled for a while. I can use the business."

Holt unlocked the door and held it open for her as she walked inside.

He had a feeling he'd have no shortage of customers for her for the foreseeable future.

CHAPTER 18

The crowd inside the Railhead Saloon was larger than Holt would have expected for that time of day. Two tables were filled with poker players who switched from whiskey to pots of coffee. Cigar and cigarette smoke filled the air, forming a dirty cloud in the morning sunlight.

Hoppy, the bartender, was propped up against the back of the bar, dozing on his feet. His eyes snapped open when he heard a floorboard creak and opened even wider when he saw it was John Holt.

"Hoppy," Holt said. "I'm not—"

Before he could assure the bartender that he had not come for a fight, Hoppy called out, "Frank! You'd best get out here."

Holt hung his head. *Why can't anything be easy in this town?*

He looked up and drew when he heard the unmistakable sound of a round being levered into a rifle.

He drew and caught Frank Peters before he could bring the rifle to his shoulder.

"I'm not here to fight," Holt told him. "I just want to

talk to Ma. That's all. Put the rifle down before you get hurt."

Frank Peters did not look as drunk or hungover as he had. His eyes were red, but clearer than Holt had ever seen them. He thought that might be due to an avoidance of whiskey but imagined the sight of a pistol aimed at his chest had an equally sobering effect.

"Do what he says, Frank," one of the gamblers said. "We've got a game going on here. No cause to spoil it over your nonsense."

But Frank continued to hold on to the rifle, even if he was out of position. "You really just come here to talk, Holt?"

Holt nodded and kept his Remington steady.

Frank slowly lowered the rifle to his side. "Now you put yours away."

Holt thumbed back the hammer. "Not until you do what I told you to do. Set that rifle on the bar and go get Ma."

Peters cursed as he placed the rifle on the bar top and stormed up the stairs to Ma's room. Holt's pistol followed him along each step until he was upstairs and out of view.

One of the old gamblers said, "For a man who's supposed to be a peace officer, you're awfully hard on the peace, mister."

Holt saw no benefit in answering him and lowered his pistol but did not holster it. He caught the bartender reaching for the rifle and raised the Remington again. "Leave it."

Hoppy backed up as if he had been shot. Hands raised as he knocked over a couple of bottles behind him, much to the amusement of the gamblers.

"Old Hoppy," another of them said. "Ain't much of a barkeep, but always good for a laugh."

Holt holstered his pistol as he grabbed the rifle and

levered rounds out of it until it was empty. He kicked away the cartridges that had spilled on the floor, bringing protests from the gamblers who feared slipping on them later.

"Mind your step and you'll be fine, boys," Holt told them.

Ma McAdam walked out at the top of the stair. A black shawl wrapped around her. "Good morning, Sheriff Holt. This is a pleasant surprise."

"I'm here to talk."

She stepped back and held out her arm toward her room. "Let's talk up here where it's more private. I hope being invited up to a lady's room doesn't offend your modesty."

Holt started up the stairs. "As long as Frank's not waiting around the corner with a shotgun."

"You won't have to worry about him," she assured him. "It's just you and me."

Holt hoped so. It was still a nice day outside and too early for a killing.

Ma McAdam had sat quietly for twenty minutes or so while Holt talked. When he finished, she poured him another cup of tea from the pot and one for herself. Cassie had been moved back to her own room last night.

"You and I haven't exactly been cordial since your arrival here in Devil's Gulch, Sheriff. I don't know why you'd think I'd be able to help you against Mullen."

Holt ignored the tea. "For the same reason anyone does anything. Because there's something in it for them."

"Ah." Her watery blue eyes brightened as she sipped her tea and laid it gently back on the saucer. "Now we get to it. You want me to help you against Mullen. What's in it for me?"

Holt opened his hands. "What do you want?"

"A free hand for starters," she said. "I've heard about how you like to run things, Sheriff, and how you don't have much use for people like me."

"I don't have much use for you," Holt said, "but as long as it's not against the law, you'll have no trouble from me."

"And what if I were to cross over that line from time to time."

"I'd be there to put you in jail." Holt leaned forward. "I'm not here to barter with you. I'm not like your lapdog Peters. I don't turn a blind eye to anyone or anything and I don't just let things slide. If you help me, it's because Mullen and Cassidy have been thorns in your side for a long time and this is your chance to push them back. I don't know what started your feud with them and I don't care to know. All I care about is Mullen and his committee men trying to turn this town into a battlefield now that Mayor Chapman's gone. You're a saloonkeeper and blood is bad for business."

Ma pulled her shawl tighter around her shoulders. "You're not really offering me anything, are you?"

"I'm offering you a chance to have one fewer enemy in town," Holt said. "Or, at least, a weaker enemy."

She tapped her fingers on the end of the armrests of her chair. "You're not an easy man to deal with, are you, Sheriff?"

"Never claimed to be. So, are you going to help me against Mullen and Cassidy or not?"

"Not until we get something straight between us." Her fingers stopped tapping. "I didn't know Hank and Em were going to hurt Cassie. I thought they might rough her up a little, but a woman in this line needs to expect unpleasantness. I never thought they'd go that far. If you don't believe that, you can get up and walk out of here right now."

Ma McAdam would never know how hard it was for Holt to keep himself calm. "It was still wrong, but I don't believe you knew how far they'd go."

She seemed to realize that was as close to an answer as she was liable to get. "And you were mighty fair and gentle with her with Les Patrick over the inquiry. Keeping certain details from coming to light and such."

"I figured she'd suffered enough," he said.

She mulled it over and made her decision. "I'll tell you what I'm gonna do. Other than Frank, I don't have any men to put behind you right now. But I'll talk you up to my customers. See to it that all of them understand that I'm on your side. My place might not draw the same numbers as the Blue Bottle, but we get a fair number of men coming in here each night. We'll try that for a couple of days, see how it goes. Some of them owe me more than a few favors. Maybe I can talk some of them into throwing in with you if you need it. I can also guarantee none of my customers will join in anything Cassidy or Mullen are planning. And if I hear about anything, I'll let you know."

Holt had expected more, but at least it was a start. "That would help."

"Working with me won't make you popular with Cassidy or Mullen, but that's the point, now, isn't it?"

She had forgotten the most important point he had talked about when they first sat down, so Holt reminded her. "Be sure to mention the part that Mayor Chapman's killer worked for Mullen. That's the main thrust of this."

She smiled thinly. "You're a crafty boy, aren't you?"

Holt held out his hand to her. "Do we have a deal?"

She spat on her hand and waited for Holt to do the same before they shook on it.

"Congratulations, Sheriff Holt. You've just gone and made a deal with the devil."

Holt was surprised by how firm her handshake was. "Depending on who you ask, the same could be said for you."

CHAPTER 19

After getting his mare from the livery in preparation of loading her down with supplies for the jail, Holt drew rein in front of the general store and climbed down from the saddle. People were more eager now to tip their hat to him and bid him a good afternoon. He imagined the gossip had already turned in his favor, perhaps due to Ma McAdam's influence.

He wrapped the gelding's reins around the hitching rail and stepped onto the boardwalk to enter the general store of Devil's Gulch. A bell above the door tinkled as he opened, then shut the door.

He found a portly man in a leather apron stretched across his girth on a ladder, pulling down a bolt of fabric from a high shelf for a woman customer. Holt did not know what concerned him more. That the man might fall, or the ladder might give way.

The heavy man took hold of the fabric and brought it down to his customer. "Be with you in a moment," he said as he offered the fabric to the woman to examine. He was telling her about its high quality when he glanced over at Holt.

The shopkeeper would have dropped the fabric had the woman not been holding it.

"Great God Almighty," he said.

"Hardly," Holt grinned. "John Holt. I'm new here."

The shopkeeper recovered from his shock. "I know who you are, sir." He told the woman to examine the cloth at her leisure while he tended to the sheriff. He scrambled behind the counter, which seemed to allow him to regain some of his composure.

"I'm Art Ross," the man told him. "Owner and proprietor of this establishment."

Holt extended his hand across to him. "Pleased to meet you, Mr. Ross. I have a feeling we'll be doing a lot of business with each other."

Ross shook his hand without enthusiasm. "You've already made quite a name for yourself in such a short amount of time, Sheriff. Things were a lot quieter around here before you showed up."

Holt had never been interested in the opinions of bartenders or shopkeepers. "Let's see what we can do about getting things back to normal."

He began to give him a rundown of the list of supplies he needed. He stood at the counter while he watched the heavy man run around the store, piling up what he needed.

When he was done, Ross wiped the sweat from his brow with his sleeve. His female customer had placed the fabric on the counter and promised to come back when he was less busy.

"Anything else?" Ross frowned at him over the loss of a sale.

Holt tapped the glass countertop and pointed at the double-barreled shotgun that was beneath it. "Let me take a look at that."

Ross lifted the weapon from the case and handed it to

Holt for examination. He cracked it open and, making sure
it was unloaded, looked down the barrels. It looked clean
enough and was in excellent condition. It would be a
good gun for Jack Turnbull to use until he learned how
to work a pistol properly. "Add this to the bill. And a box
of cartridges for it too. An empty gun's not much use to
anyone."

He enjoyed Ross's annoyance as the shopkeeper wrote
down the list of everything Holt had selected. "I assume
this is going on the town's bill?"

"You assume correctly. And some burlap sacks to put it
all in. Make it easier for me to load all this on my horse."

"Town paying means I won't see my money until next
month," the shopkeeper grumbled as he tallied up the
amount, then found a sack to place the goods in, except
for the shotgun. "Maybe even longer now that the mayor's
dead."

The shopkeeper's lack of concern over the mayor's
death annoyed him. "I'll see what I can do about getting
you paid earlier than that."

"I must say that seeing you buying so much ammunition doesn't settle my nerves any," Ross said as he put the
last of the items in the burlap sack that had once held
coffee. "You've got enough rounds there to take on a small
army."

Holt threw the bag over his shoulder and took the
empty shotgun with his right hand. "Like the man said, 'If
you want peace, prepare for war.'"

"Just make sure you wage that war somewhere other
than Main Street," the shopkeeper called after him. "I don't
want my place going up like the Chapman's store."

Holt thanked him for his time and stepped outside to
begin loading the bag on his horse. He undid the bag and
placed the boxes of cartridges and other smaller items in

his saddlebags. That allowed him to flatten the burlap some and he was able to tie the bag in place across the back of his saddle. He slid the shotgun into his empty scabbard along the right flank of the animal.

It was one of the first endeavors that had gone right for him since he had come to town. He took pleasure in what little victories he could find in Devil's Gulch.

Holt turned around when he heard boots skid to a halt on the boardwalk. He saw a stocky man with deep-set eyes that were too small for his face. His clothes had not seen a good cleaning in months, and he looked like he had not bathed in weeks. Judging from the way the wind was blowing, he imagined his assumption was right.

Holt had never seen him before, but it was clear that the stranger recognized him and did not like what he saw.

Holt's hand moved toward his holster while the man stood as if nailed to the spot. "Something on your mind, mister?"

The man responded by going for the gun on is right hip.

Holt crouched as he cleared leather first and fired.

The man got off a shot that sailed over Holt's right shoulder. His target was much faster than he appeared, and Holt's bullet grazed his left shoulder as he ducked into the general store.

Holt fired two more shots at the fleeing man. This time, his bullet shattered the glass in the door, and he heard his target yelp.

Behind him, a great thud shook the ground. Holt remained low as he looked to his right and saw his horse on the ground. Its head was lifted at an ugly angle by the rein wound around the hitching rail.

Holt grabbed his pistol tighter. The outlaw in the store had just killed his mare.

He looked up at the store as his target called out to him

from inside. "Best stay where you are, Sheriff. I've got myself a hostage now, and unless you want his blood on your hands, you'll do exactly as I say."

In the army, Holt had learned the best way to surprise an enemy was to charge straight at it before it had a chance to settle itself into position. Surprise was not as important as hitting it before it had both feet planted.

Which was why he rose from his crouch and pushed open the doors of the general store.

He found his target behind the counter holding Ross tight against him. His wounded left arm was around his neck with his pistol to his temple.

Holt kept his Remington raised high as he closed the distance between them.

The shopkeeper struggled against the outlaw's grip. His eyes wide with fear as Holt walked closer.

"I mean it," the outlaw yelled. "One more step and I—"

Holt kept closing the distance as he fired, striking the man in the left eye.

The outlaw fell back against the shelves behind the counter. His gun firing only when his dead hand hit the shop floor.

Ross stumbled away and scrambled out from behind the counter before running outside.

Holt kept his pistol ready as he rounded the counter to ensure the man was dead. The vacant look in his remaining eye assured that he was.

Holt shifted his aim to the door when he heard someone run in, but quickly lowered his pistol when he saw it was Doc Klassen.

"What happened?"

Holt nodded down to the dead man at the floor. "Guess this fella didn't like me much." He walked behind the counter and plucked the pistol from the corpse. "Started shooting at me and ran in here. Tried hiding behind Mr. Ross. It didn't work."

The doctor walked over to the counter and peered over it at the dead man. "You've sure got a knack for killing people, don't you, John."

"Got a knack for being around people who need killing," Holt corrected him. "He look familiar to you?"

"I know at least twenty men who it could be," the doctor said. "Maybe more. Can't rightly say."

Fortunately, Holt knew someone who might. He looked outside and saw a boy of about ten at the front of the crowd that had gathered in front of the store. "Boy. You know where the Railhead is?"

"Ought to," the boy nodded slowly. "Had to pull my pa out of there often enough."

"Run down there and fetch Frank Peters for me. Tell him I need him here right now."

The boy and two of his friends ran in the direction of the saloon, all too eager to carry out a direct order from the sheriff.

Holt found a box of .44 cartridges on the shelf next to him and placed it on the counter. He pocketed his spent shells and replaced them with new rounds from the box.

Doc Klassen came around the counter from the other side and took a closer look at the dead man. "Heck of a shot, Sheriff."

"I was too close to miss." He pocketed the box too. He figured Ross owed him that much for saving his life. "He one of Mullen's boys?"

"Still can't say," the doctor admitted. "Let's hope he's not."

Holt knew they were beyond hoping for anything. Hope

would not do them much good. The dead man had decided that the moment he went for his gun.

He looked up when the boys skidded to a stop in front of the store just as Frank Peters rounded the corner. He had his rifle in his hand, but lowered it before he came in. "What happened?"

Holt pointed down at the corpse. "Need you to tell me if you recognize him."

Peters came to the counter and looked down at the body. "Well, I'll be. You've gone and bagged yourself Cal Abel."

Holt had no time for amazement. "Who is he?"

"Was Bob Bostrom's right-hand man when he was alive," Peters told him. "I imagine he was Hank's right hand now that Bob and Em are dead."

Holt's mind filled with possibilities. "Think he came to town alone?"

"Never knew a Bostrom man to do anything alone." Peters was already on his way out when he said. "I'll scout the town for them. If you hear a shot, best come running."

"I will, don't worry."

He watched Peters go and regretted he did not have a man he could trust search the town instead. But as one of his fellow colonels had once told him in the war, "You don't fight with the men you want. You fight with the men you have."

Doc Klassen finished his examination of Cal and stood up. "I'll get Earl over here with his wagon to clear this one out as soon as possible. You think he came here gunning for you, John?"

Holt did not think so. "He seemed surprised to see me at first. Stood there like a deer for a couple of moments, so I don't think so. Probably was coming to town to supply his outfit. Cassie said they're running low on money and supplies up in those hills."

"I've heard the same," Klassen confirmed. "Well, if it makes you feel any better, this won't make things any worse between you and Mullen."

"And I killed the only man who could likely lead me to the Bostrom Gang." Holt slipped his pistol back into the holster and looked outside at his dead mare. " Rotten skunk shot my horse, Ralph. She was a good animal. Rode her since the war, clear up from New Orleans. Never faulted once and had a wonderful temperament. I was hoping to find a rancher to put her out to pasture. She deserved a better end than an outlaw's bullet."

"Doesn't everybody?" Klassen asked.

Holt was not so sure, so he said nothing.

CHAPTER 20

Hank Bostrom did not feel anything at first. Nothing new, anyway.

When Cal had not come back from the supply run, he felt as though his belly was filled with ice water. Cal had been the most dependable man he had ever known. Always steady and reliable, both in a fight and at camp. Bob may have been the brains of the outfit, but Cal had been its backbone. He kept the men in line and had their respect. No easy task among a group of outlaws. He was not the type who went to town and lost himself in liquor and women. Not when he was on a supply run and had the whole outfit depending on him.

Which was why Hank had ordered Charlie Gardiner to ride down to Devil's Gulch to see what had happened. Charlie was not as dependable as Cal had been, but he rarely drank and did not gamble. He was the best man in the bunch to find out what had happened to Cal.

And now that he had returned with the news, the ice water in his gut had frozen solid.

He felt the men looking at him as he digested the news like it had been undercooked steak.

Hank struggled to keep the tremble out of his voice. "You're sure he's dead?"

"That's what the boys in the Round Table told me," Gardiner said. "I stayed out of the bigger saloons out of fear of being spotted, but the story was the same. Got himself shot straight through the eye by that new sheriff they hired. Holt's his name."

Hank knew the name. He knew the reputation and the man behind it. If Cal had to die, he was glad it had been by Holt's hand.

Gardiner dug at the dirt ground of the old mine with a stick. "Said it was a fair fight if it's any consolation. Cal killed Holt's horse and took the shopkeeper as a way of bargaining his way out of there. At least he wasn't shot in the back."

Hank might have taken comfort in that if his brothers had still been alive, but he did not. "He's still dead, Charlie."

"He surely is." Gardiner tossed his stick in the fire and folded his hands across his knees. "Also heard that Mayor Chapman got himself killed last night by a miner named Ott Heller. Holt killed him right after. They say they're having a viewing for him at the county hall tonight."

Hank did not care about the mayor's death. He had troubles of his own.

He felt all the eyes of the men on him now. They were not just looking to him for answers. They were looking to him to do something. To lead. They wanted to know what he planned to do about this.

For how to avenge the deaths of Em and now Cal. For where their next meal would come from.

He looked at Duke March, who was sitting on the other side of the fire. "I want you to take Art and Jenkins with you to find some provisions at one of the miner camps up here in the mountains. You three have done some prospecting in your time, so they'll smell the mines off you. Get what you can quietly. Trade for it if you have to."

"And if they don't give it over quietly?" Duke asked.

"Then take everything they have," Hank told him. "Coffee and flour mostly, which shouldn't rankle them any. We can hunt for meat if we need to, but if they push you too far, take it all."

Ted Graham disappointed Hank by saying, "I don't know if going in hard is a good idea, Hank. We've managed to hide out here for a good long while without no one noticing on account of we haven't drawn much attention. Buffaloing a mining camp is liable to stir up trouble, especially if it's a Mullen camp. Those boys'll still be plenty sore over losing one of their own to Holt. We don't want them turning that anger toward us."

Hank sat up, his anger numbing the pain that roared in his side. "I reckon I've got enough anger of my own right now to give the whole federal army the fight of its life." He looked at the other men around the campfire in turn. "I reckon all of you have, unless I miss my guess."

The outlaws agreed with him, and the looks in their eyes made him believe it.

He spoke to Duke again, "You mind what I said about a light touch. We don't want trouble, but don't be afraid to bust a few heads if needs be. Kill only if they leave you no choice. And make sure to cover your back trail. I might not be afraid of miners, but I sure don't want to wake up one night finding we're trapped in here."

"Or having that Holt fella raise a posse to come up here and get us," Charlie added.

Hank had heard just about enough of that lawman's

name to last him a lifetime. "We're not gonna have to worry about him raising a posse. I imagine he's about as unpopular as we are right now. They won't lift a finger to help him one way or the other. Besides, unless they've found religion, I'd wager Mullen's boys will be heading down the mountain and into town to show Holt they're none too happy about him killing one of their own."

He nodded at Duke. "Them being away should make whoever's left behind more apt to listen to reason when it comes to being generous with supplies."

"We won't let you down," Duke assured him. "You can count on us."

Hank surprised them all by getting to his feet and standing tall for the first time since he had returned from town with a hole in his side. He surprised himself by how steady he was on his feet.

"I want the rest of you boys ready to ride as soon as you're able. Art, go saddle my horse for me."

Cy Wentworth was the first outlaw on his feet. "Where are we going, boss?"

Boss. Hank liked the sound of that. "With the mayor being on display in the county hall, I plan on paying another visit to Cassie. And this time, I'm not leaving until I've got some answers about where Bob hid that money. I don't know about you boys, but I'm sick of sitting around waiting to be rich."

The men cheered and went about seeing to their horses. It was not until the last one left the mine that Hank allowed himself to lean against the wall. He pulled his coat aside and felt his wound. His hand came away damp and tacky with blood. The dressing would need to be changed soon, but he would see to that later.

He could not dare show weakness in front of the men. His men. Not now. Not ever.

Because he knew if he did not find that money soon, he would not be alive much longer anyway.

CHAPTER 21

Holt silently poured out the contents of the burlap bag and his saddlebags onto his desk. His saddle sat in the far corner of the jail, a painful reminder of the animal he had lost in front of the general store.

Jack Turnbull looked on quietly as he watched the sheriff arrange the pile in some sort of order. "Was sorry to hear about your horse, John."

Holt did not want to talk about it. "Judge Cook still in the back with the prisoners?"

"Les Patrick and Ty Arbour too," he confirmed. "Was sure glad they agreed to do their hearing here instead of over at the courthouse. Bringing those three boys over there with all this going on would've been difficult."

"But not impossible," Holt said as he lugged a sack of coffee over to the stove. All that remained were boxes of cartridges and other items he imagined he would need for whatever fight was coming. "Only reason we didn't is because they're fixing up the lobby for putting Mayor Chapman on display."

"Wonder if they would've done that if his house hadn't burned down like it did," Turnbull asked. "Things like this are usually done at a man's home, aren't they?"

He knew the boy was talking just for the sake of it. He was afraid of the silence. Afraid Holt would withdraw even further into himself than he already had. If he kept him talking, he might make him snap out of the dark mood that had settled over him. Maybe dull the look of anger and determination on his face.

Holt knew no amount of talking would have any effect but appreciated the boy's determination. "You said you don't know how to handle a pistol."

"Said I could," Turnbull reminded him. "Just wasn't particularly good with one. I'm better with a rifle, but never shot a man. Never even aimed at one, come to think of it."

He gestured to Cal's gun belt on the desk. "Strap that on. I imagine you'll have to add a couple of notches in it to fit you, but it'll serve its purpose." He tossed a knife and scabbard he had purchased at the store to him. "It's sharp, so be careful. That ought to help you do the job."

Turnbull slipped the knife into his pocket and tried the belt on for size. Holt noticed the belt practically wrapped around his thin waist twice before it was tight enough. The boy pressed the tip of his new knife into the leather until he made a hole, then cinched the belt tight around his waist. He knew enough to tie down the holster around his right leg without any encouragement from Holt.

The sheriff handed the dead man's gun to him. "There's your pistol. I'd check it over and clean it and load it if I were you. I've got some oil and cleaning things right here for you to use while I'm gone."

"Gone?" Jack asked. "Where are you going?"

Holt looked out the narrow window and frowned at the darkening sky. He would have preferred to be getting on the trail after the Bostrom Boys. He did not have any idea where they were, but Cal's horse did. He imagined the animal would be anxious to head back to the hideout it had called home for the past week or so.

Relying on a horse's instinct was not the soundest tactic Holt had ever employed, but usually led him to whomever he happened to be looking for at the time.

But it was already going on dark, and he imagined it would be well on night before he reached the Bostrom hideout, if the horse led him there at all. Facing off against a passel of outlaws would be dangerous business in the light of day. It would be suicide at night.

Which was why he had ordered the hostler to feed and tend to the animal but keep it hitched to the post where Cal had left it. Holt feared that it might forget its home if it was allowed to mingle with the other animals in the livery. As soon as the mayor's burial was over the next morning, he intended on setting out after the Bostrom Boys.

He only hoped Mullen stayed wherever he was holed up and did not seek to cause trouble until after. Unfortunately, Holt imagined he would not be that lucky, hence his current preparations.

"Where do you want me to be?" Jack asked, pulling him back to the present.

"Right here in the jail, guarding the prisoners. It'll be safer for you here while people get used to the idea that you're a free man." He watched the boy rubbing his hand along the butt of his holstered pistol, getting used to the feel of it. "What game did you used to shoot back home?"

"Squirrels. Rabbits. Deer. Felled a buck once. Why?"

Holt grabbed the double-barreled shotgun and tossed it to him. The boy caught it easily. "This is good for bigger varmints. Just aim and squeeze. One barrel at a time if you can. And if you can't the result will be the same. Just remember to keep plenty of cartridges on you when you have it. Nothing quite so useless in this world than an empty gun."

"Not the way you handle it," Turnbull said. "You cut down those three fellas back there without even firing a shot. Clubbed them as I recall."

"You're not me," Holt reminded him. "Use that thing right and you won't need to club anyone. Go to your pistol only if you must. And if you do, grab it with both hands and squeeze, just like the rifle. If you try firing it single-handed like I do, you're liable to break your hand or worse, drop the pistol."

The young man looked over the shotgun and managed to crack it open without any suggestion from Holt. There was hope for the boy yet.

"To hear you tell it," Jack said, "I'd think there's a fight coming."

Holt finished sorting the boxes of cartridges and set them on the ledge of the empty rifle rack beside his desk. "There's always a fight coming, boy. Live like that and you'll live longer."

He looked up when he saw Judge Cook lead the two attorneys out from the cells. Les Patrick looked as satisfied as if he had just pushed himself away from a full meal. The man who trailed behind them looked like he had been sent to bed without any supper.

Holt had never seen the man before, but took him to be Ty Arbour, counsel for the defense. He had only heard of him from Les Patrick, but pictured him to be a small, grubby man who looked to be one meal away from starvation.

Arbour resembled Les Patrick in many ways. Tall, fair-skinned and well attired. He might have been forgiven for mistaking them for brothers had their last names been the same.

Cook ignored the lawyer as he stopped in front of Holt's desk. "I heard what happened at the general store. I'm glad to see you're well."

"As well as I can be under the circumstances. I'm just glad Mr. Ross made it out alive."

"He's doing all too well." Cook frowned. "He presented me with a bill for all you purchased and for the replacement of the two windows you shot out in defense of his life."

Cook waved off the unpleasantness and gestured to Arbour. "I don't think you two have met. This is Ty Arbour, our town's resident defense counsel who also happens to be Mr. Patrick's cousin. I suppose one might say they have something of a monopoly on all of the legal proceedings in town."

Holt had not expected to shake the man's hand, but he did when he offered it. "Pleased to meet you, Sheriff. I'm sorry the town hasn't given you a more hospitable welcome."

"They didn't hire me to run a saloon," Holt said. "I'm here to enforce the law."

"Which you appear to do with great enthusiasm, as evidenced by the condition of my clients back there in your cells."

Holt decided to ignore him before he lost his temper. It was already strained, and he did not want to risk losing it by punching the attorney in the mouth. He asked Cook, "Where do we stand with the prisoners?"

Les Patrick answered for the judge. "We cut a deal. Six months of hard labor at the territorial prison. If they behave themselves for an additional two years, they'll win their freedom. Any offense in the interim, and they go back for ten years."

Holt did not like the idea of them returning to town in

six months, but he was not an attorney or a judge. Since Cook seemed pleased by the agreement, he decided to put it out of his mind.

"How long do I have to keep them here?"

"The U.S. Marshal for this district is scheduled to come to town next week," the judge told him. He'll take them off your hands then. Hopefully things will remain quiet until he arrives." He looked at the number of boxes of ammunition and the knife Holt still had on his desk. "But judging by what I see, you seem to expect a different outcome."

"I'll take what comes," Holt told him. "When does the viewing start for the mayor?"

Judge Cook pulled a pocket watch from his vest and consulted it. "Within the hour. I'll have just enough time to change into the appropriate attire in my chambers." He looked at Holt's brown outfit. "I trust you won't be wearing that, will you?"

"It's all I've got." He gestured at Ty Arbour. "His clients burned down Mayor Chapman's store before I could buy a change of clothes."

Arbour smiled. "The only clients I have were rendered unconscious by you in front of this very jail. As for those who burned the store, no one has been charged with that crime. Yet."

"At least the man who killed the mayor is where he belongs," Holt pushed, hoping for a reaction.

"I'm only sorry he couldn't hang for it," Arbour said. "I would've defended him, of course, but did not shed a tear at his passing."

The attorney placed his hat on his head and touched the brim of his hat. "A pleasure meeting you, Sheriff. I'm sure our paths will cross again soon." He bowed to the judge. "Your Honor." He slapped Les on the back before leaving the jail. "Cousin."

Judge Cook also bid him a good evening and left soon behind Arbour, leaving Les Patrick in the jail.

And judging by the attorney's demeanor, it looked to Holt as if he had something to tell him.

"Uh-oh," Holt said. "This doesn't look like good news. Should I be sitting down for this?"

"If anything, your preparations might be proven warranted," Les Patrick told him. "I've received word that Joe Mullen and twenty of his men are headed into town. They say it's under the guise of paying their respects to the mayor and to Ott Heller, of course, but I think they have less than admirable intentions in mind."

Holt had been expecting that. "They'll probably have Heller's widow with them too. Wailing and crying, getting as much sympathy as she can from all of this."

Les Patrick let out a long breath as he looked down at his shoes. "I'm afraid not. It seems she was so consumed by grief that she too has passed on. To hear Mullen's people tell it, the poor woman died of a broken heart at the news of Ott's death."

"Mercy," Jack Turnbull said.

But there was something in what Les had told him that did not ring true. And something in the way he had said it that told Holt he did not believe it either. "Doc Klassen told me he used to beat holy hell out of her on a regular basis."

"Anyone in town could've told you that," Les said, "and they'd be right too. He was a terror when he drank, and poor Mrs. Heller was often the target of his displeasure. And, like you, I find the coincidence most suspect."

Holt agreed. "Sounds like more than grief played a role in all of this if you ask me."

"You'll have the opportunity to ask Dr. Klassen himself at the viewing this evening. He rode up to the mine after your run-in with Cal at the general store. Word is she went to sleep and never woke up. The doctor is a good man. Clever too. He'll know if there was something more to it than that."

Holt let out a long breath. "Looks like one more thing I'll have to investigate."

Les looked like he was about to say something, but remembered Turnbull was still there. "Jack, could you excuse us for a moment. There's something I'd like to discuss with the sheriff in private. No offense."

The boy was about to leave when Holt said, "The kid stays. He's my deputy now. His neck is in the same noose as mine. Anything you have to say to me, you can say in front of him."

He watched the youth stand a little taller, which only served to make him look even younger.

"Fine," Les said. "I think it might be a good idea if you remain here in the jail tonight, John. Don't risk going to the viewing. With Mullen and his men there, not to mention his committee men, you're liable to find yourself with few friends in attendance. You'll be outnumbered by more than twenty to one. And I know Mrs. Chapman would be most disappointed if her husband's viewing was interrupted by any . . . unpleasantness."

Holt did not know Les Patrick very well, but he knew that, with time, he might come to respect him. But it was still too early for him to take the man at his word. And it was too early in Holt's tenure as sheriff to back down from a fight. Les might have had a point, but it did not mean he was right.

"I'm paid to keep law and order in town," Holt told him. "On Main Street. In the saloons. And at the mayor's viewing too. There won't be any trouble. At least none started by me."

"Yes, I was afraid you were going to say something like that." Les tapped his fingers on the desk. "Well, my conscience is clear. I intend on being armed as well during the viewing tonight and at the funeral tomorrow, so if trouble does happen to break out, you can count on my support."

Holt smiled. "I didn't know you cared."

"I'm full of surprises." He gave a final knock on his desk before he turned to leave. "Well, I'll leave you to get back to whatever it was you were doing. Let's just hope for a peaceful evening for all concerned."

"Hoping never gotten me much except disappointed," Holt said.

The lawyer offered a final wave as he opened the door but jumped back when he found Frank Peters blocking his way.

"Les," Peters greeted, a bit out of breath.

"Frank," Patrick said as he moved around the former sheriff and walked across the thoroughfare.

Holt moved his hand to his belt buckle as he asked Peters. "What do you want?"

The former sheriff held out his hands away from his sides, showing they were empty. "Can I come in?"

He might have appeared unarmed, but Holt still did not trust him. "You can tell me whatever you came to say from there."

Peters looked at Jack but decided whatever he had to tell Holt was too important to wait.

"I'm here to deliver a message for you." He held up his hands again. "It's not a threat, just a message. Hank Bostrom is in the back room of the Railhead, and he wants to talk to you. Right now."

Holt looked Peters over, trying to detect any dishonesty in him. He seemed to be telling the truth.

"Said he just wants to talk," Peters went on. "And only

talk. He's got men with him, but they're out back of the place. It'll be you and him and Ma. That's all."

Holt took the knife from the desk and tucked it into the back of his pants. He did not need to check his pistol for he already knew it was loaded.

He straightened out his jacket and took his hat from the peg beside the rifle rack. "Keep an eye on the place while I'm gone, Jack. Looks like I've got an outlaw to see."

As they began to walk along the boardwalk, Frank Peters stopped and placed a hand on Holt's arm. "Look, Sheriff . . ."

Holt snatched him by the throat and pinned him against the wall of a building. "Take your hand off me, boy."

Peters again held up both hands and croaked, "I was just trying to be friendly, darn it!"

Holt let him go. "You can be friendly without pawing me."

"Fine." Peters ran his fingers over his neck, trying to get the blood to flow again. "I just wanted to tell you that you've got the wrong idea about me is all."

"Really?" he laughed as they resumed their walk to the Railhead. "I think I've got you pegged just about right."

"I'm not trying to tell you I'm a saint," Peters said as he fell in behind him. "I've done too much in my life to make anyone believe that. But I'm no back-shooter, either, and there's not a man in town who'd tell you otherwise. Drunk, yes. Greedy, sure."

"Crooked," Holt added.

"Depending on how you look at it, fine. Crooked too. But whatever I am, I'm an open book, so when I tell you that you've got nothing to worry about by walking in there tonight, it's the truth. And if trouble does happen to break out, I'll be there to back you up. That goes for tonight and against Mullen too. He's everything I am and worse, only he has enough money to put a better shine on it than me. So long as you don't find yourself on the opposite side of Ma, I'll be there to back your play. Tonight, and in the days ahead too."

Holt did not trust Peters any more than he trusted a rattlesnake. But he still might serve a purpose. "Any idea on what Bostrom might want to talk about?"

"Only that he wanted to speak to you on neutral ground. He didn't want to come to the jail out of concern you might start shooting."

Holt hoped that meant the outlaw had some common sense. That did not absolve him of the beating he had given Cassie. "He still has to answer for what he did to that girl."

"Just hear him out for now," Peters said. "He's looking for a temporary truce, not a surrender."

Holt decided to test the man's usefulness a bit further. "How long were you sheriff here, Peters?"

"Five years," he said. "Mullen and his committee men rode me out of town and Mayor Chapman let them run things. But, when Mullen wound up being worse than I was, Mayor Chapman sent for you."

Holt remembered the correspondence he had received from Mayor Chapman and Mullen in the weeks before Holt had accepted the position. Both men seemed to be honest about the problems in town. Both had blamed Ma McAdam for most of it.

But neither Chapman nor Mullen had mentioned Tony Cassidy at the Blue Bottle Saloon in any of their letters. They had not mentioned the Bostrom Gang either. Chapman may have mentioned them in one of his letters, but Mullen had not. It might not mean anything. It also might mean everything.

As they walked toward the saloon, Holt decided to put

another question to Frank Peters. "How come you and Mullen never got along?"

"Boils down to him always being a Blue Bottle man while I was always a Railhead man," Peters told him. "Don't know how it turned out that way, just that it's always been that way."

Holt knew such fault lines tended to exist in towns. Alliances only a few years old seemed to stretch back to time immemorial to those involved in them.

But to an outsider like Holt, he could see where Cassidy's slick underhanded ways appealed to Mullen while Ma's rough-yet-tender approach could reach a man like Peters.

As they drew closer to the Railhead, Holt still had a couple of questions to run by the former lawman. "Were you a good sheriff?"

Peters answered immediately. "Always did my job, Holt. Ma and her bunch might've gotten off easier from time to time. Maybe I came down on Cassidy harder than I had to, but the job got done. Whether they were McAdam boys or Cassidy boys, I brought them all in to Judge Cook's court. You can ask him yourself if you want."

Holt stole a glance back at the county hall and saw a line of mourners had already begun to form there. The clock tower of the bank said it was going on five, so he knew the doors for the visitation would be opening at any moment.

Holt decided to ask the final question. "You have any idea where that Bostrom money is, Frank?"

"What I think and what I can prove are two different things."

As they crossed Main Street, Holt said, "This isn't a court of law, Peters. I'm looking for any hint about where I can find that money."

"You and everyone else in town," Peters said. "If I knew where it was, what makes you think I'd tell you?"

"Not a reason in the world," Holt said. "Just asking a question."

Peters rushed ahead and held the Railhead door open for him. "I always thought it would be in the last place anyone would ever look, especially his brothers."

That did not help Holt narrow it down much. He remained on the boardwalk. "And just where would that be?"

Franks continued to hold the door open. "With Joe Mullen, of course."

Holt walked through the open door and found his mind filled with possibilities. Because handing off the stolen money to Joe Mullen would be the last place anyone would look. And getting it away from him would be impossible.

Perhaps his meeting with Hank Bostrom would be a good idea after all.

Peters led Holt into a back room of the saloon. He found Ma McAdam at a round table with a younger, good-looking man at her side. His square jaw was clean-shaven except for a few spots he had missed. His brown hair had been combed back, but the face beneath it was almost skeletal. It was a painfully thin and haunted face with sunken eyes surrounded by dark circles. He looked as bad as he had left Cassie upstairs, except that one could tell her scars would heal. His brow was damp with a thin sheen of sweat. He looked like he had crossed a line toward death and had passed the point of no return.

Despite the man's condition and Peters's assurances of peace, Holt knew this man was Hank Bostrom, and he drew his pistol as soon as he entered the room. "Get up, Bostrom, with your hands in the air."

But Hank didn't move as Ma McAdam stood up and came around the table to Holt. "Now, John, this ain't that kind of meeting. Just set down and listen to what he has to say."

"I can listen to everything he has to say once I have him in his cell." Holt moved away from Ma and kept his pistol trained on Hank. "Get up or die where you sit."

Ma grew anxious and looked at Peters. "Well, Frank? Ain't you gonna do something?"

"Nothing I can do," Peters said. "Hank hurt Cassie. I'd like to see him pay for it."

The outlaw flashed a smile that Holt imagined had been charming once but looked decayed now. Like an old plantation allowed to go to seed. "I wish I could oblige you, Sheriff, but I'm afraid I can't do that at the moment."

He showed him empty hands and his right palm was almost brown with blood. "Seems like Cassie's already killed me. I just don't know it yet."

Holt had almost forgotten about her wounding Hank before he managed to jump out the window. He kept his Remington level at him anyway. "How bad is it?"

"Went through and through as you know," Hank said. "Em would still be alive otherwise if it hadn't, but it did. Too bad it's taking so long to kill me."

Holt had seen such wounds before and knew they were not always fatal. In fact, they usually were not.

Holt looked at Peters. "Go fetch Doc Klassen and bring him here. He'll be able to patch up Hank just fine."

"Don't bother, Frank." Hank swiped off his hat and tossed it on the table. His scalp was soaked through with sweat, and Holt noticed his breathing was shallow.

Hank looked at him from the other side of the table.

"Come now, Marshal Holt. I hear you were in the war. Tell me what you see. And if you get a little closer, you might even be able to smell it."

But Holt could already smell it just fine from where he was. He slowly lowered his pistol. That stench only ever meant one thing. Gangrene had settled in on the wound. And given its location, it had probably already spread out through the center of him. It was not like a limb that might be cut off before the infection reached his blood. The poison from the wound in his side had undoubtedly already spread to his organs. There was nothing to amputate and an operation would not do him any good.

Hank Bostrom was right. He was already dead. His body just did not know it yet.

Holt lowered his pistol but kept it at his side. "If you're not here to turn yourself in, why are you here at all?"

"To take another run at Cassie," Hank admitted. "I was hoping she could tell us about where we could find the money my brother hid."

Holt gripped his pistol tighter. "Like you did last time?"

Bostrom shook his head slowly. "Just talking. With Ma's help, of course."

Holt sneered at the madam. "Just like last time."

"Gentler this time," Bostrom said. "More persuasive because, in case you haven't noticed, I'm not exactly spry."

"I noticed," Holt said. "Noticed the bruises on Cassie's face too. Bruises you put there." He looked the dying man over. "You're left-handed, aren't you?"

"Learned to shoot with my right," Hank said, "but the left is my dominant hand. You could tell that from the bruising?"

Holt saw no reason to tell him anything. "Among other signs I saw. None of them make much difference now. How come you're talking to me instead of Cassie?"

Ma stepped between them again. "Because he's dying, John. He's dying and wants to leave this world better than he found it."

Holt looked over at the outlaw. "Just dying will help things."

Bostrom sneered. "You law boys are all the same, aren't you? It's always your way and no other. How does it feel to always be so sure you're right?"

"Feels fine," Holt said. "Helps me sleep at night and get out of bed the next morning. So, tell me what you want or I'm leaving."

Bostrom brought his hand down on the table. "I need to know where that money is. My men and I earned it. We deserve it. We stole it fair and square."

Holt would have laughed if it was not so tragic. "If you could hear yourself now. You really believe that."

"You've lived your life a certain way and I've lived mine a different way. You don't like me or my brothers, that's fine. We earned that. But my men worked for that money."

"Stole it fair and square." Holt laughed. He thought about shooting him just to end this nonsense.

But Hank did not laugh. "I need to know where it is before I die so I can give my share to the girl. Personally. She deserves it for what she's been through, just like my men deserve their cut. The bank won't miss it. They've got plenty and have already written it off. Giving it back to them won't mean anything. But to Cassie? To my boys out there? It'll mean a new life for them. A life where they don't have to scrape the bottom of the barrel just to get by." He pointed at Holt. "Where they don't have to harm people to make a living either."

But the sheriff was not buying it. "They'll spend every

cent you give them in a month, and they'll be right back on the road, holding up stagecoaches and payroll wagons."

"Maybe," Hank allowed, "but Cassie won't. And ain't it worth giving her a chance at a new life? Bob promised her that. And I'd like to see that she gets it, especially after all that happened to her."

Holt kept looking at Bostrom until he finally got the point.

"Fine," Bostrom said. "After what *I* did to her."

Holt remembered the quiet promise he had made to her. About getting her a new start in life. If he had to use Bostrom to get it, and pay off his men in the bargain, then maybe it was worth it.

Ma McAdam handed Holt a hand-drawn map. "That shows all of the usual places where Hank and his brothers have hidden their stashes over the years. He and his men have checked every one of them since Bob got himself killed and haven't found a penny. That means Bob must've used another place. Somewhere Hank and the others don't know."

While he had been talking to Bostrom, his mind had been puzzling over what Peters had told him on the walk over to the saloon. About where the money might be.

He decided to get Hank's take on the idea. "Was your brother Bob close to Joe Mullen?"

Bostrom grew very still. "Friendly but I wouldn't say they were friends. Why?"

"I've heard a rumor floating around town that Bob might've hidden the money with Mullen," Holt said. "Or hidden it in one of his mines."

Bostrom shook his head. "Bob wouldn't have risked a miner happening on it. But giving it to Mullen for safe-keeping is a notion I never considered."

Holt was glad to see the notion taking root. "And now that you're considering it?"

"Sounds possible." Bostrom sagged a bit in his chair and Ma rushed to his side.

Holt could see his forehead drenched with sweat as if he'd just had a bucket of water dumped all over him.

Ma dabbed his forehead with her handkerchief as she looked up at Peters. "Frank, he's burning up. Help me get him upstairs to a room where he can rest."

But Bostrom gently eased her hand away. "I think we're past all that now, Ma." He looked over at Holt. "Let's say Bob did give my money to Mullen to hold. He never would've done that without getting him to promise to hand it over to me and Em if something happened to him."

Holt saw a way to make Bostrom's greed work for him. "Sounds to me like Mullen reneged on the deal. Can't imagine that sits too well with you."

He watched the dying man's look turn sour. "That's because it doesn't."

"Too bad we'll never know if he has it or not." Holt held up the map Ma had given him. "But since you didn't find the money in any of these places, Mullen's as good a place as any. Ott Heller might've been in on it too."

Bostrom looked at him as if he'd been woken from a dream. The infection had a firm hold on him now. "Heller? Mullen's foreman? The one who shot the mayor? What makes you think he has anything to do with this?"

"I didn't think he did until I found out his widow is dead too." He spoke over the gasps from Ma McAdam and Frank Peters. "They said she died of a broken heart. Maybe it wasn't as simple as that. Maybe it was from having a big mouth."

Bostrom swayed in his seat but steadied himself by placing both hands flat on the table. "It would figure, wouldn't it? Rita always had a way of saying too much, especially when she had a jug in her hand. Being married to Ott, no one could blame her for drinking so much."

Yes, the more Holt thought about it, the more he believed Bostrom just might be able to put his final moments in this world to good use. "Too bad we can't get Mullen to tell us. He was at the mayor's shooting, but so were dozens of other men. I've got nothing to arrest him for."

Bostrom's breathing was shallow now. He was practically panting as the infection took deeper hold of him. Ma comforted him as he lowered his head to summon up more strength.

"He going to be at the mayor's viewing tonight?"

Holt nodded. "With twenty of his miners, from what I hear. His committee men too."

Bostrom looked up at him. His eyes were little more than blackened circles. His face looked more dead than alive. "If you had something to arrest him for, think you could get him . . . to talk?"

Holt was glad the outlaw was coming around to his way of thinking. "I know I could. A man like Mullen isn't the type to take too kindly to a jail cell."

Bostrom slowly raised his head to Ma and whispered, "Whiskey. Get me some whiskey. Don't bother with a glass. Just a bottle. Get it for me quick."

Ma cradled his head to her bosom. "Oh, honey. Whiskey's the last thing you need right now. You need rest. Let me take care of you."

The outlaw tried to pull away from her but did not have the strength.

Frank Peters spoke for him. "Leave him be, Ma. He knows what he needs doing. And what he needs to do. I'll go get you that whiskey, Hank."

"Much obliged," the outlaw said, barely above a whisper.

Ma looked at Holt, wild-eyed and teary. She wanted him to talk Hank out of it, but Holt would do no such thing. Hank Bostrom would face justice that day one way or the other. He might not have lived well, but he was intent on dying as best he could.

"I'd best be getting up to the viewing," Holt said as he turned to leave.

"I'll be joining you in a while," Bostrom struggled to say.

But Holt already knew that.

CHAPTER 22

As he stood in line with the rest of the mourners, Holt had to admit the decorating committee had done a fine job of making the lobby of the county hall look solemn. Black bunting had been draped along the banisters of the two stairs that led up to the offices. Similar bunting had been draped around the platform on which the coffin holding Mayor Blair Chapman's remains now sat.

The American and territorial flags flanked the coffin. Flowers of all descriptions had been placed around the platform, partially to demonstrate life, partially to hide the smell of whatever chemicals the undertaker had used to preserve the body. For Holt, none of it took away from the impact of death or the guilt he felt over Chapman's murder.

Since Lincoln had been shot three years before, morticians across the country had taken to using a variety of chemicals to preserve those who had passed from this world. Holt thought it a ghoulish practice to view a man's dead body, but it seemed to give the survivors some comfort. As Holt's family had been killed during the war, he could not speak to its impact.

Mrs. Chapman sat on a chair that had been brought into the lobby for the purpose. Since he figured all her belongings had been burned along with her store during the riot, Holt wondered who had loaned her the black dress and mourning veil she now wore. He imagined it had been one of the women who now stood beside her as she quietly wept into a handkerchief. She did not seem to notice the people who took her hand and offered their condolences once they had passed by her husband's remains.

He saw Earl Sibert standing at a respectful distance to the side. His stovepipe hat in hand, his head bowed. Holt might not have thought much of the man, but he knew how to conduct himself in such environs.

Holt felt a pair of eyes boring a hole into him and saw Joe Mullen farther ahead of him in line. He was at the head of the coffin while Holt was closer to the entrance. His blue Vigilance Committee ribbon was pinned to the lapel of his black coat.

The two men eyed each other as they made their slow circuit around the coffin. Holt was reminded of a similar scene he had witnessed while leading a scouting party during the war. Two wolves snarling at each other while they circled a dead deer, each vying for who would ultimately claim the kill. Only this distant dance was for much higher stakes than a rotting body.

Mullen broke off the contest first as he led a woman to greet Mrs. Chapman. He took the widow's hand in both of his.

Holt imagined the woman with him was his wife, Sarabelle. She looked like the kind of woman Mullen would choose to marry. Dirty-blonde hair pulled up beneath an elegant black hat. Despite the veil, he could see she had high cheekbones and complexion tanned by years spent beneath the prairie sun. She was lean and used to hard labor, though her dress showed someone who had become accustomed to the finer trappings of having money.

But Holt knew all the money in the world would never change what she was. A pioneer woman at heart and a good match for a man like Joe Mullen.

As the line continued to slowly advance around the coffin, Holt felt a hand on his left arm. He was glad to see it was Dr. Ralph Klassen.

"A solemn occasion," the doctor said.

"For some of us," Holt said as he watched Mullen begin to mingle with some of the other committee men at the side of the entrance. All of them sporting similar ribbons on their lapels as Mullen.

"Not here and not now," the doctor whispered as he walked beside Holt. "Not only for Mrs. Chapman's sake but for your own as well. You'll be held accountable for any unpleasantness that happens here and I don't want that. Neither do you. Don't let him bait you, John. There'll be plenty of time to settle the business between you after the funeral tomorrow. Until then, please remain civil."

As usual, Klassen was right, and Holt decided not to glare at Mullen any further. "If trouble starts, it won't be from me."

He felt the doctor grow rigid beside him. "I don't like the way you said that. It sounds like a condition."

"No conditions," Holt said. "Just the truth."

The two of them remained silent as they followed the slow procession of mourners that snaked their way around the coffin. Some of the townspeople placed a hand on the coffin as they passed by. Men and women wiped tears away after they offered the widow their condolences. The women huddled around Mrs. Chapman made it difficult to see her as he drew closer to where she sat.

When he and Dr. Klassen finally reached her, Holt was

surprised she looked up at him and slowly got to her feet. The women surrounding her closed in to support her, though she stood on her own.

He braced himself for a slap from her as he extended his hand. "My deepest condolences on your loss, Mrs. Chapman. I didn't know him well, but I could tell he was a fine man."

Behind the veil, the widow's face remained stoic as she placed her gloved hand in his. "My husband held you in high regard, Sheriff Holt. He often said the future of this town rested in your capable hands, and despite his many faults, Blair Chapman was a fine judge of character."

Holt bowed slightly. "I'm honored, ma'am."

He thought she would let go of his hand, but she only held on to it tighter. "I didn't thank you for the kindness you showed me that night. How quickly you attended to my husband after he was cut down by that filthy coward."

Holt winced at the memory. "I'm only sorry I wasn't able to save him."

"You did all you could," the widow told him. "And I hope I can rely on you to continue to do so under my administration."

Holt was not sure he had heard her correctly. "Your administration, ma'am?"

"Indeed, Sheriff." She raised her voice and looked around the lobby as she said, "For I shall be taking my husband's office as mayor of Devil's Gulch. I will serve out the rest of his term in his stead, after which, the good people of this town can decide to reelect me or replace me."

The mourners broke into hushed whispers at the Chapman widow's announcement, none more so than the women who had been attending to her.

And although Holt could not swear to it, he thought he saw a small smile appear beneath her veil. "Well, Sheriff

Holt? You never answered my question. Can I rely on you to fulfill your oath to my husband and protect this town?"

Holt bowed slightly again. "Of course, ma'am. It'll be an honor."

"Very well, then. Please come to my office upstairs after my husband's funeral. We have much to discuss."

She released his hand and resumed her seat and Holt moved away from her. Dr. Klassen followed close behind.

Holt looked up when he heard a commotion at the entrance of the hall, followed by muddled curses as Mullen and his fellow committee men pushed their way out of the building.

Klassen was at Holt's elbow again. "Good God, John." He struggled to keep his voice down. "When she got to her feet, I thought she was going to slap you. I wasn't expecting that!"

"That makes two of us," Holt admitted. "She's got sand."

"She certainly does," Klassen told him. "She has a will of iron and when she sets her mind to something—"

But the doctor's thought was interrupted by a shout from Main Street that echoed through the hall.

"Mullen! I want to talk to you!"

Holt hid his grin for the benefit of Klassen.

"Who's that?" the doctor asked as he tried to look around the crowd that had gathered at the entrance.

But Holt did not have to look to know it was Hank Bostrom. And he was living up to his end of the bargain.

Holt edged his way through the crowd, who resented his attempts to move to the front until they saw the star pinned on his lapel.

He saw the front of the county hall was lined with

committee men standing behind Joe Mullen. Mullen's wife was off to the side with some of the other wives.

Mullen stood alone in front of his men, facing down Bostrom.

The outlaw's face was streaked with sweat, and he took another pull on the whiskey bottle in his right hand while his left rested on the pistol on his hip.

"Go home, Hank," Mullen said. "You're drunk."

"I'll go." Bostrom threw the bottle at Mullen's feet. It shattered on the boardwalk beside him. "I'll go after you tell me what you've done with my brother's money!"

Holt watched Mullen flinch. Not from the whiskey bottle, but from the question. He quickly recovered by saying, "I don't have the slightest idea what you're talking about and neither do you. Get out of here before you get hurt."

"I'm already hurt." He held up his bloody right hand, which caused the crowd to gasp.

Women looked away. Husbands gasped and gripped their wives' arms, ready to pull them from harm's way if things got any worse.

"I'm dying," Bostrom went on, "but before I go, I want to know what you did with Bob's money. My money now. And, by God, I'll hear you tell me, or I'll drag you down to hell with me."

Dr. Klassen tried to get past Holt, but the sheriff grabbed his arm and kept him where he was.

He watched Mullen slowly pull back his black coat, revealing the pistol on his right hip. "Hank, I'm telling you for the last time. I won't tolerate talk like that, not even from a dying man. If you're hurt, I'll see to it Doc Klassen tends to your wounds, but I won't stand being accused of taking anyone's money. Not even a thief's money."

Holt watched beads of sweat drop from Bostrom's brow

as he swayed alone in the middle of the street. "I asked you a question. I won't ask again."

Mullen stepped down from the boardwalk and Hank grabbed for his holster.

Mullen drew and fanned five shots into the middle of the outlaw.

Hank Bostrom collapsed and died in the middle of the thoroughfare.

Mullen took a step forward as the rest of the crowd recoiled.

Holt and Klassen forced their way through the crowd as Mullen turned to face them. His gun aloft and his arms wide, like a showman. "It was a fair fight. Anyone can see that."

Klassen broke free and ran to Bostrom's side.

Holt walked toward Mullen.

"Ah, there you are, Sheriff," Mullen sneered. "How good of you to finally show yourself."

Holt snatched Mullen's pistol with his left hand while his right connected solidly with his jaw. The blow was enough to stagger him, but he kept his feet. Holt brought Mullen's pistol butt across his temple, which dropped him to his knees.

The committee men moved forward as a group until Holt pressed Mullen's pistol against the back of their leader's head.

"There's still one shot left in this thing by my counting." He thumbed back the hammer, causing Mrs. Mullen to scream.

The sound froze the committee men in their tracks.

Holt said, "Any of you take another step and we'll find out."

Holt held Mullen in place and looked down at Klassen,

whose ear was very close to Bostrom's mouth. The doctor rocked back on his knees and said to Holt, "He's dead."

That was all Holt needed to hear. Hank Bostrom had lived up to his end of the bargain. Now it was time for Holt to live up to his.

He spoke loud enough for the crowd to listen. "Joseph Mullen, I'm placing you under arrest for the murder of Hank Bostrom."

He grabbed Mullen by the collar and pulled him up to his feet. As they were the same height, Holt dug the pistol into Mullen's side as he forced him to walk sideways. He used Mullen as something of a shield between him and the committee men.

Mullen struggled against Holt's grip as he yelled, "It was a fair fight, by God! He went for his gun first!"

Doctor Klassen picked up what had fallen from Bostrom's left hand. It was not a gun. It was a steak knife.

"He was unarmed, Joe," the doctor said.

A great clamor broke out among the crowd as Holt pulled a stunned Mullen up on the opposite boardwalk and pulled him into the jail, where Jack Turnbull quickly closed and bolted the door behind them.

The youth scrambled ahead of them, took the keyring from the peg, and opened the door leading to the cells.

Holt shoved him inside and threw him in a cell across the aisle from the other prisoners.

He slammed the door shut and locked it while Mullen charged the bars. His arm shot out from between them and strained for Holt's throat.

"You set me up! You're behind all of this! You're trying to ruin me!"

Holt grabbed the prisoner's wrist and yanked it hard to the right, causing Mullen to twist and cry out in agony.

"You ever lunge for me or my deputy again and I'll

break your arm. No one made you gun down an unarmed man, Mullen. That was all your doing."

Mullen cradled his wounded arm and sank down to the floor with his back against the bars.

Holt grabbed a handful of Mullen's hair and pulled his head against the iron. He kept his voice low so the other prisoners would not hear. "I know you told Heller to kill the mayor, you piece of filth. And before you leave here, I'll hear you say it, or you'll never spend another day on this earth without pain."

He released his head with a shove and got to his feet. He faced the three other prisoners, who backed away from the bars.

Holt stepped out into the office and slammed the door shut, where Jack Turnbull was all too happy to lock it.

"Looks like you got him, boss," Turnbull said as he hung the keys on the peg. "Looks like you got him good."

"Yeah," Holt said as he listened to the gathering crowd on the street. "Now I just have to keep him."

CHAPTER 23

From his perch by the saloon door, Frank Peters placed the shotgun across his lap as he kept his eye on what was left of the Bostrom Gang. The men were huddled around a poker table without playing cards. Usually, he would have made them stand at the bar if they were not gambling, but under the circumstances, decided to let them be.

He figured each man had drunk a half a bottle of whiskey at least. One or two were already on their second. Peters knew they were not drinking for fun. They were drinking to dull the pain of losing their leader. Peters knew Hank Bostrom might not have been as good a leader as Bob had been, but he had been a Bostrom, which gave the group a name and a reputation behind it.

Without Hank or Em or Bob, they were no longer the Bostrom Boys. They were just a group of outlaws down to their last few dollars. Funds they had decided to spend on whiskey instead of a proper burial for their friend.

Not that Frank Peters had seen fit to charge the men for their whiskey. They were armed and dangerous and grieving over Hank. In his experience, it was just best to allow men in their condition to drink themselves into a stupor until they passed out. A man with a hangover was much easier to handle than a drunk with a score to settle.

But Frank knew these men had no score to settle, which he knew bothered them something awful. Their boss had been killed days ago by the same bullet that had taken Em's life. Hank's body had just been slower about dying.

He imagined they could blame Cassie for killing two Bostrom Boys, but Frank knew none of the outlaws were particularly fond of men who were rough with ladies. They all knew Cassie and figured she had suffered enough. They had no intention of avenging Hank or Em at her expense.

Cal was dead, too, thanks to his run-in with Holt at the general store. Frank knew the news had hit them hard, what with him being the unofficial head of the gang. But, by all accounts, it had been a fair fight, so the Bostrom Gang had no quarrel with the sheriff either.

Had they been other men, Frank Peters might have felt sorry for Charlie and Ted and Duke and the others. But despite the choices he had made in his life, Frank found it difficult to work up much sympathy for men who made their living by the gun. He did not exclude himself from this principle. To his way of thinking, the only kind of justice a man could hope for out of this world is to die the same way he had lived it.

Men like Charlie and the others had lived by the gun. Frank Peters, too, in his own way. It was only fitting they met their end by the gun too. Though none of them were especially eager to reach that end any time soon.

Peters looked over the crowd of the Railhead Saloon from his elevated lookout chair at the corner of the bar and knew Ma would be pleased. Despite Mayor Chapman's viewing—or perhaps because of it—they were doing a good business. The tables were seeing plenty of action and the girls were finding willing men eager for company—both on the floor and upstairs in private.

He watched Ma McAdam pull her shawl around her shoulders as she began to walk down the stairs. Her ruffled dress trailed behind her. She was the most elegant woman Frank Peters had ever seen, not that he considered himself an expert on such things. She had seduced him ten years ago when he had watched her step down from the stagecoach on a rainy afternoon. Life had been cruel to her since. Too many customers and late nights had robbed her of her looks too soon. Rotgut whiskey and a lack of sun had given her skin a yellowish appearance that some called sickly, but Frank thought had given her a fine patina like copper or another fancy metal.

She may not have been the stunning beauty he had seen all those years ago, but Frank Peters did not care about such things. He only cared about the woman she was. She had told him years ago that she would never love him, never be his. But words had held little value for Frank Peters then. They still held little value, which was why he woke each morning with the renewed hope that she would change her mind. The possibility of it was enough to keep him close and remain at her beck and call.

He watched her grace a few of the tables with a smile and a short greeting as she made her way over to him. Peters climbed down from the lookout chair, leaving the shotgun across the armrests.

Hoppy handed her a glass of champagne as she glided by on her way to speak with Peters.

"Better than I expected for the middle of the week." She sipped her champagne as she looked at the crowd. "They're all buzzing about Hank being gunned down by Joe Mullen."

Peters eyed the table of the Bostrom Gang in the far

corner of the saloon. "They seem to be taking it better than I expected."

"Poor lambs." She frowned as she looked over at the table of dejected men. The expression made new lines in her face Frank had not noticed before. "Guns on their hips and rifles on the saddles and not a penny to their name. At least they're peaceful enough for now. What do you think will happen to them?"

Peters had seen what had happened to better men than them over the years. "They're used to being told what to do. Bob led them for a long time. Now that all the Bostrom men are dead, they'll probably break apart and go their separate ways. California. Texas. Some might join up with another outfit, but it won't be the same. In a couple of years, most of them will be dead or close enough to it to wish they were."

The lines of her frown grew deeper. "It's that war that did it. Not to them but to the rest of us. Left a whole half of the country with nothing to do except sift through the ashes and relish their own shame. It's not right to treat grown men like that. Not right at all."

"No, it's not," came a voice from behind them.

Peters turned first and saw Sheriff Holt had entered the saloon without making a sound.

"We don't want any trouble in here tonight, Holt."

Her glass in hand, Ma smiled up at the lawman. "Evening, Sheriff. I understand you've been busy."

"Too busy for my tastes." Peters watched him look around the saloon until he saw the Bostrom Gang at the table in the back corner. "Are they behaving themselves?"

"Like lambs," Ma said, repeating her earlier description. "Lost lambs, if you want to know the truth."

"I've had enough truth for one night," Holt said.

Peters did not know the man well, but thought he looked

tired. Not tired in the way a man looks from working in a mine all day or behind a plow. But tired in the way a man's soul gets when it has seen too much death and hardship. And, he imagined, Holt had seen more than he had been bargaining for since coming to Devil's Gulch.

The sheriff surprised him by saying, "I'd like to speak to them."

"That's not a good idea," Peters said. "They might not blame you for Hank, but they know what happened between you and Cal. Whatever you've got to say should wait until morning when they're hungover. A man with a big head and sour belly is more apt to be agreeable."

Ma smiled up at him and ran her hand across his cheek. "You didn't know my Frank is a philosopher at heart, did you, Sheriff?"

Peters leaned into her hand, warmed by her touch.

"What I came to say can't wait," Holt said. "I've got a town full of mourners at the hall, Mullen in jail and twenty of his men at Sibert's place mourning Ott Heller. I want to tamp down any fires before they spring up."

"An unfortunate reference," Ma said, "considering the smoke from the Chapman store still hangs in the air."

Peters could tell Holt had not thought of that and did not like Ma pointing it out to him.

"Figure of speech," he said. "But I still want to talk to those boys. Make sure there are no hard feelings."

"And if there are?" Peters asked.

"Then I'd prefer to settle it now. On the ground of my choosing."

"But it's not your ground to choose," Ma told him. "This is my saloon, and I don't fancy it being shot up on account of your pride."

Holt's eyes narrowed. "Pride has nothing to do with it. Practicality does. And I'd rather head off trouble now while they're drunk and slow instead of having to face it down tomorrow after the mayor's funeral. I'm liable to have a mob of angry miners on my hands. I don't need those boys getting riled up and making it worse."

Peters watched Ma's look soften a bit. It was a look he had seen countless times before. A look that was not caused by Holt's reasoning, but by an idea that had come to her. An idea that she could turn a situation to her advantage.

"If you insist on seeing them, I can't stop you," she admitted, "but I can insist on going over with you. They're less liable to get violent if I'm around. I'll have to insist on that."

Peters thought he had misheard her at first until she winked at him. "Frank will come along to watch your back. What do you say, Sheriff?"

Holt did not look pleased. "I'd say it looks like I don't have a choice in the matter."

She drained her glass and placed it on the bar, where Hoppy appeared and refilled it. She picked it up as she slid her arm through Holt's. "Come along, Sheriff. You too, Frank. Things are about to get very interesting in the Railhead tonight."

Frank grabbed his shotgun and held it at his side as he followed Holt and Ma toward the back of the saloon. He leaned against the end of the bar as they continued to the corner table where the remnants of the Bostrom Gang drank away their sorrows.

He was glad that none of them paid Holt much mind until he and Ma were already standing over them. They all sat up straighter then, though none of them tried to get up or go for their guns.

Ma said, "The sheriff here has something to say, and I

want all of you to hear him out. I don't want any trouble in my place, so if you can't listen to reason, I'll have to ask you to leave. I know you boys are hurting, so I don't want to do that."

Frank watched Duke swagger in his chair, about to say something, when Charlie Gardiner motioned for him to be quiet. "You come to gloat about our dead?" His Cajun accent added an edge to his words.

Holt said, "I came to tell you I'm sorry about what happened to Hank, but he died the way he wanted. I also wanted to thank you boys for agreeing to his wishes by staying out of it. Earl Sibert has him up at his shop and he'll fix him up nice for you to see him tomorrow after the mayor's funeral."

"And Cal?" Charlie asked.

"He's fixing up Cal too," Holt told him. "You'll be able to visit them after the mayor's funeral tomorrow. Ott Heller will be planted soon after."

"I'm not talking about visiting hours, Holt," Gardiner said. "I'm talking about you killing Cal."

"It was a fair fight, boys," Holt said to the group. "He shot first and took the shopkeeper as a hostage. Nothing would've happened if he hadn't started it. He went out like a man, and he went quick if that's any consolation."

Duke pounded the table, causing the glasses of liquor to overflow. Art grabbed the bottle before it fell over.

"It's no consolation," Duke slurred. "Ain't no consolation at all. We lost two fine men today and you had a hand in both. You've got a lot of sand to stand there and tell us it wasn't personal, Sheriff. I'll give you that."

"Sand has nothing to do with it," Holt told him. "I came here to tell you it wasn't personal and that I'm sorry things turned out the way they did. I'm not sorry about doing my job, but I don't want any ill feeling between us over it."

Charlie eased Duke back in his seat. "You here to arrest us, Sheriff?"

"Got nothing to arrest you for," Holt said. "Just rumors about what you boys may have done." He cocked an eyebrow. "I didn't come for a confession, and I don't want one. Didn't come here expecting to make friends either. Just wanted to let you know that, as far as I'm concerned, there's no trouble between us."

Ted Graham grinned into his glass. "That's right neighborly of you, Sheriff. But your concerns don't concern us. We decide if it's over or not. You don't."

Holt nodded. "I know. You get a say in this. I'm not here to threaten anyone or warn you. Just wanted you to know you've got no trouble coming from me."

Ted looked up at him. "And if we decide you've got trouble?"

Frank watched Holt grow very still. "Then you boys will get more than you can handle."

Ted began to get up, but a sharp bark from Charlie kept him in his seat. None of the other men tried to get up, either, including Duke.

"That all of it?" Charlie asked.

"That's all I came to say unless you've got something to add."

Frank watched Charlie slowly reach for the bottle and refill his glass. "Well, can't say we accept your condolences or appreciate the kind words, but we heard you. Now, we'd appreciate it if you clear on out of here and let us drink in peace."

Frank watched Holt eye each of the men before he backed away from Ma and turned to leave.

"Evening, Peters," the sheriff said as he passed by.

"Sheriff," Frank said as he watched the lawman leave the saloon.

For once, he found himself agreeing with Duke March. It had taken a lot of sand to stand before a table full of men who wanted him dead and offer his version of condolence.

Ma toasted the outlaws. "You boys handled yourselves better than I expected just now. Here's to Hank and Cal. They died like men."

The gang lifted their glasses, joined her in her toast and drained their drinks before Art began to refill them.

Charlie Gardiner was the only one who did not drain his glass. Frank knew he had never been much of a drinker and was not surprised he was the most sober in the group.

He said to Ma, "Fine toast."

Ma waved away the compliment. "Think nothing of it. Nor of the whiskey either. You boys are drinking on the house tonight."

The group's mood brightened a bit. Duke got up and staggered over to the bar and demanded another bottle from Hoppy. After a nod from Ma, Hoppy gave it to him.

But Frank noticed Charlie had not taken his eyes off Ma. "I'm not kicking a gift horse in the mouth, but what's with the sudden good will? Near as any of us could see it, you were a might sore at Hank for his poor handling of Miss Cassie."

Ma smiled at her guests as Duke returned with the bottle and dropped into his chair. "Let's just say that I've been in this business long enough to know that everyone in it gets their knocks eventually. I've had mine. Cassie's had hers. You boys have had yours. Recently too."

Ed Volk refilled his glass. "Never took kindly to hurting women. Any kind of women. Sporting or otherwise."

Ma rested a hand on his shoulder. "You boys were always more respectful than Hank or Em. All my girls say so. You all took after Bob in that regard, and I'm grateful."

Frank watched the men change a little at the mention

of their fallen leader. Bob had not died like Cal or Hank or Em. He had been gunned down by a cavalry unit armed with a Gatling gun. He had never even had a chance to defend himself.

He watched Ma use that to her advantage. "I've been watching the way you boys changed after poor Bob met his end. You're different now and, if I might be allowed to say it, not for the better."

Stew Adams wobbled in his seat. "Hank and Em were a different sort from old Bob. Can't expect a leader to change without the men who follow to change along with it."

"That may be true," Ma allowed, "but you boys were quite the outfit when Bob was running things. And recent events have made me wonder if you might not be ready to be like that again."

The gang grumbled among themselves as Charlie said, "We'll find our footing. Don't worry about us."

Frank watched Ma smile. "My girls call me 'Ma' for a reason, boys. I worry about people. People like you. I suppose that's why I'd like to help you find your footing sooner rather than later. Could be best for all concerned. You as well as me."

Now Frank understood the look he had seen on Ma's face when Holt first walked into the saloon. She had only agreed to help him because she thought there was a way she could help herself too.

Tony Cassidy already had Mullen's committee men and, likely his miners. She must figure the remnants of the Bostrom Gang could work for her to even the score.

Frank had always admired the way her mind worked, and it made him love her even more, if that was possible.

Charlie had clearly caught on too. "What did you have in mind?"

Frank knew they were already roped. All she had to do

was lead them into the corral. "If you don't mind me joining you boys, I'll be happy to tell you."

She did not have to ask Frank to bring a chair for her, which he did. She warmed his heart by saying, "Grab one for yourself, Frank. This involves you too."

She did not have to ask him twice.

CHAPTER 24

Holt stood in front of the jail and watched the crowd that had assembled in front of County Hall. Townspeople playing the role of mourners and gossips. Their grief over the tragic loss of their beloved mayor forgotten amid the bloodshed many had witnessed that very evening on Main Street.

Although he was too far away to hear any of their conversations, he knew what they were saying. The outlaw Hank Bostrom had been shot dead in the middle of the street by Joe Mullen. He should have been given a medal, not arrested for performing a civic duty. He was head of the Vigilance Committee after all. It was his duty to stop a mad killer and Hank had it coming. How was he supposed to know the outlaw was unarmed?

Holt knew that soon the conversation would take a nasty turn, at least as far as he was concerned. And where was Sheriff Holt when it was going on? Why hadn't he stopped it before it got that far?

If town gossip had not already taken that direction, Anthony Cassidy up at the Blue Bottle Saloon would make sure it did.

Which was why he intended on making sure his next

stop was to Cassidy's place. As with the Bostrom Boys at the Railhead, if trouble came, he wanted it to come on ground of Holt's choosing.

He turned when he heard Jean Roche call out his name and saw her crossing Main Street with her wicker basket over her arm. Two other women from her café trailed behind her with baskets as well.

He grinned for the first time since he had last seen her. "Looks like I'm good for business."

She did not grin as she stepped up onto the boardwalk. "What's good for me looks pretty bad for you. I'm glad to see you're not hurt."

He unlocked the door and called in to Jack. "Dinner's here."

Jean handed her basket to one of the women, who quickly brought it into the jail. "I'm worried about you, John Holt."

"I didn't know you cared."

"I care about my business," she said. "If you get yourself shot, who'll be around to keep the jail full? Just about the only one in town who's making more from you than me is Earl Sibert. His mortuary's running out of room thanks to you."

He had not thought of that. "Just doing my job."

Jean kept up her teasing. "Word has it he's planning on cutting down half the trees around town just to keep up with demand for coffins."

Holt threw up his hands. "I surrender. You win."

He liked that she enjoyed teasing him. She seemed to be the only person in town who did not either fear him or want him dead.

She nodded over at the townspeople in front of the county hall, who had begun speaking in earnest now that the sheriff was talking with the young Negro woman from the café. "Looks like we've given those old hens something else to talk about, as if they didn't already have enough. I'm not doing you any favors, talking to you out in the open like this. I'd best be about my business."

As she began to head into the jail, he heard himself say, "Don't go. Not just yet."

She stopped, seemingly unsure of what to do next. "Why?"

He was not sure himself. "Just like seeing a friendly face is all."

She seemed to take that as an answer and stood beside him, hands folded across her apron. "Why, John Holt. I didn't take you for the sentimental type."

He leaned against the porch post. "Not sentimental." He did not know how to describe it himself. "Just need to be reminded of why I do this kind of work."

"Because you get paid," she reminded him. "Quite a bit, too, if what I heard is right."

With Mayor Chapman gone and with Joe Mullen now against him, he was not surprised that his fee had become public knowledge. "I'm worth it. Quality doesn't come cheap."

"I just hope the people will be willing to keep paying." She looked at the blood spots that Hank Bostrom had left behind in the thoroughfare. "Your kind of justice is mighty expensive."

"It's worth it in the end," Holt said with conviction. "I've been through this before. You can't make breakfast without breaking a couple of eggs."

"Can't get bacon without slaughtering a pig neither," she added. "People love bacon, but don't have the stomach for the blood that goes with it." She nudged him with her elbow. "Guess that's why they hire men like you."

Holt liked the way she thought. "I guess you and I

aren't all that much different. People go to your place for a meal. They don't pay much mind about all the hard work that goes into making it. They just order their food, and someone brings it to them." He looked out at the towns-people. "Same thing in my line of work. They don't like seeing justice done. They just want it taken care of." He had been through this before. In other places, other towns. "It'll get better if they give me the chance."

"You might want to start by giving yourself a chance, John Holt," she said. "Walking into a saloon full of men looking to kill you isn't the best way of going about that."

He imagined word of his trip to the Railhead had reached her quicker than he had expected. "You're the one who told me to reach an agreement with Ma in the first place. All I did was smooth things over with Hank's boys. As much as they could be smoothed over, considering."

"I'm not talking about what you've already done," she said. "I'm talking about what you're fixing to do now. You're going up to the Blue Bottle, aren't you?"

If he had not already been leaning against the porch post, he might have fallen over. "How did you know that?"

She smiled at her own intuition. "You're not as tough to figure as you think, John Holt. You're a balanced man. It stands to reason that you spoke to one group of men against you that you'd want to talk to the other. And right now, too, before the liquor gets to working on them. You already visited the Railhead, so the Bottle is the only place left. With Mullen in jail and not around to rile them up, you figure you can bring them around to your way of thinking."

Holt could not argue with her, but her ability to read his thoughts was troubling. "You sure you're not a gypsy? You remind me of a Creole woman I used to know in

New Orleans. She had a knack for knowing things before they happen."

"I don't need that heathen nonsense to know you, John Holt. Just two good eyes and a dash of common sense." Her mood darkened a little. "I don't like the idea of you going to the Bottle, but if you do, best go in ready for trouble. They'll have no welcome for you up there."

Holt did not expect they would, but it did not change his mind. "Tell me something I don't already know."

He felt her look up at him. "You're not as tough as you pretend to be, but I'm the only one who can see that. Guess that makes me special."

"It certainly does," Holt said. "Just make sure you keep that to yourself."

She rocked up on her toes as she continued to stand next to him. "Just hope I don't get shot standing this close to you."

He wanted to tell her she was safe but did not like making promises he was not sure he could keep.

CHAPTER 25

From his spot at the corner of the bar, Cassidy made sure Bobby Simpson and the other bartenders were keeping every glass filled, and every drink paid for before the customer thought better of it.

Cassidy did not mind that the tables were full of drinkers instead of gamblers that night, for he knew that whatever he lost at the tables, he would more than make up for in beer and whiskey. Every one of his girls had found a willing lap to sit on and bawdy jokes to pretend to laugh at. Each jokester was a potential customer willing to take a trip upstairs, further lining Cassidy's pockets.

Had he been a more cheerful man, Cassidy might have smiled at his good fortune that evening. Anger was good for business, and he intended on making the most of it while he could.

He had not expected Sheriff Holt to be crafty enough to set up Joe Mullen the way he had. He had underestimated the lawman. It was a mistake he would not repeat.

If anything, Holt had been too smart for his own good, though he did not know it yet.

The twenty miners Mullen had brought to town with him were already well on their way to getting drunk. He had planted the seeds of discontent following their viewing of Ott Heller at Sibert's mortuary. How their dear friend was forgotten while his remains sat in disgrace and forgotten at the edge of town. He told them of how Mullen had thought Holt had framed poor old Ott for killing Mayor Chapman. He told them it was mighty suspicious that Holt arrested Mullen for murder when Mullen had begun to tell the city elders of his suspicions at Chapman's wake.

The fact that poor Rita Heller had died soon after her husband only stoked the embers of rage already glowing in their bellies. He knew the whiskey would only make the flames grow even higher and hotter.

He then moved on to spread his false gospel to Mullen's committee men. He poured his poison in their ears as they sat stunned about Mullen's arrest at the various tables around the saloon. They sat together in conspiratorial clusters, hunched over the tables while Cassidy asked open questions about how much they were willing to take from Holt and his kind.

Now he stood at the corner of his bar and watched his seeds take root. Alcohol had made their minds fertile ground for insurrection and resentment. He had done his best to sow resentment within them. Now it was time to stand back and allow nature to take its course.

With Mullen in jail, Cassidy knew it was only a matter of time before these different groups began to think that something ought to be done about this Holt problem. But these were not deliberate men. They were used to being told what to do. They were used to being led. And in the absence of Mullen, there was only one man to whom they could turn to lead them.

Which was why he was not surprised when he saw Ed Chase rise from his table of committee men and begin to make his way through the crowd toward him. Marty Barry, one of the miners, reached Cassidy first, but he beckoned both men to join him.

Cassidy already had a fresh bottle of whiskey and two glasses waiting for them. He filled them when they joined him in the corner.

The miner was the first to speak and the most direct. "That stuff you said about Mr. Mullen real? I mean, was it true?"

Cassidy handed the glass to him. "As true as I'm sitting here, sad to say."

Ed Chase said, "That ain't right. Holt taking us on like that. He doesn't know how this town works."

Cassidy handed the second glass of whiskey to Chase. "Sounds like someone ought to educate the man, doesn't it?"

"But how?" Marty Barry asked. "He's got the law on his side. All we've got are numbers."

"Sometimes, numbers are enough," Cassidy told him. "Ed here was in front of the jail when Chapman got shot. Ask him how many men were there."

"About thirty or so," Chase said. "I'd had a bit too much whiskey to count for certain, but I reckon that's a fair number."

Cassidy knew it was. He had counted them, from the safety of the front of his saloon, of course. "By my count, you boys have more than forty of you in this bar right now."

"Nearer to fifty with my men," the committeeman said. "And every one of them madder than hell over Joe rotting in that jail over something any man with a conscience would've done."

"Hank Bostrom was a mad killer," Marty added. "And that's a fact even a blind man could see."

"A blind man could see more than that," Cassidy went on. "He'd see that you mining boys don't have a boss. Who's gonna pay you when you're back digging in the ground tomorrow? Holt has leveled quite a charge against him. He's not liable to get out of jail for weeks. And he's got a town full of witnesses who can testify at trial that Joe shot an unarmed man."

Ed Chase balked at the idea. "It was self-defense. There's not a man in town who'd convict him."

Cassidy knew that was true, but he was not interested in truth just then. "Sure, when it comes to trial. Eventually. Until then, who's going to see to the mines? To his ranch? Who's going to keep the Vigilance Committee together while he's stuck in jail."

Both men agreed with him but did not look ready enough to do much about it.

"What can we do?" Marty Barry asked. "I heard about what happened in front of the jail the other night. Folks just broke and ran when Holt set to shooting. I don't think they've got the stomach for a fight."

Cassidy was about to answer that when Ed Chase spoke first. "That's because we didn't know what we were up against. Now we do."

Cassidy was glad to see his seeds of discontent had taken root. It was time to see just how deep those roots were. "Knowing what you're up against is one thing. Doing something about it is something else. Either you're willing to allow an outsider to come in here and tell us how to live, or you're willing to do something about it. What's it going to be, boys?"

The two men were thinking it over when Cassidy heard a deafening silence fall over the saloon. He looked up just as Simpson was coming over to get his attention.

Sheriff John Holt had just walked into the Blue Bottle Saloon.

Alone.

Some of the men at the front had backed away from him, forming something of a ragged arch in front of the sheriff.

Cassidy could see the man in brown take his time looking over the crowd as if he was soaking in the silence. At a shade over six feet tall, he was taller than most of the customers. He seemed even taller standing alone as he was. He had not brought his Henry rifle with him, but his right hand rested on his belt near the Remington on his hip. Cassidy could not say he looked relaxed, but he did not look afraid either. If he had to describe how the lawman looked, he would have to say he looked confident.

Cassidy decided to remain where he was while Holt said what he had come there to say.

He did not have to wait long before the sheriff said, "Some of you don't know me yet. My name is John Holt and I'm the new sheriff of Devil's Gulch. I'm the law in this town and in this county. The law's not always popular with folks, but that's for a judge to decide. Not me. Not you either."

He drove his point home by looking several men in the eye before continuing. "I know most of you are friends of Joe Mullen. You work for him and with him. You think he's a good man. I'm not going to try to convince you otherwise. But he gunned down an unarmed man in the middle of Main Street tonight. A lot of the people I see here saw him do it. You can expect to be called as witnesses at the trial and trust me when I tell you there will be a trial. He'll have a chance to make his case in court before Judge Cook. I'll abide by whatever judgment a jury makes. So will all of you."

He paused again and looked around the bar. "I suspect some of you are angry that I arrested your friend. I imagine some of you are even thinking about doing something about it. That's the liquor talking. I came here tonight to tell you to think again. Some of you saw what happened at the jail last night when a mob tried to force my hand. Three men are in jail and one's over at Sibert's mortuary. I don't like killing, but I won't hesitate if it comes to it. Don't make me prove it again."

One of the miners pushed himself away from the bar and through the crowd toward Holt. Cassidy recognized him as Nels Stewart, a hotheaded Welshman and miner who had been close to Ott Heller.

When Stewart pushed his way through the crowd, he stood fewer than five feet from Holt. Cassidy did not think the saloon could get any quieter, but it did.

"Mister," Stewart slurred, "Ott Heller was a good friend of mine. Joe Mullen is a fine boss. You've hurt a lot of good people since you came here and I, for one, have had a bellyful of it. I left the old country to get away from men like you and I'll be dipped in snuff if I'll put up with it now."

He turned his head and yelled to his friends. "Come on, boys. Let's rid ourselves of this filth once and for all."

Cassidy watched some of the miners begin to move, only to freeze when they saw Holt aiming his Remington at Stewart's head.

Stewart seemed to be the last one to see it but straightened when he did.

Holt's gun glinted in the dull lamplight of the saloon. "Next step's your last, boy."

The miner balled his fists at his side as he raged at the sheriff. "You wouldn't dare. You squeeze that trigger, and my boys will tear you apart."

Holt thumbed back the hammer. "You willing to bet your life on that?"

The men at the front grabbed Stewart and had quite a time pulling the angry Welshman back into the crowd.

Holt's thumb rode the hammer down before he slid the pistol back into his holster. Cassidy noted how smooth Holt was with a gun. And fast. The kind of skill that only came from practice and not the kind that came from shooting old bottles either.

Holt looked at the crowd again and Cassidy felt any resentment in them begin to wilt under his glare.

"I know he's raw over Mullen," Holt said, "so I'll let his insult pass. Chalk it up to the swill they serve in here rotting his brain. But any man who tries to spring Mullen will find themselves against me. And next time, I won't be so forgiving. Keep that in mind before anyone tells you otherwise."

Cassidy did not know how Holt had spotted him but felt the sheriff's glare bore into him from across the saloon. "Anything you'd like to add, Cassidy?"

Cassidy reddened as he saw all the men in the saloon turn to face him. He had never been one for making grand declarations. Mullen had always been willing to make those. Cassidy had always preferred to conduct his work in the shadows.

But now that the light was on him, he had no choice but to say something. He stood up straight and held a glass aloft, as if he was giving a toast. "Let justice prevail." He smiled. "Gulcher justice."

He was surprised when the men of the saloon got to their feet and joined him in the toast, speaking as one as they said, "Gulcher justice!"

As his glass was empty, Cassidy could not join in his own toast, but beamed with pride down the bar at Holt.

The lawman had turned them with his actions, but Cassidy had turned them back with his words.

He sneered at the lawman as Holt waited for the toast to end before he slowly backed out of the saloon and into the street.

The men resumed their drinking and went back to the conversations they had been having before Holt had made his declaration.

Those around Cassidy patted him on the back and raised their drinks to him. They may have backed down for a moment while Holt was there, but they had rallied at the end. He could not say he was proud of them, but something close to it.

Ed Chase got between Cassidy and the rest of the men and spoke over the cheers. "What do we do now, Tony?"

Cassidy chose his words carefully, for he knew once he said them, there would be no way of taking them back. He said them anyway. "Looks like we'll have to get rid of John Holt."

CHAPTER 26

Holt slammed the jailhouse door behind him, and Jack Turnbull rushed to bolt it shut.

"What happened?" asked his young deputy.

Holt pulled down the shotgun from the rifle rack and tossed it to Turnbull. "We've got a fight coming."

He was glad the boy did not check to see the gun was loaded. He remembered that it was and, instead, opened a box of shells and began stuffing them in his pockets. "Then I say let 'em come."

Holt pulled down his Henry. "This is my fight, Jack. Not yours. I practically forced you to take this job, so if you want out, now's the time. Just say the word and I'll have the livery stake you to a good horse and supplies so you can ride out of here before it gets thick."

The boy continued to stuff his pockets with cartridges. "Got nowhere to go. Besides, after how they came to get me, someone's liable to shoot me if I step outside the door anyway."

Holt's mind filled with ways to shore up the jailhouse when he saw a plate of food on his desk. It reminded him of Jean. "I need you to run over to the café and warn Jean off from coming here anymore. Tell her we'll come fetch the food when we need to. I don't want her anywhere near here."

Jack headed for the door. "I'll knock twice if it's clear and three times if I've got a gun to my head. An old trick my daddy taught me."

"Better trick is to not get caught. Just get back here as soon as you can," Holt told him as he bolted the door behind him.

He knew sending him out there was risky, but few people in the town had seen the lad cleaned up. They knew of him, but not what he looked like. It was a chance Holt had no choice but to take.

He unlocked the door to the cells and heard deep laughter coming from Mullen's cell. The other three prisoners were on their cots, eyeing Holt carefully as he passed them.

Mullen's laughter only grew as Holt examined the back wall of the jail. It seemed sturdy enough and there was no back door to worry about. It was one of the few advantages Holt had going for him.

Mullen continued to laugh. "Sounds like you've got yourself a bit of trouble, Sheriff. Guess my boys aren't taking too kindly to you grabbing me up like this."

"Nothing I haven't been up against before," Holt said as he continued to look over the space. The narrow windows high above the cells were closed and protected by thick bars. The glass might break, but the bars looked sturdy.

"You've never been up against the likes of my boys," Mullen said. "I've got more than fifty men working my mines for me. Another fifty or more working my spreads. All of them relying on me to keep their families fed and their pockets full. That's not counting my committee men. Throw them all in together and you and that boy out there are facing fifty-to-one odds between the two of you. And when you get that boy killed, it'll be just you against all of them."

Holt did not need the prisoner to tell him what he was facing. "If it comes to that, you'll be beyond caring."

Mullen ignored the threat. "That's what I'm trying to tell you, Sheriff. It doesn't have to come to that. I'm a reasonable man and so are you, so let's come to something of an understanding."

Holt was tired. It had been nothing but hard going from the moment he'd hit the trail for Devil's Gulch and this night had been no exception. He had not known a minute's peace since coming to town. Some of that was his doing, but most of it was thanks to the man who was taunting him now.

He decided to do some taunting of his own. "What kind of understanding?"

"You talk to Judge Cook and get him to release me pending trial," Mullen said. "It's been done before and I'm sure you can convince him to do so in this case. I'll agree to stay out of town until my trial, then I'll come back nice and peaceful. We both know you won't be able to find twelve men in town to convict me, so I'll go free anyway. That way, you've done your job, and no one else has to die."

Holt leaned against the wall. "You'll promise to come down for trial. With those hundred men you claim will die to protect you. Just like that?"

"Got no reason not to," Mullen said. "Seeing as how things'll go in my favor and all. What do you say?"

"I say Judge Cook knows as well as I do that you'd take off the second you step out of this jail. Maybe head over to the next county where people will be more than happy to hide you out. I'd find you, of course, and shoot you when I did, but not after a whole lot of fuss and bother."

He smiled down at Mullen. "No, I think I'm gonna keep

you right where you are until trial. You might go free after that, but that's beyond my control. If you care about your men as much as you say you do, you'll send word through your lawyer that they're to stay back and not cause any trouble. Because if they do, you die. If they try to shoot it out or burn me out of here, I put two in your belly on the first whiff of smoke. I won't let Doc Klassen work on you, and you'll suffer every second until you die. Ever see a man die from a belly wound, Mullen? It's an ugly way to go."

Mullen stamped his foot in frustration. "If so, then, by God, I'll see you in hell!"

"And I'll enjoy your company." Holt pushed himself off the wall and walked out into the office. "Make yourself at home, Mullen. You're not going anywhere."

Holt shut the door and locked it over the sound of Mullen's curses.

He hung the key on a peg when he thought he heard someone outside calling his name. He grew very still, listening, until he was sure of what he had heard.

"John Holt," yelled a man out in the street. "Come on out. I've got something you want to see."

Holt gripped his Henry tightly as he slowly approached the door. He slid the iron peephole aside and looked out.

He had not recognized the voice but recognized the man he saw. It was Ed Chase, one of Mullen's committee men. His ridiculous blue ribbon on his lapel blowing in the night breeze along Main Street.

He had Jack Turnbull in front of him and a pistol to his head. The boy barely came up to Chase's chin, but the man stood as proudly as if he had just captured a Sioux chief.

"There you are," Chase mocked from across the thoroughfare. "I was getting awful lonely in my grief, so

I was glad to find someone to commiserate with. Your friend Jack here. The same one who helped get the mayor killed."

Holt slid the iron slat shut. He remembered Chase had been one of the men in front of the jail when he had brought Jack and the other Turnbull men into town. He had gotten a good look at Jack and knew what he looked like.

Holt had been counting on Chase to still be up at the Blue Bottle with the others instead of roaming the streets. It looked like trouble had come faster than Holt had anticipated.

Chase kept talking. "Don't go getting all shy on me now, Sheriff. Not after that grand speech you made. I might get to thinking them hard words were just for show. I know how much you prize your reputation as a hard man and all, so how about you come out here so we can talk things over?"

Holt knew Chase could have men waiting on the other side of the door, just waiting for him to undo the lock so they could rush him. He thought about going back to the cells and dragging out Mullen as cover. But he did not think Jack had that kind of time.

He thought about shooting Mullen in the belly as he had promised but knew the gunshot would probably cost Jack his life.

There was only one way to handle this.

Holt's way.

He dropped to a knee and opened the jailhouse door just wide enough to get a good view of Chase across the thoroughfare. His boot kept the door from opening any farther.

"That's more like it," Chase said. "Now come on out and let's talk some sense."

Holt raised the Henry to his shoulder and took careful aim. The ribbon on Chase's lapel helped him gauge the strength of the wind.

Chase's eyes went wide when he realized he should have taken a taller hostage.

Holt fired and the bullet slammed into the committeeman's face.

Jack ducked and dove away as the dead man's gun fired into the air before he bounced off the wall and sagged to the boardwalk.

Holt saw the blur of a rifle barrel lower through the opened door and threw his weight against it to shut it. The gunman's rifle went off, sending a bullet into the jailhouse floor.

The man on the other side pushed against the door, sending Holt sprawling onto his back. The door slammed open, and a man stumbled inside.

Holt racked in a fresh round and shot the man in the chest, sending him back out into the street, where he fell off the boardwalk and dropped to the thoroughfare.

A pistol appeared from the left side of the doorway and fired blindly into the jail. Holt rolled away from the bullets biting into the floor and kicked the door closed. The man withdrew the pistol before it was caught in the door.

A loud blast sounded from outside and he heard a man cry out as buckshot bit into the wall and door. Holt knew that must be Jack cutting loose with the shotgun he had given him. He only hoped the boy found cover while he reloaded.

Still on his back, the door was pushed inward, and Holt kicked it shut again. He levered in another round as the door burst open and two men rushed inside.

Holt ignored the pain in his right leg as it was pinned between the door and the wall while he dug his rifle barrel into the belly of the first man through the door. He squeezed the trigger and looked away as the spray from the impact filled the air.

A second man tumbled into the jail behind the first as both men fell into the jail.

Holt pulled his leg clear of the door and got to his knee as he shouldered the door shut. He fell back against it as the second man—his face covered in the first man's blood—rolled onto his back and blindly raised his pistol in Holt's direction. He managed to get off a shot that struck the top of the door while Holt levered in another round and shot him under the chin.

Holt reached up for the bolt and slid it shut.

The door shook again as more men put their shoulders against it. A rifle sounded from somewhere outside and was quickly followed by another blast from Jack's shotgun. More buckshot hit the outside of the jail, but the wall held.

An uneasy silence fell over the outside. The thudding against the door stopped. Whether or not that was due to Jack's shooting or common sense from whoever was trying to get inside the jail, Holt had no way of knowing.

The lawman used his Henry as a cane to help him get to his feet. His right knee was on fire, but after feeling at it, he was glad to see he had not been shot. It was not broken, either, just sore.

He looked down at the two men he had just killed. The second man was already dead. The first man through the door was gasping as he reached for the ceiling. His fingers were clawing at something that Holt could not see, but perhaps only the dying could.

He watched as the man's eyes dimmed and his hands dropped to the floor. His struggles were at an end.

When Holt thought he had caught his breath, he called out to Jack. "You hit?"

He did not hear a response and realized the door was too thick to be heard through. He hobbled to the side of the door as he threw open the iron slat. "Jack! You hit?"

"I'm fine," Turnbull answered. "Can't say as much for the four prairie dogs in the street, though."

Holt felt winded, but he was glad Jack was still alive and unhurt. "Get over to the café, then get word to Judge Cook. I won't open this door until I hear him outside. Stay in the café until I come get you."

He took Jack's silence that he understood Holt's order and Holt slid the slat shut again.

He tried to put some weight on his injured leg as he hobbled over to the rifle rack. He took down a box of cartridges and began feeding new rounds into the Henry. Figuring he was as safe as he could hope to be for the moment, he took down the keys from the peg and opened the door to the cells.

Mullen was on his feet. "Boys? That you?"

"It's them," Holt said as he limped over to one of the dead men, grabbed him by the collar and began to pull him back into the cells.

Mullen recoiled from the bars as he watched Holt drag one of his committee men into the aisle. "Figured you boys ought to keep each other company."

He ignored Mullen's threats as he went out into the office and dragged in the second dead man, dropping him next to the first. "Maybe it'll serve as a reminder that—"

But Holt had not been paying attention and had gotten too close to Mullen's cell. The prisoner grabbed him by the throat and pulled him back against the iron door. He felt the prisoner reach down for his pistol, but Holt managed to pull it and let it drop to the floor out of Mullen's reach.

Mullen's thick hand squeezed his throat as his right hand joined his left around his throat. The other prisoners cheered as he brought his left arm around Holt's neck while he used his right to lock it in place, pinning him back against the bars.

Red and blue bursts of pain and light fired off in Holt's brain as it became more difficult to breathe the harder Mullen gripped him. Holt used both hands to try to break the hold, but felt his strength begin to wane.

Mullen used his free hand to begin clawing at Holt's eyes.

Holt stopped trying to break Mullen's grip and twisted the prisoner's right hand away from his face. The pain caused him to cry out—the squeeze on Holt's neck that much harder.

Mullen tried to bring his right hand down on Holt's face, but the lawman had it at an angle and sank his teeth into the side of his hand.

The prisoner screamed and his grip around his neck loosened just enough for Holt to pull free. He kept hold on the hand and pulled Mullen's arm all the way out of its cell.

The arm was already at an ugly angle and Holt brought up his elbow to break it, which would render the man a cripple for the rest of his days.

But the coppery taste in his mouth made him remember who he was. This was not a saloon, and this was not a bar fight. Mullen was a prisoner. *His* prisoner. *His* responsibility.

Holt released his grip on the arm and allowed Mullen to sink back into his cell. He fell back against the rear wall of the jail and tried to get a lung full of air. He managed to do so after a few tries, though the pain in his throat now matched the pain in his knee.

He picked up his pistol from the floor and slid it back into the holster on his hip. He looked down at Mullen, who had ducked his head as he cradled his bleeding hand.

"Next time I'll kill you," Holt told him, before walking out into the office and locking the door behind him.

CHAPTER 27

Holt woke with a start when he heard his name being called from the street.

He had leaned back in his chair and kept his legs crossed on the desk after his death struggle with Mullen. He wanted to keep his leg elevated and stretched lest stiffness settle in. He knew he would need all the flexibility he could get and could not afford to be hobbled.

"I say again," the voice from outside repeated. "Hello, the jail! This is Judge Cook with Les Patrick and Ty Arbour. We are unarmed and mean you no harm, John. Open up."

Holt pulled his legs from the desk but found they had gone numb while he slept. He tried to rub them to get the circulation flowing again, but only got pins and needles for his trouble.

"Just a minute," he called out as he willed feeling back into his legs. As soon as he had feeling in his legs again, he hobbled over to the door and slid back the iron slat. He saw the judge and the two lawyers outside.

He opened the door and allowed the three men to enter. Judge Cook walked in first and was careful to avoid stepping in the blood streaks on the floor. Holt had meant to clean them up but had fallen asleep before getting around to it.

The two attorneys did likewise, and Holt quickly bolted the door behind them.

The judge cleared his throat as he did his best to not look at the blood. "I'd ask you how you're doing, but I don't think I'd like the answer."

"I've had better nights," Holt admitted. "Did Jack tell you I wanted to see you?"

"He sent word late last night," Les Patrick said. "Sent one of the women from the café to get us. We spent the night in the county hall. Figured it was safer that way, with things being as raw as they were."

Holt could not blame the men for being cautious. After all, they were lawyers, not gunmen. "What time is it?"

"Just after one o'clock," Ty Arbour told him. "You missed the mayor's funeral, though no one could blame you for that. You had a horrible night. I'm ashamed of not coming to check on you sooner." His eyes narrowed as he looked at the bruises on Holt's neck. "What happened there?"

Holt winced as he ran his hands along his throat. "Your client tried to kill me last night. Don't worry. He's still alive. Took a chunk out of his hand, though."

Only Cook managed to be able to find the words to say, "You two go in and talk to Mullen. I'll stay out here with the sheriff."

Holt said, "Mind the dead men in the aisle."

Patrick and Arbour hesitated before reaching for the keys on the peg.

Holt shrugged. "I had to put them somewhere."

Patrick took down the keys and opened the door before

stepping inside. Both men held their hands to their noses as they went back to the cells.

Holt felt the judge take his arm and guide him back to his seat. "Sit down, John. You look like you might fall over."

Holt did not like being handled, but he did not have the strength to fight him, so he sat down. "How many did we get last night?"

"Four, not counting the two you seem to have in there." Cook sat on the edge of the desk. "I'm afraid I have some bad news for you. News you won't like but I know you can take."

He remembered his appointment with the mayor's widow. "I was supposed to meet with Mrs. Chapman today."

"She understands, trust me," Cook said. "I came here personally to let you know I'm letting Mullen go."

Holt felt the weariness drain from him. "Let him go? You can't do that."

"I can and I am," he said. "Les and Ty are working out the details with him now. He'll have to sign over all his holdings to the town as collateral for his release. He'll also be forbidden from entering town until his trial date next week. None of his men will be allowed into town, either, except a few for supplies."

Holt said, "If you do that, he wins."

"This isn't about winning or losing, John," Cook told him. "It's a matter of practicality. Of life and death, if you'll allow me to be dramatic about it. A fair number of Mullen's miners are still in town and are worked into quite a bother over Mullen being in jail. A lot of people work for him, people who are more than willing to come down from his mines and ranches to raise trouble here in town until he's released. I know you have a reputation to protect, but no man's reputation is worth the price of a town."

Holt resented that. "I'm not talking about my reputation. I'm talking about the law."

"And we both know a law is only good if it can be enforced," Cook said. "The law also does not exist on its own. It must first serve the community it was created to protect. I don't like seeing Mullen go free any more than you do, John. I know he's a flight risk and I have no doubt we'll be tacking up wanted posters for his arrest within the week. But if he flees, he's practically admitting guilt and we can enlist the territorial marshals to help us. That'll take the burden off you."

Holt did not like the inference. "You haven't heard a complaint from me yet."

"Nor would I expect to," Cook said. "But look at all that has happened since you've come to town. Your style is partly to blame for it, yes, but the citizens of this community certainly share part of the responsibility. They've performed less than admirably." He pointed back toward the cells. "You killed six committee men last night and you have two of their bodies still in there. Do you think that's where it will end? These aren't hardened criminals, but family men with wives and children. They're shop clerks and business owners who volunteered to keep order in this town."

"Attacking me is a bad way to keep order." He thumbed at the door over his shoulder. "Those men in there came here to free Mullen. Ed Chase took Jack hostage. They quit being a committee and became criminals the moment they crossed that line. And if Chapman had disbanded them when I told him to, those men would still be alive."

Holt saw the frown on Cook's face and immediately regretted what he had said.

"Sounds like you're blaming everyone for what happened except yourself," the judge said. "That's a dangerous train of thought for men in our position."

"I feel plenty of guilt over what happened." Holt looked away. "But anyone I killed was asking for it. I gave the Bostrom Gang fair warning about looking for vengeance over Hank's killing. Last night, I gave the same warning to Mullen's men up at the Bottle right after. I don't play favorites, Judge. And I think you need to keep Joe Mullen exactly where he is until you're ready to put him on trial. His men will think twice now that they've seen we're not pushovers."

"At what cost?" Cook asked. "How many more men have to die to keep your sense of honor intact?" He shook his head. "You may be right about all of the fight having gone out of Mullen's men, but it's a risk I'm not willing to take. It's a miracle no innocents have been killed and I won't risk it again. My conscience won't allow it. Mullen will sign the agreement Les and Ty put before him and, when he does, he'll be set free. I've made up my mind. I don't expect you to like it. I also don't expect you to stand in the way of it either."

Holt had never liked being backed in a corner. Not by a judge either. He liked to have room to maneuver. He liked to be able to find another way to win.

But he could tell Judge Cook had made up his mind and there was no point in trying to talk him out of it. He was not an unreasonable man and Holt could understand why he believed releasing Joe Mullen was best for the town and the county. Holt did not have to like it, but he had to obey. Just like back in the army.

He knew the judge wanted him to say he agreed, but Holt could not bring himself to say the words. The closest he could get was, "You'll get no trouble from me."

The judge tried a smile. "I already knew that, John, but I thank you for saying it. I know it wasn't easy."

Holt got to his feet when he heard the unmistakable rattle of keys and the squeal of an iron door swinging open. He stood next to the judge as Les Patrick led Joe Mullen and Ty Arbour out from the back. At least Les had the good sense to bring him around the other side of the desk.

Holt kept his hand flat against his holster. If Mullen so much as looked at the rifle rack, he would cut the man down, no matter what Judge Cook said.

But Mullen was smart enough to keep his head down as Les opened the jailhouse door and ushered the two men outside.

Holt relaxed and resumed his chair. "That went better than I'd expected. I figured Mullen would try to get in a parting word before he left."

"Ty told him you'd shoot him if he did," Les said as he handed Holt and the judge the agreement. "He signed over everything he owns to the town. He's worked his claims too hard to forfeit them, so I don't think he'll run. Besides, Ty doesn't think there's a jury in the territory that would convict him for killing Hank, and I tend to agree. I doubt the inquest will allow the matter to go to trial."

Holt sneered, "That doesn't exactly inspire confidence, Les."

"My case against him is solid," the prosecuting attorney said, "but your shootout last night has turned a lot of people against you, John. I'm not saying you're wrong, just telling you the way things are. The men you killed had families and businesses, just like the three you've got locked up back there right now." He opened his satchel and dug out some papers that he handed to Judge Cook. "I've got the paperwork you requested right here, Your Honor."

Holt did not like what he was seeing. "Don't tell me you're letting them go too."

"I am," Cook said as he examined the papers. "They've agreed to plead guilty to disturbing the peace and inciting a riot. I'm leveling a heavy fine on them. More than a year's wages. They'll be a long time paying and if they don't, they face arrest and a five-year sentence in territorial prison."

Before Holt could protest, the judge took Holt's pen from the inkwell and signed all six pages.

Les placed the ring of keys on the desk. Holt knew he had not intended it to be an insult, but it certainly felt that way.

The judge placed three orders on Holt's desk and handed the others back to Les. "See to it those are filed properly. There's liable to be some questions once they're released and I want those orders as part of the public record."

Les placed the orders in his satchel before speaking to Holt. "After you let them go, Mrs. Chapman—I mean Mayor Chapman—wants to see you in her office."

Holt took the keys from his desk and went to the back to release the prisoners. Each of the three men ducked their heads and ignored the two bodies in the aisle as they left and quickly walked outside to freedom.

Holt hung the keys on the peg beside the door. "Can I go like this, or do I have to wear a sackcloth and ashes first?"

Judge Cook laughed. "I wouldn't worry about her. She's probably your biggest defender right now. You're a hero to her, remember?"

Holt let out a long breath. He was not so sure of that. He imagined her decision to serve out the rest of her dead husband's term would not sit well with many of the people in Devil's Gulch. Being his ally would not serve to make her any more popular.

"Might as well get it over with."

He pulled on his hat and opened the door for the judge and the town attorney. He found Earl Sibert standing on the boardwalk in front of the jail. He quickly removed his black stovepipe hat and held it over his heart.

"Solemn greetings, Sheriff," the undertaker said. "I have come to collect the remains of the departed men I understand you have in your cells."

He had seen more of Sibert than he would have liked since coming to Devil's Gulch. And he had a feeling he would be seeing more of him before things quieted down.

Holt pointed at one of the two men with Sibert. "I need you to go over to the café and tell Jack Turnbull to come over here."

Sibert motioned for the two men to enter the jail. "I'll be happy to deliver that message personally, Sheriff, while my men tend to their work. I'm afraid rigor has set in and moving the bodies will take time. Don't worry. We won't leave the jail unattended."

Holt waited for Sibert to leave before he walked across Main Street to the county hall. Judge Cook and Les Patrick trailed behind him.

He felt like a man being led to the gallows but decided to keep his feelings to himself.

CHAPTER 28

Joe Mullen pushed away the plate of food his cook had placed before him. He had not eaten since his arrest and food held no appeal to him now.

Sarabelle Mullen laid her hand on top of her husband's. "You have to eat, Joe. You need to keep up your strength."

But the kind of hunger growing in Mullen's belly could not be sated by food or drink. Only revenge could quell his hunger. Revenge and blood. The blood of John Holt.

"He had no right to arrest me," Mullen grumbled. "He had no right to show me up in front of the entire town like that. He made me look like a fool."

"He'll only make you look like a fool if you let him," Sarabelle said. "You know how people saw it. The whole town saw that Hank gave you no choice but to shoot him. How were you supposed to know an outlaw would only have a knife instead of a gun?"

But Mullen was not worried about the inquest, much less going to trial. Ty Arbour all but assured him he would be acquitted at the inquest. And even if they agreed to hold him over for a trial, the next jury was bound to set him free. He had too many friends in town to allow himself to think otherwise.

No, it was not his legal woes that troubled him. "This is about prestige, Sarabelle. It's all I have." He looked around at the large dining room of his home. The silver that gleamed in the corner. The fine china on his table and the heavy drapes on the window. "All of this was built on my control of the town. Not even Frank Peters dared to cross me in public and he would've done anything the McAdam woman told him to do. But Holt? He's a madman who's every bit as crazy as Hank Bostrom was. He's got a name to protect. A reputation. And he's looking to build his reputation in town on my back." He brought his free hand down on the dining room table. The silverware and china jumped, though his wife remained still.

He looked at Sarabelle. "You saw what happened when I was in jail. How quickly things spun out of control. Those boys should've known better than to come for me. I knew I'd be out in the morning. Instead, they made fools of themselves trying to rescue me and got killed in the process. Good men too." He ran his free hand over the stubble that had grown on his chin. "Men who helped me keep control of this town, like Ed Chase."

Sarabelle drew closer and rubbed his back. "You still control it, darling. You're still the man everyone looks to. You've still got about a hundred boys with you who'll put that town to the match if you just give them the word."

But Joe Mullen was not so sure. "They're loyal because I pay them. The committee only follows me because they're too afraid not to. I've always been the one to fix things. To get men sprung from jail. Last night, Holt showed them I'm only a man, just like them. He taught them a lesson they won't soon forget. Cassidy won't forget it either."

That was his biggest fear. He had no doubt that Cassidy had worked them up to attack the jail. A foolish notion. Even if they had killed Holt and managed to free him,

Mullen would have been in more trouble than before. He'd have Holt's blood on his hands and be a fugitive from justice. Everything he had spent the past twenty years of his life building would have been ruined by the actions of a greedy panderer in a seedy saloon on the outskirts of the town he controlled.

The town that Joe Mullen controlled, not Cassidy.

"I always told you to be mindful of that man," Sarabelle said. "Of Cassidy, I mean. He was never your friend, only an ally of convenience if you ask me."

Mullen had not asked her but decided not to test her temper. She had handled Rita Heller for him, and he was grateful. Thanks to her efforts, that drunken sot no longer posed a threat to him or to the stolen money Bob Bostrom had given him. His secret about setting up Bob with the army had died with her.

Sarabelle drew herself closer to him and rested her head on his broad shoulders. "I know you're disappointed, Joe, but that's just your pride talking. They'll clear you at the inquest in a couple of days and then things will be able to go back to how they were. Why, by the time all is said and done, you'll see that John Holt was the best thing that ever happened to you."

He pulled away from his wife so he could look at her. "What are you talking about? Holt threw me in jail and killed my men."

"Yes, he did," she agreed, "and created martyrs in the process. Good, brave men who died trying to avenge an injustice." She shook his shoulders. "Don't you see? You're a hero, Joe. You're the man who killed Hank Bostrom and rid the town of his kind forever. *You* did that, not John Holt. You were the only one brave enough to confront him and do what needed doing. And Holt arrested you for it out of pure jealousy. There's just no other way anyone can look at it. Or will look at it after I'm done spreading the word."

Mullen had been too angry to think of it that way and cursed himself for it. He could always be counted upon to see things clearly and use them to his advantage. He had been too consumed by anger and resentment of Holt to see it any different.

As usual, she saw what he had missed. "I wasn't thinking of it that way."

"I know you said you're forbidden from going into town until the inquest," Sarabelle went on. "But I'm not. I'll head down there later today. I'll be your eyes and ears, especially now that poor old Ed Chase is gone. I'll poison the well so bad against Holt that the good people of Devil's Gulch will lay rose petals at your feet when you show up for the inquest. You don't worry about a thing. I'll be back here tomorrow night with a fresh look on things and we can decide how best to proceed."

Sarabelle held him close to her bosom, assuring him everything would turn out just fine. He did not like to be coddled, but it made her feel better, so he did not resist.

He also did not tell her there was only one way he would believe that everything would turn out fine.

John Holt lying dead in the middle of Main Street.

Mayor Elizabeth Chapman surprised Holt by selecting a cigar from her late husband's humidor, cutting it, and thumbing a match alive to light it. She looked at him through the thickening smoke.

"I understand you don't partake," the widow said.

"Don't drink and don't smoke," he told her.

"You a religious man, Sheriff Holt?"

"Just don't like the taste of either."

She continued to draw the flame deeper into the cigar before waving the match dead and tossing it in the ashtray. "Does a woman smoking a cigar offend you? Surprise you?"

"I haven't been surprised by anything since the war."

"I believe that." She sat back in her late husband's chair as if it had been made for her. "I suppose you're wondering why I'm not prostrate with grief over the death of my late husband. After all, he was only buried this morning."

The first time he had seen her, she had been in nightclothes with a robe hastily tied around her middle as she tended to her dying husband on a cot in the jail. Now, she was wearing a black dress that showed her thick frame.

"I learned a long time ago that people mourn in their own way, Mrs. Chapman. How they do it is none of my business."

"It's Mayor Chapman," she corrected him. "At least until the town gets around to trying to replace me."

Holt caught that. "Sounds like you don't think they'll do it."

She allowed some of the smoke to escape her nose. "They'll grant me something of a pardon for now. They'll wait an appropriate time to let me play at being mayor until they think they've been gracious enough and demand to hold an election." She grinned. "The fools. They didn't know that I was more of a mayor than Blair ever was."

The more Holt saw of the widow, the more he was inclined to believe that.

"My husband was a wonderful man, Sheriff," the mayor said. "He was kind and good and loved me very much. I suppose I loved him, too, in my own way. He was a different sort from me. He came out here with the best of intentions. To carve a life out of the rugged wilderness. Quite admirable. I'm a Baltimore gal myself and I come from a long line of Baltimore politicians. I know it takes more than just a haberdashery to make a mark in the world. More than just good intentions too. It takes power—real power—to change things, which is why I don't intend on going anywhere." She pointed the cigar at him. "And neither do you."

Holt's pride was still sore from having to let Mullen and the other prisoners go. He had overslept and still felt groggy. His right leg hurt from the previous night, and it hurt every time he swallowed.

Mrs. Chapman's praise did little to improve his condition. "I'm glad you think so."

"I more than just think so, Sheriff," she said. "Blair didn't want to hire you at first. Joe Mullen had done a good job of working on his insecurities about crime in town, but he'd done his job too well. He'd hoped he was talking Blair into giving the Vigilance Committee more power. I was the one who convinced my husband to hire a man like you. Someone from the outside who could change this town for good. Mullen fought him at first but stopped when he realized he wasn't just going up against poor Blair. He was really going up against me."

Holt was not particularly interested in the history of the town or listening to gossip. He needed to be back on the street. The people needed to see that he was fine after last night's ugly events, and he could not do that by sitting here listening to the Chapman widow relive past glories.

"This is all mighty interesting, mayor, but—"

She spoke over him. "Doing the right thing isn't always popular, Sheriff, but it's necessary. I'm always surprised by the number of enemies one can make by going about the people's business. You learn a lot about people when you govern. More than you might otherwise as a civilian.

My husband used to dismiss it as pure gossip. He rarely saw it for what it really was. A way to gather information."

Holt suppressed a yawn. "I imagine you know this town better than anyone else."

"Don't be insolent," she said. "Such information is just about the only way we'll keep control of this town. Keep it away from the likes of Mullen and McAdam and Cassidy."

Holt was beginning to get interested. "How so?"

"Blair Chapman wasn't the only man in Devil's Gulch who had a good woman doing his thinking for him. Take Joe Mullen for instance. He's nowhere near as clever as he thinks he is. His wife, Sarabelle, does most of his thinking for him."

Holt had not known that. "He puts on a good act."

"Which is all it is," she told him. "An act. Just look at what he does when left to his own devices. Take last night, for instance. From what I heard, Hank Bostrom could barely stand up, yet Joe was dumb enough to allow himself to be goaded into a fight. He's a proud man, our Joe. And if we play him right, we can use that pride against him."

Holt moved to the edge of his seat. "How?"

"I don't know yet," Mrs. Chapman admitted, "but I'll think of something. This inquest will put him ill at ease. He's not a man who is used to being held accountable for his actions. Your predecessor, Frank Peters, tried to fight him but he was too busy mooning over the McAdam strumpet to do much good. Give me a day or so to think it over. We'll come up with something. In the meantime, I want you to concentrate your efforts elsewhere. On the main reason you were hired in the first place. Finding the missing money that Bob Bostrom is supposed to have hidden."

Holt felt his confidence in her abilities begin to fade. "Just about the only person who might know that is Cassie over at the Railhead and she swears she has no idea where it is. Hank, Em, and their boys looked all over for it and came up with nothing. I don't think I'll do any better than they did."

"That's where you're wrong," she told him. "But I wouldn't be too hard on myself if I were you because no one else has been able to figure it out either."

"But you have."

"Possibly," she allowed. "After Mullen succeeded in running Frank Peters out of a job, Mullen and his committee were the only people we could count on to enforce the law around here. He did a good job of making everyone believe he was single-handedly responsible for keeping the gang from striking the town. But, as you learned firsthand, the Turnbull Gang was able to rob our bank quite easily."

Holt felt his weariness go away as his instincts began to go to work. On his way to Devil's Gulch, he had heard the town was a tough nut to crack thanks to Mullen and his men. That was why he was surprised the Turnbulls had seemed so intent on robbing the bank. Their plan to do it at night might make their job easier, but their plan had not been foolproof.

But the Chapman widow had given voice to something that had been nagging at him since he had learned of the Turnbull plot. If they thought the bank was a pushover, why had the Bostrom Boys passed it up?

That question came to the fore of his mind and caused him to ask others. "The Bostrom Gang hit stages and mines all over the territory, didn't they?"

The mayor nodded slowly through the smoke of her cigar. "Go on."

"How many Mullen mines did they hit?"

"None," she told him. "Not a single one. Awfully convenient, don't you think?"

Too convenient. He had asked Cassie plenty of questions, but perhaps he had not asked her the right questions. He got to his feet. He did not have a moment to lose. "I know someone who might be able to tell us why."

"Wait," the mayor said, before Holt reached the door. "I'm going to need you to tread lightly around town, Sheriff. Your actions last night might've been justified, but there are a lot of people who'll be looking to goad you into a fight. Don't let them. And I won't be pleased if you do. You're a sheriff, not a gunman. Had I wanted a mercenary, I would've told my husband to hire one."

Holt opened the door. "Sounds like we're the only friends either of us have right now."

"You have me outnumbered," she said. "Earl Sibert wants a statue erected in your honor. You're better for his business than the plague."

Holt did not know how to respond to that, so for once, he said nothing at all and went on his way.

CHAPTER 29

As he left the county hall, Holt saw a group of townsmen clustered together on the boardwalk. None of them were armed and all of them looked beyond fighting age, though Holt did not like the way they looked at him as he approached.

One of the men held a walking stick aloft as Holt approached. "Sheriff Holt. Might we have a word with you?"

Holt almost preferred men trying to kill him over men trying to talk to him. He found exchanging shots easier than exchanging words. Still, he stopped walking and waited for the men to have their say.

The man with the stick said, "We just wanted to thank you for all you've been doing for this town since you got here."

He listened for sarcasm in his voice but all he heard was sincerity. When the old man extended his hand to him, he shook it.

The other men in the group offered their hands as well.

"This town is like an old rug that's been in need of a good beating for some time," one of the other men said. "Glad to see you doing that."

After offering his thanks, he continued heading for the

Railhead where he hoped to find Cassie. He imagined she would still be recuperating from her injuries at the hands of Hank Bostrom.

He was surprised to see her sitting on a plank bench in front of the saloon. A blanket was wrapped around her shoulders, and she angled her head toward the afternoon sun. Her pretty face was a mess of blemishes and swelling.

She smiled up at him when he drew closer. "Afternoon, Sheriff."

"Afternoon, Cassie." He touched the brim of his hat. "Glad to see you're out of bed."

"Ma told me the sunshine would do me some good. I told her the sight of me all banged up like this would only serve to scare off customers, but she and the doctor insisted."

Holt knew her swelling and bruises would go away soon enough. As for the cuts on her cheek, only time would tell if they would leave scars. "Mind if I join you?"

"I don't mind if you don't," she said. "Can't see as how sitting next to me could hurt your reputation any. From what I hear, you're not too popular with a lot of folks right now."

Holt sat beside her on the bench. "You'd be surprised how easy a man can become used to being unpopular. If you don't have affection to lean on, you have to learn other ways to survive."

"Sounds like you've had plenty of practice at that." She pulled a thin whisp of hair from her face and tucked it behind her left ear. "I hope you're not here again to ask me about that money, Sheriff. I already told you that I don't know where it is. Bob never told me."

"That's not why I'm here," he assured her. "I'm here to

talk about something related, but different. How well did Bob Bostrom know Joe Mullen?"

Her eyes opened wide, and she was about to say something when she quickly thought better of it and looked away. "I really can't say, Sheriff. I never knew much about Bob's dealings."

Holt did not want to scare her, but knew she was holding something back. "That's the first lie you've ever told me, Cassie. Why?"

She looked up at him and he saw tears racing down her cheeks. "Please, Sheriff. Don't make me talk about that. It won't do either of us any good."

Holt knew he was on to something, and Cassie was close to breaking. He hated putting her through more trouble, but he had to know. He knew his life may depend on it.

"I know you've had a hard time of it," Holt told her, "and I wouldn't be asking you about this if it wasn't important." He decided to try to make it easier for her to answer his questions. "I already know Bob and his gang never hit Mullen's properties. Do you know why he left them alone?"

She wept as she buried her swollen face in her hands again. "Please go, Sheriff. I don't know how much more of this I can take."

"Then tell me about Mullen and Bostrom and I promise I'll leave you alone. Did they have some agreement? Mullen has some of the biggest mines and ranches in the county. Why did his gang leave them alone?"

She lifted her face from her hands. "Because they're brothers!"

Holt sat back on the bench as if he had just been slapped. He had not been expecting that. "Brothers? How's that possible? Does that mean Hank and Em—?"

"Bob and Joe were half brothers," she told him. "Same mother but different fathers. He died in one of the mines he owned, and the mother married a Bostrom man. He had money and a big ranch, so she took up with him. He adopted Bob before Em and Hank came along. At least that's what Bob told me once. He was very drunk at the time. Afterwards, he swore me to silence. Now that they're all dead, I guess it's not much of a secret, but a promise is still a promise, whether or not the man you made it to is above ground or in it. Don't you think so, Sheriff?"

But Holt was no longer listening to her. He was too lost in his own thoughts and conclusions. Mullen and Bostrom were brothers. That explained why the gang had left the rich Mullen properties alone. "Did Em and Hank know?"

She shook her head slowly before burying her face in her hands.

Holt felt as if a fog had been lifted. Everything became much clearer now. Hank and Em had not been told they were related to Mullen. They had probably pushed Bob to his Mullen properties over the years and may have wondered why he had refused.

Holt knew Bob had not told them his reasons. For, if he had, they would have known where Bob had hidden the stolen money. With the last person anyone would ever suspect of being a crook.

Joe Mullen. The Chairman of the Devil's Gulch Vigilance Committee. His own brother.

Holt sat forward and removed his hat. For a moment, he thought he might be sick.

"Are you all right, Sheriff?" Cassie asked. "You look worse than I do right now."

He had never been one to rely on the word or goodwill of a sporting woman, but Cassie was the only person in town who could appreciate his dilemma. "You think Bob gave Joe Mullen the stolen money?"

She looked away and grew very still. "I didn't say that."

"I know you didn't. I did. Just answer my question."

"I think it's likely, since the brothers couldn't find it in his usual hiding spots," she said, "but I don't know for certain."

Holt believed her. "Judge Cook made me cut him loose. If I still had him in jail, I could lean on him. But now that he's back up in the hills?" He left the question remaining open. He had never been one to shirk his responsibilities but confronting Mullen on his ranch or at his mines would be suicide. He could not do anything about bringing Mullen to justice if he was dead.

He looked up when he realized a sudden silence had fallen over the town. He quickly understood why.

Earl Sibert was driving a four-horse team ahead of his hearse down Main Street toward the cemetery. The undertaker sat up straight as he gently urged the horses to quietly move along.

Holt saw another wagon trailing behind the ornate hearse and a thick column of men following it. As the group drew closer, he saw the hearse was followed by the remaining members of the Bostrom Gang. Charlie Gardiner was in front. He imagined that must have been Hank Bostrom and Cal Abel's remains. His suspicions were confirmed when he looked through the glass of the hearse and saw two coffins inside.

He recognized the group behind the wagon as some of the miners he had seen in the Blue Bottle Saloon the previous night. Their wives walked with their husbands. Holt imagined the wagon held the bodies of Ott Heller and his wife, Rita. Although it was already afternoon, each of the men looked worse for wear. He imagined they were still suffering from sore bellies and aching heads from the amount of whiskey they had consumed the night before. He hoped the presence of their wives and their hangovers would make them less likely to cause trouble.

Since it was too late to duck out of their way, Holt got to his feet and placed his hat over his heart out of respect for the dead and the mourners. He thought it was a bit hypocritical on his part to show such deference for men he had killed, but he saw no other choice.

Cassie remained seated as the procession rolled slowly by.

Holt stood still and eyed the mourners as they passed. Some of the Bostrom Boys looked his way but remained dignified. None of the miners or their wives seemed to notice him as they struggled to walk in a straight line behind their dead friends' coffins.

Holt stood until the procession made the left turn toward the cemetery on the outskirts of town, then took his seat next to Cassie.

"Well," he said. "At least they didn't spit at me when they passed."

"Why would they?" she asked. "Charlie won't do anything to you. Ma wouldn't allow it."

Holt had not been expecting that. "What does Ma have to do with it?"

She was about to explain when Ma McAdam stepped out onto the boardwalk. "Come along, Cassie. That's enough sun for one day."

Cassie offered him a weak smile as she stood and went back into the saloon. Ma strode over and grunted from the effort of joining him on the bench. "My old bones are tired, John. Does my heart good to see Cassie healing so quickly. The benefits of youth."

But Holt did not want to talk about Cassie. "What did

she mean about you not allowing Charlie Gardiner to stand against me?"

"You've been too busy for me to tell you the good news." She pulled her shawl tighter around her shoulders. "Charlie and his boys work for me now."

Holt had not been expecting that but was far from surprised by the news. "You didn't waste any time getting an army of your own."

The aging madam gave him a hoarse laugh. "This town doesn't reward people who pass up opportunities, Sheriff. Besides, I figure you'd be happy with the outcome. Having them work for me is a lot better than having them roaming the county getting into trouble. They might even get it into their heads to come back here and settle the score with you. This way, we're all one big happy family."

Holt did not like being thought of as one of Ma's men, but he admired her ability to take advantage of a situation. "Mullen and Cassidy have their guns and now, you have yours."

"Sounds kind of ugly when you put it like that," she said, "though I imagine it adds up to the same thing. Sorry they couldn't be much help to you when those idiots took a run at you last night, but next time will be different."

Holt rubbed his sore knee. "Let's hope there won't be a next time."

"Don't count on it," she said. "Mullen might've left town with his tail between his legs, but he'll spend the time licking his wounds. And when he comes back for the inquest, you can be sure he'll be bringing plenty of trouble with him."

Holt had been thinking about that from the moment Judge Cook had told him he would be cutting Mullen loose. Half of him hoped the man took the opportunity to leave the county to avoid the inquest. As a fugitive, he would be the territorial marshal's problem. Holt would not care where he wound up. Knowing he was no longer in town would be enough to put Holt at ease.

Half of him hoped Mullen stuck around for the inquest and made another run at him. He would see to it that Mullen died first and when he did, no one could accuse him of prejudice.

Holt knew the third option would be for Holt to resign his position and leave town once Mullen cleared the inquest. But running had never been his style, so he quickly dismissed it.

But a better third option came to mind. One that Ma McAdam had given birth to without realizing it.

"Gardiner and his boys give up any hope of getting that money Hank hid from them?"

"Don't think I could ever get them to do that," she said. "Wouldn't expect them to either."

Holt grinned. "Because you'd lose out on your cut, too, wouldn't you?"

She turned to face him. "Don't you sit there grinning at me like a fool. You know something, so you might as well spit it out."

Holt let it out slow. "Just remembering something Mullen said back in the jail when he tried to kill me is all."

He pulled his collar down so she could get a good look at the bruises on his neck. "Said no one could stop him from spending all that money once I was out of the way. Now, he might've been talking about something else, but I don't think he was. Made me wonder if Bob hadn't struck a deal with Mullen to hide the money from his gang."

Ma sat back and seemed to chew that over for a moment.

"Can't say that I ever knew of any friendship between them."

Holt decided to sweeten the pot. "Ever know Bostrom to hit any Mullen mines or properties? Because I did some checking, and it doesn't look like they did."

She appeared ready to tell him he was wrong but stopped herself. "Can't say that I have. Mullen certainly would've called out a posse if they had. He always threatened to if they ever came near town, but never did."

Holt was glad his words were beginning to take hold with her. "Sounds like more than a coincidence if you ask me."

"Sounds like you're trying to get my boys to do your dirty work for you," Ma said. "Well, if you're thinking I'm going to turn them loose on Mullen looking for that money, you're dead wrong. I'm not sending them after him on a rumor. I've got plans for them and they can't do me much good if they're dead."

Holt shrugged as if it meant nothing to him. "If they're not as tough as I heard, then it sounds like a good idea."

Ma fixed her shawl. "You're a crafty one, aren't you, Holt? Thinking you can goad their pride into taking care of Mullen for you. Well, forget it. They're plenty tough, but I'm not going to waste them on a fool's errand. We've got no idea where the money might be. Could be in his ranch house. Could be buried deep in one of his mines. Could have it at the bottom of his privy for all we know."

"Only one way to find out," he said. "When the moment's right."

Ma was quick to catch on. "You mean while he's here in town for the inquest."

Holt looked up Main Street and nodded. It was already getting darker and, before long, the sun would be setting.

He imagined sunsets were quite an event in this part of the world. He hoped the town would be quiet enough for him to enjoy it.

"I figure a man like Mullen will keep that kind of money close. He wouldn't leave it to chance in a mine or a hole somewhere. He'd keep it close so he could get his hands on it if he needed it. But I imagine you know him better than I do."

"You might not know him, but you know his kind. The ranch house is a good place to start. Most of his men will be out tending to the cattle, so I expect the house will be lightly guarded if at all. I just hope Sarabelle is with him. Ever see her?"

"At Mayor Chapman's wake last night. Pretty woman."

"Don't let her looks fool you. She's just as ruthless as he is, maybe even worse. Comes from pioneer stock, that one. Why, when I heard poor old Rita Heller died, my first thought was that Sarabelle had done her in. I didn't have a reason for it then, but I do now."

Holt had not thought of that. "Think her and Ott knew about the Bostrom money."

"Makes sense considering what you just told me. Ott was full of cancer and near the end anyway. Mullen wouldn't have had to promise him much to shoot Chapman and I'd wager Rita got drunk and held her knowledge about the money over Mullen's head. She was always a devil when she drank, not that I could blame her. Poor soul didn't have an easy life with Ott."

Holt stood up and pulled his hat back on his head. He did not know why he stood up, but considering all that he had just heard, it seemed like the right thing to do. For suddenly, everything fit. Not neat enough for a court of law, but enough for his purposes.

Ma remained on the bench. "I sure hope you're not

planning on asking Judge Cook for a warrant because you won't get one. I'm no lawyer, but even I understand that knowing a thing happened is different from being able to prove it. And you won't find much appetite in town for raising hell over a dead miner and his drunken wife, especially against the likes of Mullen."

Holt knew she was right. He could not do much for now, but if the right moment presented itself, the implication could be a more powerful weapon against Mullen than anything he had in the jailhouse.

But for this to work, he had to deepen his agreement with Ma. A fact that did not exactly put him at ease. "Do we agree to keep all of this between us until we know more?"

"We agree," Ma said, "as long as you don't breathe a word of this to Charlie and the boys without talking to me first. I'll be mighty cross with you if you do."

"I wouldn't dream of it." Holt touched the brim of his hat as he began to walk back to the jail. "I've already got enough enemies."

CHAPTER 30

L ater that night, Holt wiped his mouth with a napkin and set it down next to his plate. "That's the first real supper I've enjoyed in quite a while, Jean. Thank you."

She smiled at him from across the table. Her café had long since closed for the evening, so it was just the two of them at a table. A candle providing spare light in the quiet dining room. "Glad you liked it. Figured you deserved a proper meal after all those jailhouse dinners I brought you."

"The setting is much nicer," Holt said. "And I don't have to worry about any prisoners breaking your dishes."

"It's the utensils I always fret over. Before you, Frank Peters only let me bring over soup and a slice of bread. Since you didn't say anything, and since the town's paying for it, I decided to tack on a little extra. The town can afford it, believe me."

"They can certainly afford me," Holt said. "Come to think of it, this is a pretty prosperous town. Guess I haven't had time to notice that much until today. It's the first day I haven't killed someone since coming to town."

She held a finger up to her lips. "Don't spoil it. It's just passed nine o'clock. Still, plenty of time to keep your streak going."

He took another sip of wine. He usually did not drink but decided this was something of an occasion. His first real meal in his adopted town. He had never developed a taste for wine or port like his fellow officers in the army but figured a little now could not hurt.

He felt himself blush when he noticed Jean was studying him. "What? Did I forget to clean my face properly?"

She rested her chin on her hand. "No. Just looking at you. The real you, not the sheriff with the big reputation."

"He's still here," Holt said. "I'm just more than that is all."

"I wouldn't have gone to all this bother if I thought otherwise," she said. "Not that it's been a bother. I had to eat anyway."

Holt grinned as he set his glass back on the table. "You always know how to make a man feel special."

He felt horrible when he saw her smile disappear and wished he had kept his big mouth shut. He had never had a way with women, and it showed. "I'm sorry if I said something wrong, Jean. I didn't mean anything by it."

She shook her head as she glanced down at her lap. "It's nothing you said or did, John Holt. If anything, it was my doing." When she looked up at him again, he noticed the traces of tears in her eyes. "You ever wish you could be different than what you are? That you could go back somehow and undo some of the things you've done?"

"Never gave it much thought," he admitted. "Not much future in the past for a man in my line of work. Can lead to regret, to second-guessing myself. That kind of thinking can get a man killed and dying's not something I look forward to."

Her smile returned and warmed him. "I'd bet my deed to this place that you've got quite a history."

"Everybody's got history," he said. "Not everyone's history matters. Mine sure doesn't."

"You had a life before the war, fought in the war, lived through it and after it," Jean said. "There's got to be something that matters in all of that life."

"Just a lot of death," he told her. "Some at my hand, some around me. Some I couldn't save no matter how hard I tried. Guess that's why I keep at this work now. To save those I can."

"In your own way."

"I don't know any other way of doing it."

Holt did not know why she looked around until a moment later when he heard it too. Something that sounded like a group of women's voices raised and growing louder. It was not a chant like he had heard outside the jailhouse the night Mayor Chapman had been killed. This was more disorganized.

"What is it?" Holt asked Jean as she got up from the table. She plucked the carving knife from the chicken and moved to the door.

Holt quickly got to his feet and joined her. "Probably best if you stay—"

But Jean had already unlocked the café door and headed out onto the boardwalk. She kept her carving knife flat against her leg, hidden by the folds of her skirts.

Holt looked up the street at the growing racket and saw a line of women linked arm-in-arm that spanned the width of Main Street heading this way. The torches some of them held cast unsettling shadows across their faces.

He watched Jean shrink back into the darkness of the boardwalk. She had held the knife so she could strike down in a stabbing motion or bring it across to slice an attacker. It was clear to him that she had not moved back out of fear, but to gather her strength. She was coiled like a rattler, ready to strike if she had to.

Holt took his Remington from his holster and held it against his side. It was clear Jean wanted to handle this her way. He hoped the line of women would continue to walk past the café but was disappointed when the line broke apart as they stopped on the thoroughfare.

Jean spoke loudly from the darkness. "What do you ladies want here?"

A woman he recognized as Sarabelle Mullen stepped forward. She held a torch, which revealed Jean and the knife at her side.

"Well, if it ain't the town traitor," Sarabelle said. "Thought you'd be in bed by now."

Jean did not shrink away. "I'm a light sleeper. Now answer my question. What do you ladies want here?"

"Can't say we had a reason." Sarabelle glanced back at the other women who had crowded closely behind her. "We were up at the Bottle when some of us got to thinking about Ott and Rita's passing. Got to talking about who we could call to account for them dying. That scoundrel Holt came to mind, but there's not much a group of us ladies could do to a man like that. Then Marcia here reminded us that you're the one who feeds the jail when they've got prisoners. Another woman told us you and Holt have gotten mighty close lately. Figured we ought to come down here and see about that."

Holt watched Jean point at the torches. "Which I suppose is why you came here after dark with fire and such. Which one of you has the rock you were gonna throw through my window?"

He watched a woman step forward holding a brick. "Can't throw it very far, but far enough to get the job done."

Holt stepped out of the shadow of the doorway. "And that's as far as you'll go too."

The torches shifted his way as the women fixed their eyes on a new target.

"Well," Sarabelle said. "Isn't this cozy?"

"This is what they call unlawful assembly," Holt told them. "You ladies best get on back to the Bottle before someone gets hurt." He pointed at the woman holding the brick. "And you'd better drop that right now."

She jutted out her jaw at him. "Or what?"

Holt remained perfectly still. His finger remained aimed squarely at her. He allowed the silence to speak for him.

The woman took a step back and allowed the brick to fall from her hand.

Holt quit pointing and looked over the women. "You lost some friends because of a gathering like this. I'd hate to see you lose any more for the same reason. I know some of you are hurting, so I'll put this down as something akin to grief. Leave now before it gets out of hand."

The woman who had been holding the brick looked up the street, brought her fingers to her lips and cut loose with an ear-piercing whistle.

Holt followed where she was looking and saw a group of miners come out from the shadows of the boardwalk a bit farther up the street. He counted about twenty of them, though they were not holding torches, so it was difficult to be sure.

Holt watched the men come toward them. A group of twenty women had just turned into a mob of about forty or so. He had never worked a town so fond of forming groups. Not even New Orleans had been able to assemble a crowd of rabble so quickly.

Holt would have given anything for his Henry rifle just

then and cursed himself for leaving it at the jail. He promised himself he would not make the same mistake again.

He watched the group swagger toward him. Their bravery enhanced by numbers and a fair amount of whiskey. He looked for any sign of Mullen's committee men or perhaps even Cassidy but could not see them. These boys appeared to be working on their own this time.

One of the miners at the front called out, "Didn't expect to find you here, Sheriff. Didn't take you for a man to have a taste for Creole women."

Holt brought up his Remington and thumbed back the hammer. The sound was enough to make the group stop.

"And it'll be the last thing you see if you take one more step. I told your women to head back to the Bottle and I'm telling you the same thing. You're all drunk. No need for you to wake up dead in the morning."

The man held up his hands, as did the rest of the miners. "Why, that'd be murder, Sheriff? Shooting unarmed men just doesn't go here in town. Ain't that the reason why you arrested Joe Mullen?" The man smiled. "You wouldn't want to wind up a guest in your own jail, now, would you?"

Holt shifted his aim to the man who was talking. "Take one more step and find out."

"I'd kind of like to see that myself," came a man's voice from his left.

Holt kept his eyes on the miner as he saw Charlie Gardiner and the seven remaining members of the Bostrom Gang walk past the women. The sight of the outlaws sent the women back to their husbands. Sarabelle trailed behind them with her torch.

Gardiner was in front and, like the men with him, had a rifle at his side. "The sheriff told you to get moving, so get."

The lead miner kept his hands raised. "Never thought I'd see the day when Charlie Gardiner backed a lawman's play."

"Not backing his play," Charlie said as he led his men closer. "Not wearing a deputy's star or one of them fancy blue ribbons from the committee men either. We work for Ma McAdam now and she doesn't want you or your womenfolk causing trouble in this part of town. If you set Jean's place to the torch, the flames could reach the Railhead. We can't have that."

He and the seven men with him kept walking closer and the miners began moving backward.

Charlie continued, "So heed what the sheriff told you and move along."

"And if we don't?" the miner said as he kept stepping backward.

"Then we'll just have to move you."

One of the men behind the leader pulled on his shirt, but the lead miner pulled free and pointed up at Holt. "This man killed Cal. Cut him down in cold blood."

"Was a fair fight," Gardiner said. "But this won't be if you try to stand your ground."

The miners and their wives had already backed up more than two storefronts away before they turned and headed back to the Blue Bottle Saloon.

Only Sarabelle remained standing in the street. Her torch seemed to burn from more than just the oil, but also from her anger. Holt thought she might force the issue until she turned and slowly joined the others.

The outlaws stopped walking in front of café and stood still, joining Holt in watching Sarabelle and the mob until they entered the Bottle.

Charlie looked back at his men and nodded for them to

go back to the Railhead. The outlaw hung back and tipped his hat to the sheriff. "No cause to thank us, Sheriff. Just doing our duty."

Holt lowered his pistol but kept it at his side. "No cause to thank you because I didn't need your help."

Gardiner grinned. "You can tell yourself that if it makes you feel any better."

Holt resented the idea of being indebted to the outlaw. "Maybe you're forgetting I held off bigger crowds than that since I've been here."

"You surely have," Charlie said, "but with us around, you won't have to. As long as Ma likes you, that is."

"And if she doesn't?"

The outlaw seemed to give some thought to it before shrugging. "Then I guess I'll promise to put flowers on your grave."

Now, it was Holt's turn to grin. "You can tell yourself that if it makes you feel any better."

Charlie Gardiner threw back his head and laughed. "I'm gonna like you, Sheriff Holt. Yes, I do believe I will." He looked at him and Jean and tipped his hat again. "Good evening to you both."

Holt watched Gardiner take his time as he walked back to the Railhead, whistling a tune to himself as he went.

Holt realized Jean had moved to his side. "We could've handled them together, you know?"

"Together," he said. "I like the sound of that."

Even in the dim light of the boardwalk, he saw her smiling up at him. He holstered his pistol and was about to bring her closer to him when he heard a woman call out Jean's name.

They turned around to see Ma McAdam hurrying toward them along the boardwalk. She had bunched up her skirts as she moved to avoid tripping over them in her haste.

Holt was surprised when Jean backed into him and felt her begin to tremble.

She ducked her head when Ma drew closer. "I sent the boys up here when I heard those fool women coming this way." She stroked Jean's arm. "Are you hurt, child?"

Jean kept looking down as she silently but quickly shook her head. When she spoke, her voice was small. "No. I'm fine."

She smiled at Jean and looked up at Holt. "I'm glad you were here, Sheriff. Those women would've set this place to the torch if you hadn't been."

Jean backed farther against him and almost knocked him over. *What was she so afraid of?*

"That was all Jean's doing," Holt said. "She had them turned before I even opened my mouth."

Ma smiled at Jean. "This one's always been a fighter, haven't you, honey?"

Jean slipped away from her touch and moved back inside. "I've got cleaning up to do. Morning won't come any later because of this."

Holt had never seen Jean flustered. He had just watched her face down a torch-bearing crowd with nothing more than a carving knife to protect her but ran away from an aging madam trying to console her.

Ma looked after her with a look of concern on her face. "Poor thing's rattled by all of this. She hasn't had it easy, God knows, but she's as stubborn as her father was."

Holt decided any questions he had would be answered by Jean, not Ma. "I'd best go in and check on her. I didn't need the help, but thanks for sending the boys around anyway."

"Think nothing of it," Ma said. "After all, we're friends, remember? Friends do things for each other."

Holt liked the idea that they were allies less than he liked Charlie thinking he owed him something. But he decided there was nothing to be gained by making the point now and bid her good night before going into the café. He quietly locked the door behind him as Ma put her face to the glass and looked in.

He was surprised that Jean had already gathered up all the plates and cleared the table. He found her back in the kitchen, already soaking the plates in a bucket of water.

He leaned against the doorway and watched her place the carcass of the chicken in a large pot. "Not much to pick off these bones. Going to boil it down for stock tomorrow. My customers are gonna eat mighty well."

But Holt was not concerned about the café's menu. "You want to talk about it?"

"Nothing to talk about." She picked up one of the dishes and began scrubbing it with a brush. "Just stopped another group from burning me out is all. It happened before you got here, and it'll probably happen again after you leave." She offered a weak smile. "When folks around here get drink in them, they seem to resent a woman of my persuasion being uppity enough to own her own place."

"I'm not talking about that," Holt said. "I'm talking about what happened between you and Ma just now. You're upset, and if you'd like to tell me why, I'm willing to listen."

She finished scrubbing away the leavings of the dinner from one plate and took the other. "None of my girls like cleaning the dishes, but I don't mind. Want to know why? Because if you scrub it hard enough, you get it clean. You see the result of your work right in front of you. Makes you feel like you've done something with the day the good Lord has given you. Wish I could do that with myself sometimes. Doesn't seem to be a brush strong enough for that, though, at least none that I've seen."

Holt began to understand. "You worked for her once, didn't you? There's no shame in that."

She set the plate down in the water. "Is that what you think?"

Holt did not know what to think. "It's none of my business, but it's nothing to be ashamed of either. We all have to do what we need to do in order to survive, Jean."

She returned to her scrubbing. "Can't blame you for thinking that. After my daddy died, Ma took me in, but not how you think. She put me to work in the kitchen where the customers couldn't see me, much less offer a price for me. Learned a lot about how to fix a meal and make the most out of the slop she bought for her customers. The way I figured, even men like that have a right to a good meal."

Holt hung his head. He felt like a fool for thinking the worst. "Jean, I didn't mean—"

"She had plenty of offers for me," Jean went on, "but she never took them no matter how much they were willing to pay. She's always been fond of money, but I guess she never could figure out a price to place on her daughter's services."

Holt eased himself off the doorway before he fell over. "You mean—"

"That's right, John Holt. I'm the only woman in town who can rightfully call Ma McAdam 'ma' and have it mean something." She kept scrubbing the dish, even though it was spotless. "After a year or so, she staked me to this place. I'd already saved enough and didn't want her money, but she went ahead and bought the building right out from under me. Still owns it, too, despite me trying to buy it from her. Said she won't hear of it."

Holt realized this was the second surprise revelation about family he had heard that day. First, Bob and Mullen, now Ma and Jean. For a tiny town, Devil's Gulch certainly had an odd forest of family trees.

He stepped over to her and gently took the clean plate from her. "Looks like neither of us like to be indebted to anyone, especially her."

He set the plate down as she looked up at him. He thumbed away the tears that had begun to stream down her cheeks, though her voice did not waver.

"You're the third person in town who knows who I really am," she said. "I'd appreciate it if you kept it that way."

He smiled. "And you're the only person alive who knows what I really am. Guess we'll have to trust each other with our secrets, won't we?"

And as they kissed, Holt decided a kitchen was not the most romantic setting in which to fall in love, but it would have to do.

CHAPTER 31

Just after dawn the next morning, Holt tried to shut the jailhouse door quietly behind him without waking Jack Turnbull. But the boy was already awake, sitting on the edge of the bed in the office. He had pulled one of the mattresses from one of the cells for his bedding.

"Well," Jack said. "Wonder where you've been."

Holt refused to allow himself to blush in front of the boy. "Maybe I'll tell you when you're old enough."

"I was plenty old enough to cover you last night out on the street," Jack said. "Had my shotgun and your Henry with me when those fools tried to surround you."

Holt could not remember seeing the boy. "You were there?"

"Hung back in the shadows while those drunken fools walked by," Jack told him. "Even covered you when Charlie Gardiner hung back. You two are going to tangle one day."

Holt hung his hat on the peg by the rifle rack. "Tell me something I don't already know." He decided thinking about the future was pointless, considering what he was facing now. "Anything interesting happen while I was . . . out?"

Jack got up from the bed and handed him a piece of

paper from the desk. "Les Patrick stopped by last night. Dropped these off for you. Said it should make you happy but looks like Miss Jean already did that."

Holt backhanded the boy before he realized he had done it. The youth fell back on the bed, holding the cheek where Holt had struck him.

He immediately regretted it but dared not apologize. "I won't have you talking about her like that. Not to me, not to anyone else."

The boy looked up at him, anger in his eyes. For a moment, Holt thought he might lunge for him, but the moment passed, and he said, "Guess I had it coming for running my mouth like that. I'm sorry."

Holt turned his attention to the papers Les Patrick had left for him. "It isn't right for me to hit you. I'm not your pa."

"Darn right you're not." Jack grinned. "Pa would've broken my jaw. You hit like an old lady."

Holt let the insult pass and focused on the documents instead. The first one was a decree from the mayor's office, declaring the Vigilance Committee disbanded until further notice. Holt had not been expecting that and held it up for Jack to see.

"Les tell you about this?"

"Spent the better part of last night tacking them all over town," he said. "Told me to make sure people saw it first thing in the morning when they woke up. Made sure the first one I put up was in front of the Bottle so those boys could see it."

Holt knew he must have passed several notices on his way back to the jail that morning, but his mind was warm with the memories of the night he had spent with Jean. He would have to remind himself to be more careful in the future. Too many people in town wanted him dead to be able to afford such distractions.

He set the notice aside and read the second document Les had left for him. It was a court order signed by Judge Cook, ordering an inquest into the murder of Hank Bostrom.

While the order itself was not a surprise, the day for which it was scheduled was. And for once, it was a pleasant one. "Mullen's inquest is set for the day after tomorrow."

Jack rubbed his sore cheek as he nodded. "Mr. Patrick thought you might like that. Said they wanted to haul him into court before he got it in his head to run for it or dig himself in up at his ranch."

Holt set the document down on his desk. "He say if Mullen knows about this?"

Jack nodded. "His lawyer does. Said Mr. Arbour even agreed to it."

Holt was glad. That meant he did not have to ride out to the Mullen spread or the mines and deliver the document personally. "This is turning out to be a better morning than I expected."

Jack got up and began to make a pot of coffee. "I'd bet Joe Mullen doesn't think so."

Up at the JM Ranch ten miles away, Joe Mullen rocked back on his heels from the impact of Sarabelle's slap across his face.

"How dare you think of running out on me at a time like this!"

Mullen shook off the blow but felt the imprint of her hand already begin to blister on his face. His wife was a deceptively strong woman who knew how to hit. "I'm not running out on you. I'm trying to protect what we have. You tried to rally the men in town last night and look all the good it did you."

"Running away like a guilty man won't make it any better," she yelled. "What good will that do either of us. You staked this place for your freedom. All the mines too. Are you willing to give all that up just so you can dodge a trial you're going to win?"

"That's just it," Mullen told her. "None of this is in my name, remember? You own all of this. That agreement I signed is meaningless. If I disappear now, they won't be able to lay a finger on me or the mines or the spread."

"Do you think a detail like that will stop Judge Cook?" she asked. "They'll take this place over faster than you can spit. And where will that leave me? You think your men will stick by you if you run? Your miners. The men here on the ranch. The committee in town? They'll see you for the coward you are, and they won't lift a finger to help you whenever you decide to return."

But Mullen had already thought of that. "Trials are tricky things, Sarabelle. Just because I stand a good chance of winning doesn't mean I'm willing to risk it." He pointed down to the three satchels against the wall. "I'm not willing to risk Holt getting his hands on that if they lock me up either."

"That money is the best defense you have against Holt, you fool," Sarabelle told him. "With that, I can make sure you get the best defense money can buy, way better than Ty Arbour can give you if it comes to it. If you run away now, they'll swear out a warrant for your arrest. Put a bounty on your head. I know you think you're a tough man, but you're not the fugitive kind. You like your comforts and how long do you think it'll be before they find you and that money you plan on taking with you?"

He dared not tell her that his time in Holt's jail had changed him. He had been locked up for less than a day, but it had been long enough to show him that he could not risk a life behind bars again. He knew how the town felt about him. He knew there were not twelve men in Devil's Gulch who would allow him to go to trial past the inquest. And there certainly weren't twelve men who would convict him should he go to trial. They would not risk his wrath should he eventually get out. And if convicted, he would get out, one way or the other.

But he could not take that risk. Despite the tough talk he had thrown at Holt, he had been terrified every moment he had spent in that tiny cell. He had spent his time with three men frightened of him and guarded by a boy barely old enough to shave. The cot had been reasonably comfortable and the food more than edible.

But the territorial prison would not be so forgiving and the men he could serve time with would not fear him. The mere prospect of being in prison was enough to make his blood run cold.

No, he decided. Running was the only safe way he could ensure his freedom. That much was certain.

Sarabelle took his face in her hands and forced him to look at her. "You're not going to jail, Joe. You run this town and everything about it. You have ranches and the mines and more money than anyone in this part of the territory. And with that Bostrom stash, I'd wager you're the richest man in five hundred miles. Men like you don't run because they don't have to. They stand strong and fight. They fight for what they have, and they don't let anyone take it from them. Not Judge Cook and certainly not Holt."

Mullen still was not convinced. He just needed to get away from her so he could make his escape.

But she seemed to sense his fear and gripped his face

even tighter. "You're a strong man, Joe Mullen. Stronger than you know. And together, we're even stronger. I took care of Rita Heller for you. For us. And I'll never let anything happen to you. No one can beat us. No one."

She let go of his face and wrapped her arms around the middle of him.

She was so convincing, he almost believed it himself. Almost.

CHAPTER 32

Holt and Jack Turnbull had their hands full on the morning of the inquest. A long line stretched from County Hall all the way down the boardwalk of Main Street.

At first, he had been surprised that Judge Cook had decided to hold the inquest on a Saturday, but now he understood the old man's thinking. Most of the town worked a half-day on Saturdays, and everyone who could be there would be. It would increase his jury pool, though Holt did not think it would matter. There were few people in town who would put a word against Joe Mullen. He could not blame them. They had families and businesses to think about. And even if the Vigilance Committee had been disbanded by Mayor Chapman's decree, it was still only a piece of paper. Holt knew no piece of paper could erase what people held in their hearts.

The crowd was growing anxious as the bank's clock tower chimed one o'clock. Many had been in line since before eleven, with the hopes of a prompt seating at noon. Les Patrick had told Holt to not allow anyone in until he gave the word, which was easy for him to say. He was not out here with a group of restless townspeople.

Mr. Ross from the general store had been first in line and said to Holt, "Can't you let some of us in, Sheriff? We're not used to standing this long and it's been hours already."

"I'll be happy to let you in as soon as the court says so," Holt told him. "I've been out here as long as all of you and I'm anxious to sit too."

He could not believe the change in his own tone. A week ago, he would have ignored Ross and the complaints of anyone else standing in line. No one had asked them to be there. They had come of their own volition to see a spectacle. To gather oats for the rumor mill that would grind for days following the events in the courtroom. Everyone in town wanted to be able to say they had seen it all with their own two eyes, as if witnessing it would make them something special in the eyes of those who had not bothered to come.

But Holt had softened his tone over the past couple of days. He supposed he had Jean to thank for that. She had managed to take some of the starch out of him and he found himself chatting with some of the people he was paid to protect. He even smiled more, which should have troubled him, but did not.

He watched Jean as she rolled a cart along the board-walk, selling warm coffee to those in line. She stole a wink at him from time to time. Another reason for him to smile. She was an industrious woman, that Jean.

He knew Joe Mullen was not smiling. He had looked nervous when Ty Arbour had led him and his wife into the courtroom just before noon. He imagined the wait must be killing him and wondered if that was not reason for the delay.

The crowd grew louder as the county hall door opened and Les Patrick slipped out beside him. Jack Turnbull continued to hold his shotgun across his chest and called for the crowd to be quiet.

Holt watched Les Patrick strain his neck to check the bank's clock tower.

"Can we let them in now?" Holt asked him.

"Not yet," Patrick said. "Still waiting on some folks."

He pointed down Main Street and said, "Finally. There they are."

Holt saw a stagecoach barreling up Main Street. The four-horse team was lathered, obviously from a brisk pace. The driver pulled back on the reins, bringing the team to a skidding halt, which kicked up chunks of dirt on the waiting crowd.

Les Patrick pushed past Holt and walked down the steps to greet the stage. He opened the door and six men piled out. At first, the sheriff thought they might be extra guards Les had requested from a neighboring county. But none of the six men he greeted looked like gunmen. They looked like all the other men now standing in line. Short, tall, skinny, and heavy. Some consulted pocket watches after they reached the boardwalk before Les held the door open for them and allowed them inside.

Holt and Jack kept the townspeople in line as they protested the admittance of the new arrivals.

After the sixth man entered the hall, Holt grabbed Patrick's arm and lowered his voice as he asked, "Who are they?"

"Our jury," Les grinned. "The judge had them brought in from Golden City to help balance things out." He nodded toward the crowd before Holt could say another word. "You can let them in now, Sheriff. We're ready to begin."

Holt signaled Jack to open the other door and allow the impatient crowd inside. He had to hand it to Judge Cook. He was much craftier than he had given him credit for.

He kept a close eye on the people as they filed past him. He made sure none of them were armed with a pistol or any other weapon that might disrupt the proceedings. None of them were.

He was about to check the next person in line when he saw Ma McAdam clad in black with a white shawl around her shoulders. He had not noticed her in line before and imagined she had paid someone to hold her place in line.

Holt remembered their discussion about the missing money and the outlaws' search for it. "Surprised to see you here. Guess Charlie and the others are minding the Railhead for you."

"They're out running an errand," she said. "You never know what those boys will get up to when I'm not around to keep an eye on them."

But Holt knew they were probably already up at the Mullen ranch looking for their stolen loot.

He ushered her past him and continued to check the remaining townsfolk as they filed into the hall.

Holt and Jack sat on benches at the back of the courtroom while the proceedings took place. Jack nodded off from time to time. Holt allowed him to sleep until he began to snore. An elbow to the side woke him up for a time until he drifted off again.

Holt had seen his fair share of inquests and court proceedings and knew they could be boring affairs to someone like Jack. But he could not help but be impressed by the eloquence of Les Patrick for the prosecution and Ty Arbour for the defense. Even Judge Cook appeared appropriately pious and in charge as he oversaw the proceedings. Some of the judges and attorneys he had seen at work in New Orleans could have learned a thing or two from how these frontier barristers conducted themselves.

The jury selection had gone smoothly and, while the presence of six men from Golden City had raised a stir at first, the selection of six townsmen calmed the spectators. Holt even recognized some of the men who had been selected for the jury. Three of them had stopped him on the street earlier in the week to commend him on the job he was doing in town.

He began to think this might not be as easy for Mullen as he had thought.

Holt's own testimony was mercifully quick. He had told them what he had seen, confirmed that Hank Bostrom had been unarmed and that Joe Mullen had shot him. Arbour had no questions for him and Holt's part in the proceedings was over.

Dr. Klassen had verified the cause of death and was dismissed without any questions from Arbour.

Others had testified similarly, though Arbour made sure they added Hank's status as an outlaw and a dangerous man.

Holt thought the event was beginning to wind down when he saw Les Patrick rise once again. "Your Honor, I would like to call one final witness to the stand."

Ty Arbour rose. "Objection, Your Honor. We have no other witnesses on our list."

Les continued. "This is a witness who came forward

only today, Your Honor. We were just as surprised as the defense."

Judge Cook leaned forward in his chair and said, "Approach the bench."

The crowd began to murmur as the two attorneys stood on tiptoes to speak to the judge. Ty Arbour grew animated while Les Patrick remained calm.

Holt found himself at the edge of his bench as Jack began to snore again. Holt left him alone as he strained to hear what was going on at the front of the courtroom.

It was impossible to read Judge Cook's expression as he dismissed the attorneys. Les Patrick remained calm.

Ty Arbour looked pale.

"Order!" Judge Cook called as he banged his gavel. "I'll have order in this court, or by God, I'll have Sheriff Holt clear it."

Silence fell upon the packed room. Holt was already on his feet. Too taken by the proceedings to think about sitting.

Les Patrick remained standing, too, as he took his place behind his table. "Your Honor, the town calls Mrs. Mullen to the stand."

Holt thought he had misheard Les Patrick and, judging by how quiet the spectators were, they must have felt the same way.

He watched Joe Mullen turn as if he had been shot as his wife rose from the gallery and walked past his table on her way to the witness stand.

Arbour got to his feet again. "Your Honor, I must repeat my objection to the prosecution calling Mrs. Mullen to the stand. As you know, a wife cannot be compelled to give testimony against her husband."

"Nor can it compel her from testifying *against* him if she

so choses," the judge told him. "Your objection is overruled. The witness will be sworn in."

The dam of silence that had been holding back the spectators finally broke and the court was filled with shouts and questions.

Judge Cook pounded his gavel and yelled for Holt to clear the court. The ruckus had been loud enough to wake Jack without any prodding from Holt and the two of them headed up the main aisle and began to pull people out of their seats and move them toward the door.

Holt was pulled backward by his collar and would have lost his footing had the low barrier between the spectators and the attorneys not been in the way.

Instinct caused him to fire an elbow straight back at his assailant, which broke the grip on his collar.

Holt brought the Henry rifle to his shoulder as he turned around and aimed at whoever had grabbed him.

He found Ty Arbour and Les Patrick struggling to push Joe Mullen back.

Behind him, the townspeople yelled as they suddenly broke for the door on their own accord.

Despite the chaos behind him, Holt kept his rifle trained on Mullen's face.

"It's over, John," Judge Cook yelled from the bench. "Lower your rifle immediately!"

But Holt could not lower his rifle. Nor could he look away from the hate in the eyes of the man that glared at him now. He had seen that look before. On battlefields and in barrooms and dance halls. The look a man gets when he is ready to kill or be killed. The look when all else is lost and his death is the only hope he had of salvation.

Ty Arbour pressed his hand against Holt's chest. "John, please."

Holt's grip on the rifle tightened. "Best let me end it now. It's gonna come to this eventually. You all know it."

"Not here," Judge Cook said. "And not in my courtroom. Lower your rifle, Sheriff. That is an order."

The steel in the judge's voice pierced the roar of his own blood raging in his ears and Holt slowly lowered the rifle.

Judge Cook said, "See to it the court is empty and bar the door. I will not allow any further outbursts, either from the spectators or from the defendant."

Holt forced himself to turn around and help Jack clear the last of the people from the court.

As Cook told the jury to disregard the outburst, Jack asked Holt what he wanted him to do.

"Go outside and make sure they stay clear of the entrance," Holt told him. "I'll stay here in case Mullen gets out of line again."

"I'm here if you need me," Jack said. "For anything. I mean that."

Holt knew he did and patted the young man on the back. "Go on like I told you."

He locked the door behind his deputy and stood with his back to the door. His rifle held across his chest as he listened to Mrs. Mullen get sworn in.

Les Patrick approached the witness stand. "Mrs. Mullen, you have sworn to tell the truth, the whole truth and nothing but the truth, have you not."

"Yes, I have," she said flatly.

"And you have agreed to testify against your husband in the matter before the court today. Against him in the charge of the murder of Hank Bostrom?"

She brought a lace handkerchief to the corner of her eye. "Yes, I have."

"And you have not been coerced or threatened in any way by me or anyone else to give such testimony?"

"No, I have not. I'm here of my own free will."

Joe Mullen began to get up, but Ty Arbour forced him to remain seated before Judge Cook could admonish him further.

Holt hoped Mullen acted out. He'd like the chance to put a bullet in him.

Les Patrick continued. "Were you present the night of the incident in question?"

"Yes, I was," she said. "I was standing only a few feet away from my husband when he drew his pistol and shot Hank dead in the street."

"But other witnesses have already testified to that," Les said. "What further evidence do you have that could change what the jury has already heard?"

"The reason why he killed Hank Bostrom." She paused and raised her handkerchief to her eye again, though Holt had not seen any tears. "When he first saw Hank in the street, he told me this was finally his chance to kill him."

Ty Arbour rose to object, but Mullen rose with him, screaming, "Why are you lying like this, Sarabelle? Why?"

Holt ran up the aisle and reached over the barrier to grab Mullen by the collar and pull him down hard into his chair. The sheriff kept a handful of Mullen's collar and squeezed, slowly choking him in the process.

Though Mullen and the rest of the court were too busy to notice.

"Objection, Your Honor," Ty Arbour said. "This is nothing but hearsay."

"The witness is Mr. Mullen's wife," Judge Cook said. "I'll allow it. Objection overruled. Proceed with your testimony, Mrs. Mullen."

Holt watched her cringe in her seat and knew she was

playing to the jury. "He hated the Bostrom family for years. I never knew why, but there was always bad blood between them. When he saw Hank staggering in the middle of the street, he told me this was his chance to get rid of him once and for all."

Despite Holt's tight grip on his collar, Mullen cut loose with a savage cry worthy of a wounded animal. He stood with a force strong enough to carry Holt over the barrier with him.

Holt let his rifle fall as he used his leverage to press Mullen down across the table and hold him in place as Les Patrick took shackles from behind the bench. Arbour helped Holt place them on Mullen's hands as Judge Cook said, "Mr. Mullen, I hold you in contempt of court. Sheriff Holt, I direct you to remand the accused to the jail until further orders from me."

Holt got his footing and pulled Mullen up from the table and forced him toward the swinging door. He strained as he tried to get at his wife, but Holt yanked the shackles high, forcing his arms back and up at an impossible angle and sending Mullen to his knees.

"I'll drag you like this if I have to," Holt yelled, "or you can walk out of here like a man. Your choice."

He let up just enough pressure to allow Mullen to get to his feet. Holt used the chain to push him through the swinging door, holding him in place as he picked up his rifle and continued to move Mullen down the aisle.

He quickly unlocked the doors to the courtroom and shoved Mullen outside.

Jack was in the empty lobby standing guard. His eyes grew wide at the sight of Holt gripping the sobbing Mullen by the neck.

"Clear a path to the jail," Holt told him. "Then get back here and make sure that door is locked. Check with Les if he needs you for anything and don't come back until he tells you."

Mullen tried to dig in his heels on the smooth floor, but Holt did not relent. "Come on, Joe. We've got a nice warm cot just waiting for you."

The prisoner's screams were drowned out by the cries from the townspeople gathered outside.

CHAPTER 33

Holt sat in his chair as Dr. Klassen slowly closed the door to the cells behind him. The doctor looked as tired as Holt felt, though the sheriff did not know why. Klassen had not spent the afternoon and the better part of the night listening to Mullen's terrors. Holt was only glad Klassen had finally found a way to quiet him down.

"How is he?" Holt asked.

Klassen dropped his medical bag on the bed and sat beside it. "He's had a conniption which has led to complications."

"Complications?" Holt's eyes narrowed. "How bad?"

Klassen pointed to the bottom drawer of Holt's desk. "You wouldn't happen to have a bottle of whiskey in there, would you?"

"No," Holt said. "Answer the question."

Klassen let out a heavy sigh. "Mullen appears to have worked himself up into quite a state. His heart was strained, and his entire left side is paralyzed, John. I believe he either had a heart attack or a stroke at some point during his incarceration here."

"A stroke?" Holt repeated. "That's impossible. He's around my age and I'm not even thirty yet."

"It's possible given certain circumstances," Klassen explained. "And I suppose having your own wife testify against you in open court and learning you'll be held for trial on a murder charge qualifies as such a circumstance. You might not like him, but you can't deny he's had a rather unpleasant day."

Holt did not care about the reasons, just the effects. "Is he going to die?"

"I don't know," the doctor admitted. "I don't think so, but such conditions are tricky. In my experience, heart events can happen in swarms, so he may have another episode. The next twenty-four hours are critical. That's why I think it's best if I stay here tonight to keep an eye on him, provided you have no objections, of course."

Holt remembered seeing Klassen in court. "I think we've both had enough objections for one day."

"Is that a joke?" The doctor's eyebrows rose. "That's awfully human of you. I thought you were above such things."

Holt decided to ignore the doctor's teasing. "Is Mullen's condition permanent?"

"It could be," Klassen said, "though it's just as likely that he'll recover at least some range of movement." He offered a weak smile. "I'm not being intentionally vague, John. I simply don't know. It depends on how his body reacts. In the short-term, his speech will be impaired due to the paralysis of half his mouth. He may not be able to walk fully or tend to his natural functions as he once did."

Holt did not like the sound of that. "I won't play wet nurse to him. I'll keep him in a tub if it comes to that."

Klassen shook his head. "I don't doubt you would either. No sense in fretting about it now. I won't know much more until the morning at the earliest."

Holt was already thinking far beyond that. "Do you think it's enough to make him get out of standing trial?"

"Not as far as Judge Cook is concerned. Mullen will stand trial for murder if he has to be tied down to a board and propped up in court." Klassen wagged a finger at him. "And I know what you're thinking. He's not faking it either. I dug a needle into the base of his foot, and he didn't so much as wince. If he's acting, he has a higher tolerance for pain than I do."

Holt ran his hand across his chin in thought. Having a murder charge hanging over him was bad enough. Having his wife turn the tables on him was another. No one had expected her to set him up like that, least of all Holt. He wondered why she had done it.

Mullen did not strike him as the type to run around on her. He had not kept a woman in town and did not seem to visit the girls upstairs at the Blue Bottle.

No, Holt decided it probably had something to do with the Bostrom money that Mullen had been holding on to. She must have known about it and decided the inquest was her chance to get it free and clear. He figured she had been planning on leaving now that her husband was in jail. There was no reason for her to stick around for the trial now. He probably would not be convicted and she would not dare wait for him to come back home.

The question of whether or not Charlie Gardiner and his boys had found it first would be answered soon enough when he paid a visit to the Railhead.

But first, he had to make an important visit.

Klassen looked at him as Holt began to get up. "Where do you think you're going?"

"Checking on the prisoner," Holt said. "Like any good sheriff would."

Klassen watched him remove his Remington from his

holster and place it in the top drawer of the desk. "You be careful in there, John. It's impossible to overstate the severity of his condition. I don't want you doing or saying anything that will make it worse."

"Why, Dr. Klassen." Holt locked the drawer and put the key in his shirt pocket. "How could you think I'd be capable of such a thing." He tried a smile. "That was a joke too."

Klassen began to fluff up the flat pillow on the bed. "And not a funny one, I'm afraid."

Mullen held a rag to the side of his face. It kept him from drooling on himself and soaking his pillow. It was one of the few dignities allowed him as he rotted in this miserable cell.

His left arm was completely dead. He only knew it was resting against his body because he saw it was there. His left leg was just as bad, still poking out from the bottom of the sheet from Ralph Klassen's test. It remained there, uncovered as if to mock his condition.

He had tried to use his right leg to push him farther back on the bed so the foot would fall into place, but he could not do it alone. He was forced to lay there alone in the dark with only his dreadful thoughts to keep him company.

Sarabelle's betrayal had brought him to this. The day before, her adamance about his remaining for the inquest had taken him by surprise. He had not expected her to support his decision to run, but he expected her to understand it. She had always been a cautious woman. She never sought to risk more than she had to and attending the inquest had been a risk.

But now he understood her reasons. She had wanted

the money. The Bostrom money. And now that he was in jail, it belonged to her. He had no idea where she would go with it but knew she had probably already prepared to leave town. She would want to be underway before his attorney got word to his men to stop her. She would not risk them taking matters into their own hands once word of her treachery reached them.

She was a smart woman, his Sarabelle. Cunning too. Her betrayal had struck him at his core. He had not believed that his wife had been capable of such a thing, but now that she had shown her true self to him, he would not forget it. He would find a way to make her pay for it one way or the other.

Mullen looked when he saw the door to the cells open and watched Sheriff John Holt enter. He had a candle in a holder and pulled the door closed behind him. He watched the lawman walk down the aisle, only to stop before his cell. He set the candle within a small niche that had been carved away from the stonework in the back wall of the jail.

When he faced him, Mullen saw his left side was in shadow. At least they had that much in common.

"The doc tells me you're in a bad way," Holt said. "No feeling in your left side. Some might call that bad luck. Not me. Guess you won't try strangling me again any time soon."

Mullen did not know how much of him Holt could see and chose to remain quiet. The only thing worse than being in his present condition was that Holt had to see him like this.

Holt went on. "You're in a bad way, Mullen, and I'm not just talking about your left side. Your wife sold you out for money. The Bostrom money you were holding on to for your brother, Bob."

Mullen's good eye widened in the darkness. *How had he known about that?*

Holt said, "Your men aren't coming to get you. Not your miners. Not your ranch hands. Mrs. Chapman has disbanded the Vigilance Committee and Cassidy has already begun to take your place. Whatever power you used to have in this town is gone after today. Judge Cook bringing in outsiders to serve on the jury saw to that. He'll do it again for the trial, so don't fool yourself into thinking you'll be freed then. Ty Arbour will be by tomorrow and will likely tell you the same thing. My advice? Throw yourself at the mercy of the court and plead guilty. The quicker you start your sentence, the sooner you'll be out. True, you'll be sixty before they let you go, but it's better than dying in prison. Until then, it'll just be you and me, Mullen. You lying on that cot like a dead fish with me and Jack tending to you."

Mullen felt his heart begin to pound in his chest again. His breathing became quicker, but he willed himself to remain silent. He would not give Holt the satisfaction of knowing the impact of his words.

Holt was undeterred. "I know you're a proud man, Joe, so part of me hopes you don't take a plea. The marshal will take you to the territorial prison if you do and that'll rob me of the pleasure of watching you suffer every time I come in here. Suffer not only in body, but in mind. Knowing that every day you're here, your grip on this town becomes that much weaker and there isn't a thing you can do about it. All alone, with only your hate to keep you company."

Holt moved away from the cell and began to walk up the aisle. "I'll leave the candle burning for you. Give a shout if you want me to blow it out."

He stopped at the door as if forgetting something. "I guess you can't shout, can you? Ah, well. I'll be back in to check on you later. I can always blow it out then if you want me to."

Mullen fought to calm himself as Holt opened the door, then stepped outside. The heavy door's hinges creaked in the darkness and the lock rattled shut like a thunderclap. Mullen felt as if he had just been sealed inside his own tomb but decided that was not quite right. He was already entombed in his own body.

No. He felt like he had just been cast into hell, though instead of eternal flames, he only had the flickering light of a distant candle to keep him company. He looked at the flickering flame now and saw his future. A future where he got back all that he lost. His speech and the use of his arm and leg. A future where he exacted revenge on Sarabelle. A future where he rode back to Devil's Gulch and regained what he had and more. A future where John Holt's broken and bloody corpse hung from the nearest tree.

Yes, Joseph Mullen looked at that flame until he felt as though he had become one with it. A flame he knew would burn brightly within him until that glorious day when he could exact his vengeance upon all those who had betrayed him.

Sleep may have evaded him, but his strength did not.

CHAPTER 34

John Holt was surprised the Railhead Saloon was so quiet. Most of the tables were empty except for a few of the regular gamblers he had come to recognize. The men looked up from their cards and nodded in greeting to him as he passed. It was not a friendly greeting, but one of respect and acceptance, which was enough for Holt.

Hoppy the bartender eyed him nervously as Holt walked to the back of the saloon where Charlie Gardiner and the rest of the remaining Bostrom Gang were sitting. Their table was littered with empty whiskey bottles and glasses. They were in the middle of a toast when Charlie spotted Holt heading his way. The men quickly downed their drinks and Duke March quickly refilled them.

Holt stopped about ten feet away from them. He rested his hand flat against his holster. Not drawing it, but ready to do so if necessary.

"Looks like quite the party," Holt said to Charlie. "What's the occasion?"

"A change in fortune, you might say." Gardiner grinned. "One long awaited and hard earned. You'll forgive me if I don't say more than that, won't you, Sheriff?"

Holt did not need them to say it. They had found the

Bostrom money up at Mullen's ranch after all. He would have loved to see the look on Sarabelle Mullen's face when she got back home and found her fortune gone. He wondered if she would throw herself at her husband's mercy or be smart enough to leave town. He did not know Joe Mullen well but knew him well enough to know he was not one to forgive her betrayal. Especially now that she had cost him more than just his freedom. She had cost him a fortune.

"I hear good things come in threes," Holt told them, referring to the three bags Bob Bostrom had left in Mullen's care.

"You might be right about that, Sheriff," Charlie said. "They do indeed."

"Good because I'll be taking one of them," Holt told him. "And I'll be taking it right now."

The merriment went out of the outlaws as each of them slowly lowered their drinks on the table.

Charlie tugged his ear. "Forgive me, Sheriff, but me and the boys have had more than our fill of drink this evening. I don't think I heard you correctly."

"You heard me," Holt said. "I want one of those bags."

The men began to stir but stopped when Charlie held up a hand. "That wasn't part of the bargain, Sheriff. Now, me and the boys are awfully grateful to you for letting us know where to find them. Why, we're even willing to give you what you might call a donation to your office." His smile faded. "But there's no way on earth that we're giving you a third of what we have."

"I don't want a donation," Holt told them. "And you're not giving it to me. You'll be paying off a debt."

"A debt?" Charlie slowly rose from his chair and squared up to Holt. He swayed a bit, but not enough to make him any less dangerous. "We don't owe you or anyone else a darn thing."

"Maybe you don't," Holt said, "but Hank and Em do. They're dead and buried, but their debt didn't die with them. And I'm here to collect." His hand moved higher up on his holster. "One way or the other."

Holt watched some of the fire go out of Charlie then. He became less angry and more curious. "You've got no idea of how much is in there, Sheriff, so you won't know if we've held any back."

"If you do, that's something you'll have to live with, not me."

Charlie looked past the sheriff and at the men playing cards behind him. Holt looked in the mirror above the outlaws' table and saw the men were too taken with their respective games to pay them any notice.

Charlie turned toward Cy Wentworth and pointed into the dark corner behind him. Wentworth frowned as he got up, lifted a canvas satchel from the floor and handed it over to him.

Charlie handed it over to Holt but did not let it go. "Good thing you didn't ask for all of it."

"A very good thing." Holt took the bag with his left hand, keeping his right on his holster. "For you boys."

With Jack Turnbull keeping an eye on things at the jail, Holt helped Cassie into the waiting stage.

"I don't know how you did it all so quickly." She fluffed out the frills of the new dress he had bought her for the ride to the train that would take her to California, "but I'm forever grateful to you, Sheriff. I truly am."

"Nothing to thank me for," he said as he tossed up

one of her bags to the coachman. "I made you a promise, remember? All I'm doing is living up to it."

"And all these new clothes?" She watched him toss up another bag to the coachman. "I don't know what to say, except to thank you."

"No need." The coachman waited for Holt to throw up the final bag, but he waved him off. Holt placed that bag in the coach with Cassie and whispered, "I fit as much of this as I could in the luggage, but this is the rest of it. Don't open it and be careful. It's heavy. Make sure the porter takes it for you when you get to the train, but that you keep it with you at all times."

He watched a questioning look appear on her scarred face. "What . . . ?"

He kept his voice low. "It's part of what those men were looking for, remember? I'm just returning it to its rightful owner."

He watched her eyes begin to fill with tears and decided that was his cue to leave. "Have a safe journey, Cassie. And if you think to write once you get to town, please do. We'll all be anxious to hear you're well."

He stepped down from the coach and shut the door, walking back up the street before her gratitude could embarrass him further.

He was glad to see Jean waiting for him in front of her café. Despite the chilly morning, she had a mug of coffee waiting for him.

She offered him a smile as she handed him the mug. "Figured you could use this after all your hard work."

He took the mug and was glad it was still plenty hot. "That was no bother at all. Just a few bags."

"They looked awfully heavy to me," she observed. "Why, I never knew a sporting lady to have so much luggage, unless she ran the place, of course."

He knew she was aware that he had bought a few things for Cassie for the trip. He could not allow her to begin a new life in a new place with old clothes. "Just a few things to help her on her way. And a little extra that she had coming to her."

Jean folded her arms across her chest. "That little extra doesn't belong to her. It belongs to the bank, John Holt. Why, some might say you broke the law by handing it over to her."

"Some might," Holt allowed. "I wouldn't."

"And you have the final say in what's right and wrong in Devil's Gulch, is that it?"

"Not yet." He sipped some of the coffee. "But I'm getting there."

"Yes, you certainly are." She rubbed her hand along his arm. "Just don't get any ideas about telling me what to do. Your authority in this town ends with me."

He toasted her with his coffee. "Yes, ma'am."

She slapped him on the backside before going back into her café. He did not know if anyone saw her do it, but he did not care either.

He heard the driver cut loose with a yell as he released the break and snapped the reins. The four-horse team came to life and pulled the stagecoach along Main Street.

Holt waved to Cassie as she rolled by, her ruined face streaked with tears. He continued to watch the stage until it was out of sight. He hoped he had done the right thing by giving her all that money. It was not as much as she would have had if Bob had lived, but it was close enough to make things right by his accounting.

He knew her scars would heal, at least on the outside. And, in time, he hoped those on the inside faded too. He had no idea what would become of her in California, but at least he had given her a chance at a new life somewhere. And he knew that, sometimes, a chance was all it took.

Holt walked across the thoroughfare until he reached the jail. After unlocking the door, he found Jack Turnbull inside, reading the report Holt had written about all that had happened concerning Mullen. He looked like a boy just then, studying his lessons.

Jack looked up when he saw Holt and said, "You've got an elegant hand for a killer."

Holt dug some coins from his pocket and slapped them down on the desk. "That's enough reading for one day. Head on up to the general store and have Ross give you some suitable clothes to wear. Can't have my only deputy going around looking like a rag doll, now, can I?"

The boy quickly scooped the coins into his hand and pocketed them. "You sure about this, Sheriff? That's a lot of money."

Holt set his mug on his desk and looked at the door leading back to the cells. Behind that door was Joe Mullen. Not just a man, but all the hate and rage a man like that could harbor.

"Make sure you spend every penny of it," Holt told Jack. "Something tells me this isn't over. Not by a long shot."

TURN THE PAGE FOR AN EXCITING PREVIEW!

**Before the Sugarloaf Ranch became legendary
across the western frontier, the Jensens had to survive
a Wild West infested with barbaric men who sought
fortune and glory while killing with violent glee.**

JOHNSTONE COUNTRY.
WHERE DYING AIN'T MUCH OF A LIVING.

Building a ranch takes heart and grit. Smoke and Sally
Jensen are more than capable of meeting the challenges of
shaping the land, raising the livestock, and establishing
their brand. But Smoke wasn't always an entrepreneur.
He's more apt to settle accounts with a fast draw than a
checkbook. And when he learns his old friend Preacher
has been ambushed by outlaws, he wastes no time
saddling up and hitting the vengeance trail with his fellow
mountain men Audie and Nighthawk.

Preacher's attackers have taken over the town of
Desolation Creek deep in Montana Territory. Their
scurrilous leader, Vernon "Venom" McFadden, has his
men harrassing terrified homesteaders and townsfolk to
get his hands on nearby property that's rumored to be rich
with gold. Smoke and his helpmates drift into town one
by one with a plan to root out Venom's gang of prairie
rats and put the big blast on each and every one.

**National Bestselling Authors
WILLIAM W. JOHNSTONE
with J.A. Johnstone**

DESOLATION CREEK
A Smoke Jensen Novel of the West

Live Free. Read Hard.
www.williamjohnstone.net
On sale June 2023, wherever Pinnacle Books are sold.

Visit us at www.kensingtonbooks.com
Western

CHAPTER 1

When a bullet zipped past Smoke Jensen's ear, leaving a hot, crimson streak in its wake, he had a realization.

Trouble sure had a way of following him.

He hadn't come to Big Rock with anything on his mind other than taking care of his business, maybe saying hello to a few friends, chief among them Sheriff Monte Carson and Louis Longmont, and then getting on back to the Sugarloaf.

Of course, his wife, Sally, had it in mind to do some shopping, but that was harmless enough, except for the damage it did to his pocketbook. So, no reasonable explanation existed as to why he found himself smack-dab in the middle of a shooting scrape.

Or rather, *another* shooting scrape.

The last thing he wanted was trouble. He wasn't the type to just stand idly by when bullets were flying, though. He might catch one of them. Or worse, innocent folks might get shot. So, he drew his Colt with lightning speed and took aim at the man who had just emerged from the general store.

A wisp of powder smoke still curled up from the muzzle of the gun in the man's fist. He had already shifted his focus elsewhere after firing that first round. Evidently, he caught Smoke's movement in his peripheral vision and turned his attention back in that direction. He leveled his weapon and sneered.

"I wouldn't," Smoke said.

The warning fell on deaf ears and the man's finger twitched, ready to squeeze off another shot. Smoke's keen eyes saw that, and his gun roared first.

The bullet hammered into the fella's chest, sending him backward as his feet flew from beneath him. He landed flat on his back. His fingers went slack, and he released the revolver. Smoke ran to the gun and kicked it away. One quick glance told him the gesture hadn't been necessary, although erring on the side of caution was always better.

A scarlet ring was spreading on the man's dirty, tattered shirt. Dull, glassy eyes, with the life fading from them, stared up at Smoke.

"Who in the—" Smoke began, wanting to know who he had just shot, and why.

He didn't have time to finish the question as another shot rang out from inside the general store.

"Sally," he said, working to rein in the worry he felt rising in his chest. He swung his gun up, while quickly stepping away from the dead hombre, who lay sprawled out in the middle of the street. Eager to check on his wife, who'd gone inside the store a few minutes earlier, Smoke was about to close the gap between himself and the structure, when the door flew open again.

Another gunman burst onto the store's porch, spinning wildly as if trying to assess his surroundings, but not moving cautiously enough to gain a true lay of the land. This gave Smoke all the time he needed to dive behind a water trough. He reached the cover just in time as the panic-stricken gunman sent two wild shots into the air. As far as Smoke could tell, no one was hit. Most of the folks who had been on the boardwalks or in the street had scrambled for cover when the shooting started.

Just who was this fella and what was he all fired up about? Maybe, Smoke thought, he could end this without any more bloodshed. He didn't care for the fact that a fresh corpse was only a few feet away. Smoke didn't hesitate to kill when necessary, but he didn't take any pleasure in it. If he had his way, he'd never be mixed up in gunplay again.

Smoke rested his arm on the trough and drew a bead, his hand steady, his aim sure.

"Put that gun down!" he called. "No one else has to get hurt. Or worse."

A few townspeople were hustling around, trying to get out of the line of fire. Two old men who'd been sitting on a bench, enjoying the shade the boardwalk's overhanging roof offered, dove off the side and onto the ground. Smoke had to chuckle, realizing the impact had probably jarred the old-timers. They were in one piece, though, and didn't have any bullets in them as they crawled beneath the porch. Thankfully, it seemed as if everyone was out of harm's way.

Until the little girl dashed past.

Smoke hadn't even noticed her before now. She couldn't be any older than six but might have been as young as four. She was a little thing, and scared, as she screamed for her ma. She tried to make it off the porch, but the gun-wielding hombre extended his free arm and scooped up the child, jerking her back onto the porch before Smoke could react.

The man held on to the girl tightly, using her as a shield as he swept his gun from side to side. She squirmed and kicked her legs as she continued screaming, but she had no chance of escaping the man's brutal grip.

Smoke regretted not having put a bullet into the wild-eyed varmint as soon as he laid eyes on the man. That would have ended this before he had a chance to grab that poor child.

"I'm gonna get out of here!" he yelled. "You all hear me?"

Smoke caught a glimpse of movement up the street and swiveled his head to see Sheriff Monte Carson hurrying toward the scene, with two deputies following him. Unfortunately, the crazed gunman on the porch noticed them, too, and sent a shot in their direction. Monte and the deputies instinctively split up as the bullet whistled between them. Monte took cover in one of the alcoves along the boardwalk, while the two deputies crouched behind a parked wagon.

The little girl screamed even louder after the shot, but her captor only tightened the arm he had looped around her body under her arms.

"Shut up!" he snarled at the girl. He turned his attention back to the sheriff and yelled, "Stay back! I swear I'll put a bullet in this here child's brain!"

Smoke's blood was boiling. He'd encountered some low-down, prairie scum in his day, but anyone who would hurt a child was the worst of the worst. He had to smile, though, when the girl started writhing even harder beneath the man's arm. She tried throwing her elbows back and even sent a few more kicks toward him, but his strength put an end to the struggle quickly. Still, Smoke admired her fighting spirit. He aimed to tell her as much too. He'd get a chance, since he would never let that little girl die.

"What is it you want?" Smoke called.

He wasn't the law in Big Rock, but with the sheriff and his deputies pinned down and unable to get closer, he was in the best position to act.

"I want out of here," the gunman said. "I want to make it to my horse down yonder, climb in the saddle, and get out of town without any trouble!"

"Sure, friend," Smoke replied in an affable tone. "Just let the young'un go and you can mosey on out of here. No one will stop you."

The man's lips curled back, revealing jagged yellow teeth. "That ain't how this works. She comes with me. I'll leave her down the trail when I'm free and clear."

Smoke's back stiffened. He couldn't let the hard case ride out of town with that little girl. If she was carried off by him, she was probably as good as dead.

"My daughter!" a loud, terror-stricken voice screamed. "He has my daughter!"

The hard case swung his gun hand around to cover the panicking woman who ran out of the store next door, holding her dress up as she sprinted. Her feet kicked up gravel and dust, but she didn't slow down any, until the man jabbed his gun toward her.

"Don't come any closer! I'll shoot her!" He jammed the hard barrel back against the child's skull, causing her to cry out. She tried reaching for her mother, the gesture causing the woman to cry even louder and stretch her arms out, too, as she skidded to a stop in the road.

Smoke had seen more than enough. He couldn't get a shot off, though. He was good—probably one of the best there was—but even he couldn't guarantee a clean shot under these circumstances. It was just too risky. And he'd be darned if any harm came to a child because of him.

But he couldn't *not act* either.

The street was eerily silent. Smoke could see the two old-timers crawling quietly beneath the porch, headed toward the gunman, obviously intent on intervening. There was an opening where they could get out, not far behind the man. Smoke hoped it wouldn't spook the varmint, causing him to shoot the child.

Smoke cast his eyes toward the sheriff. Monte Carson peered around the corner of the alcove where he had taken cover, but he made no move toward the gunman. His deputies stood motionless behind the wagon, following his example.

The tension was thick. Normally, Smoke was as calm as could be in situations like this, but now his heart felt as if it might beat right out of his chest. Perhaps the child's presence did it. Or maybe his not knowing what had happened to Sally. Had that shot he'd heard earlier hit her? Was she okay? Heaven help that crazed outlaw if she wasn't. Whatever the reason, his nerves were a bit more frayed than usual.

He fought hard to control his emotions. He needed to proceed with a clear head. He didn't give a hoot about his own life.

Right now, that little girl was all that mattered.

And Sally.

Smoke drew a deep breath, exhaled slowly, and fought down his anger. Now wasn't the time to be blinded by rage. A wry smile tugged at his lips as a plan began to take shape inside his mind. What he needed was a distraction. Maybe those two old-timers would give it to him. They were edging closer, shifting beneath the porch, and looking as if they were ready to scramble out and spring up at any moment.

Just like that, though, in the blink of an eye, the old men and Smoke's plan became irrelevant.

The outlaw had taken a few steps back on the porch, toward the store's door. He never bothered to check behind him.

That had been a mistake.

A bottle broke into a dozen pieces as it crashed against his head. One jagged shard tore into his scalp, slicing away the flesh and leaving a hot, wet, bloody streak.

Out of instinct, he dropped the child. She leaped off the porch as quickly as possible and into her mother's arms. For a moment, Smoke feared the outlaw would trigger his gun, but the man just pawed at his flowing wound. Confusion registered in his eyes as he swayed unsteadily on his feet. His gun slid from his fingers.

"What the—"

He tried spinning around but didn't have a chance before a second bottle smashed into him, sending him to the ground, out cold.

Smoke was already at the porch now, his gun still drawn, when he realized who had saved the day.

There in the doorway, with the neck of a broken bottle in her hand, stood Sally.

CHAPTER 2

"What on earth is going on here?" Monte Carson asked.

Smoke finished thumbing a fresh cartridge into his walnut-butted Colt and then pouched the iron. "I was wondering that myself." He looked to Sally and arched an eyebrow. "Here I was worried about *you*, and I should have been worried about *him*." He jerked his head toward the unconscious gunman who lay on the porch's puncheon floor.

One of the sheriff's deputies was standing over the downed man, relieving him of his weapons. A small derringer was up his right sleeve, along with a knife in one of his boots. The deputy then rummaged through the man's pockets and pulled out a wad of greenbacks and waved them toward the sheriff.

"Those are mine!" Don Baker said.

He was a large, easygoing man who ran the mercantile, along with help from his clerk, Ike Hairston. Ike was out on the porch now, too, and hurried to the downed brigand. He reared his foot back, but Sheriff Carson stopped him.

"You can't kick him now. He's laid out cold!"

"Well, I oughta," Ike said, and then his voice trailed off

into a consortium of jumbled curse words. "They tried to hold up the store."

"They didn't *try*," his boss corrected him. "They did rob us. Would have gotten away with it, too, if it hadn't been for Jensen."

"Which one?" Smoke said with a smile. His eyes darted to Sally, who was now off the porch and checking on the terrified mother and child.

"Thank God she's okay," Sally said, rubbing the girl's back.

The two old-timers had rolled out from under the porch and, after considerable effort, were finally stumbling to their feet.

"Sheriff, I think Walt done broke his backside," one of them said.

The other groaned as he rubbed his rear end. It took considerable effort for Smoke to control his laughter, and one look at Sally told him she was having the same struggle.

Monte seemed somewhat annoyed when he said, "Will someone just tell me exactly what happened?"

"I'll tell you," Ike said, still red-faced with anger. "Those two no-accounts came in the store, acted like they were shopping, but then drew their pistols and demanded the money from the register. They were also trying to take off with a few supplies, jerky, and coffee, mostly." He jabbed a bony finger toward the dead man in the street and said, "He got spooked and told his partner they had to get out of there. That's when he came out shooting!"

"That explains your ear," Monte said, looking at Smoke.

Smoke remembered the close call and touched his ear. It stung a little, but the blood had dried now. He'd had a lot worse done to him over the years.

"Guess I was in the wrong place at the wrong time," Smoke said with a chuckle.

"Or the right place," Monte said. "He may have hit someone with those wild shots, had you not taken him down. Reckon the town is obliged to you for that. Once again."

Smoke nodded.

It seemed as if Monte took every opportunity he could to state how much the town of Big Rock owed Smoke. In fact, Smoke was mostly responsible for the settlement's founding, having led an exodus here of folks escaping from the outlaw town of Fontana, several miles away. They had fled to escape the reign of terror carried out by brutal mine owner Tilden Franklin and his hired guns.

Now, a couple of years later, Franklin was dead, and Fontana was an abandoned town, nothing left but moldering ruins, while Big Rock was growing and thriving. Monte Carson wasn't the only one who gave Smoke a lot of the credit for that happening.

Smoke, however, wasn't interested in accolades. He was thankful when the storekeeper started talking again.

"Anyway," Ike Hairston continued, "that spooked his partner inside the store, and he started shooting too."

"Anyone hit?" the sheriff asked.

"No, but he plugged the dang cracker barrel!" Ike said. He looked as if he wanted to kick the man again. His anger subsiding, he shrugged and said, "That's when he came out onto the porch, and, well, you saw the rest."

Sally was at Smoke's side now. They joined Sheriff Carson in examining the two outlaws. Both wore dirty, torn homespun clothing and it seemed as if neither had bathed in a long while.

Smoke thumbed his curled-brim hat back, revealing

more of his ash-blond hair, and scratched his forehead. "Looks like these two had fallen on hard times."

"Explains why they were so desperate," Monte said with a frown. "Still doesn't give them call to carry on like this."

"Sure doesn't," Smoke agreed. "Reckon they could have gotten a meal just about anywhere here in town."

Smoke wasn't exaggerating. Big Rock was a friendly community, where folks could find plenty of help if they needed it. Smoke might have even given the two work at the Sugarloaf, had they dropped by. Of course, the fact that one had held a little girl hostage showed he was *not* simply a good man who'd fallen on desperate times, so Smoke doubted if they'd had any intent on working for an honest day's wages.

The one Sally had laid out was now starting to groan as he came to.

"Let's get him on down to the jail," Monte told his deputies. "I'll send for Doc Spaulding to patch him up."

"He needs to take a look at my rear too!" Walt said, still rubbing his derriere.

"Maybe he can get you one of those sittin' pillows," the other old-timer said. "Feels better than resting your cheeks on a hard chair, that's for sure!"

Monte rolled his eyes and mumbled, "Lord, help me." He turned his focus to the corpse, which lay in the street, and winced as he saw that flies had already started to gather. "I'll get the undertaker down here too. I'll look through the wanted dodgers I have back at the office. Could be that you have some reward money coming, Smoke."

Smoke snorted. "A bounty-hunting Jensen? Now that's a thought."

"Don't you go getting any ideas. We don't need any more trouble," Sally said. "Besides, you're a rancher. Remember?"

Smoke held up his hands in mock surrender. "Believe me, I've had my fill of trouble. I'm not looking for more." His smile disappeared as he turned his gaze toward the sheriff. He scratched his strong, angular chin and asked, "Do I need to stick around and appear before Judge Proctor?"

"Nah," Monte said. "This is pretty cut-and-dried. The way I figure it, you did the town a favor. You too," he said, smiling at Sally. "Smoke, you sure married one with a bit of sass in her."

Smoke laughed, nodding in agreement.

He certainly couldn't argue that point.

The ride back to the Sugarloaf was seven miles and Smoke didn't mind the journey one bit. The country was mighty pretty, and he had an even prettier woman by his side. As he guided his black stallion, Drifter, beside the buckboard Sally drove, he took a moment to soak it all in.

She had an infectious smile, which he never tired of. Her brown hair hung in bouncing curls. With Sally set against the backdrop of the rugged Rocky Mountains, Smoke wondered if he'd indeed been shot back in Big Rock and was now in heaven.

"What are you looking at?" Sally said, though her smile hinted that she already knew the answer.

"The woman of my dreams," he said without hesitation.

She smiled even wider. "And what are you thinking about?"

Smoke laughed. He made a show of looking around and said, "Well, I suppose I could tell you, since there's no one else around."

Now Sally laughed loudly. "Easy. We've got a few miles to go before we're back home."

"Like I said, there's no one else around."

Sally cast him one last devilish grin before turning her attention back to the trail before her. Smoke did the same.

They rode in silence for a few minutes before he said, "That was some stunt you pulled back there, walloping that owlhoot like that. You could've been hurt."

"And that little girl could've been killed."

"True," Smoke admitted. "Reckon I can't be too upset."

"Upset? You knew I was a handful when you put the ring on my finger."

Smoke chuckled. "That I did. And I wouldn't have you any other way. I just want you to be careful, is all. I intend to grow old with you."

"Of course," she said. "I'll be sitting by your side on the porch in our rockers. We can look out over the Sugarloaf. It will be massive by then."

"You have big plans," he said.

"*We* have big plans," she said.

"Yep. And they don't include gunfighting, that's for sure."

She gave him a pointed stare. "It really bothered you, what happened back in town?"

He nodded. Drifter continued to pick his way over the trail, staying beside the buckboard, moving at a measured pace. It seemed as if the horses were just as content as Smoke and Sally to enjoy the pleasant evening as night fell around them.

The falling sun painted the picturesque landscape in pink and yellow hues. A cloud of gnats hovered just off the road. A few grasshoppers leaped in the brushy grass to Smoke's left. Smoke sucked in a lungful of air and held it a moment, enjoying the smell of the upcoming summer. Something about this time of year called to him. Something peaceful. Thinking about peace, he said, "I just hope this valley is tamed one day, and sooner rather than later. I've had more than enough gunplay to last me a lifetime."

"There will be peace around these parts soon enough," she said. "Men like you and Preacher have worked hard to make this land safe for decent folks. One day, our children will thank you for it."

Smoke smiled once again. He sure liked the sound of that.

Children.

Of course, if they turned out anything like their pa—or ma, for that matter—they'd keep him and Sally on their toes.

They finished their trip in silence, content to simply be in each other's presence. The relaxing ride did wonders in washing away the unpleasantness that had occurred back in town, and by the time they arrived home, it was already nothing but a memory.

That peacefulness didn't last long, though. Upon riding up to the house, Smoke realized they had company. Two saddle mounts he didn't recognize, along with a couple of pack animals, were tied in front of the log ranch house.

Something stirred deep inside his stomach, telling him that all was not well. He remembered that realization he'd had back in town when the shooting had started.

Trouble just had a way of finding him.